The Fire This Time

Book III
Redemption Price Series

Catrina J. Sparkman

The Fire This Time

Published by:

The Ironer's Press
PO Box 1122
Madison, Wi 53701

Also by Catrina J. Sparkman

Non-Fiction:

*Doing Business with God: An Everyday Guide to Prayer &
Journaling*

Intimacy the Beginning of Authority

Intercession 101: The Heartbeat of God

Divine Revelation for a Twitter Generation

Doing Battle with the Names of God

The Fourth Watch

Fiction:

The Redemption's Price series:

Passing Through Water

Opening the Floodgates

DEDICATION

*This book is dedicated to every child that
has ever been hurt in the household of faith.
For your future—*

A demand

Who can endure the day of his coming? Who can stand when he appears? For he will be like a refiner's fire or a launderer's soap. [3] he will sit as a refiner and purifier of silver; he will purify the Levites and refine them like gold and silver. Then the LORD will have men who will bring offerings in righteousness, [4] and the offerings of Judah and Jerusalem will be acceptable to the LORD, as in days gone by, as in former years.

MALACHI 3: 2-4

He knows the way that I take; when he has tried me, I shall come out as gold.

Job 23:10

The Fire This Time

Catrina J. Sparkman

CHAPTER 1

Present Day, 2006

Michael Dutton didn't understand how the Creator of the Universe spoke to his brother. He only knew that He did and that He had, ever since they were children. Joshua claimed it was easy. That all a person had to do was open up their heart. That's exactly what Mike was trying to do now. Open his heart. *I need to find him. Show me Jabari.* Jabari had left his cell phone at home making it impossible to track him. *You know my brother has been through a lot. You know this family has had enough pain.* Mike drove in silence, no radio, no noise, nothing, just listening. That's when he heard a still, quiet voice say, **Go to Hope House.**

☙ ☙ ☙

"That'll be $37.50," the cabbie said.

Jabari reached into his pants pocket and pulled out a five, a ten, seven ones, and a ball of lint. He handed the cab driver the money. "That's all I have."

The cab driver counted the money quickly. "This ain't enough, kid."

Jabari spotted Marcus on one of the outside courts playing ball with a group of youth. "My cousin is right over there. He'll pay you the rest."

The cabbie stared at Jabari hard. "If I let you out, how do I know you won't up and disappear on me?"

"I won't. I promise."

The cabbie looked as if he didn't believe him, so Jabari added, "I can just call him over."

The driver got out of the vehicle and motioned for Jabari to follow. "Okay, stand right here and call him."

Jabari yelled Marcus' name and waved frantically in the older boy's direction. "Man, he can't hear me from all the way over here. Just let me walk over there to him."

"No, we both go together." The cab driver grabbed Jabari by the arm and dragged him towards the fence.

Marcus caught sight of Jabari and the man and abandoned his game. He picked up his shirt lying on the ground, threw it on quickly, and hurried towards them. "Yo, we got a problem here?"

"This young man can't pay his fare. If nobody pays, he's going to jail."

"Dude, chill, I got your money right here."

"Yeah, dude, chill," Jabari said, snatching his arm away from the cab driver.

"How much?" Marcus asked.

"$37.50."

Marcus reached into his back pocket and removed his wallet. He handed the cab driver two twenties. "Keep the change."

The cab driver shook his finger in Jabari's face. "Next time don't flag a cab if you can't pay the fare." He walked back to his cab and drove away.

Marcus looked Jabari up and down. "Yo, Shorty, what you doing here?"

So Jabari told him everything. The link his dad's secretary had sent to him. The information he'd found about his folks on the Internet. The confrontation with his mom. Marcus didn't say a word, not one, single word, and Jabari took the older boy's silence to be affirmation. Jabari didn't know exactly what words of comfort would come out of Marcus's mouth. Maybe something along the lines of, "Keep your head up, Shorty. What your parents did to you was straight up foul." What he hadn't expected was to be dissed.

"Jabari, nothing you said explains why you ran away."

"They lied to me, Marcus. My moms, my pops, everybody."

"So you perfect now? You never made no mistakes."

"No but—"

"It's people in this world dealing with real s@#$t Jabari, and you trippin' about your daddy not being your daddy and your mama lying to you. At least they want yo black a#$." Marcus shook his head in disgust. "We can't hang no more. I thought you was smart."

Jabari turned his face into stone and attempted to shrug off the pain of Marcus's dismissal. "I just need to crash here for a few days, till I figure out my next move."

"Do you, superstar," Marcus said as he walked away.

Jabari wanted to call to him, to ask him to keep his secret, but he knew he wouldn't have to. No matter what, even if Marcus really was done with him, he'd never snitch.

CHAPTER 2

Tonya sat in her office at the church holding the phone up to her ear listening to the irate mother whose child had been turned away last Sunday from children's church.

"It was cruel the way they did it too. And Bobby was really looking forward to the Bible lesson."

Tonya suspected that what Bobby was really looking forward to was snack time and recess, because he never paid much attention to the lesson. Still, she remained silent and allowed the woman to have her say.

"I really am sorry, Sister Debra. I can speak with Bobby if you think that would help. We want him to feel welcomed in children's church. It's for the safety of all the children that policy has been put in place. We cannot receive a child who has a contagious virus. And I know it doesn't seem like it at the moment, but that rule protects Bobby as well."

Tonya looked down at her watch as Debra continued to talk. If she didn't hang up right now, she would officially be late to the staff meeting, but rushing the woman off the phone would only reinforce the very thing that the woman had been implying throughout the entire call: that she and her son were non-entities at the church because they were poor.

"Every member is a valued member of the Now Faith International Church community. It doesn't matter what you bring to the table, it only matters that you come to the table," Tonya had asserted during their phone conversation more than once.

As the head of the children's ministry, Tonya understood that parents often saw themselves as extensions of their children. Children's ministry was as much about ministering to them as it was about ministering to their children. So Tonya listened, and when Debra was done airing her grievances Tonya asked her politely if she could pray.

"Lord thank you so much for my sister, Debra. Thank you that she is a good mother, who works hard and advocates for her son. Let her know how loved she is by you and every minister here at our church."

The woman cried and thanked Tonya. With bitterness and offense finally broken, Tonya could hang up the phone with a clear mind and heart.

෫ ෫ ෫

Ted, the senior pastor at Now Faith International Church, looked up from his position at the head of the conference table as Tonya walked into the conference room. "You're late, so glad you could join us at the very tail end of the meeting."

"Sorry, I was speaking with a parent by phone. Had to listen, couldn't rush her off."

"Is her child in peril?" Ted asked sardonically.

"No, Pastor Maxwell, he's not in peril, however her son was turned away from children's church last Sunday, and the mom was extremely upset about it."

Karen, one of the staffers around the table, spoke up. "Sister Debra. Her son had ringworm, right?"

"Actually, it was pink eye. She had already started the course of antibiotics, so Bobby was no longer contagious. I explained to her our policy and took a moment to pray with her. She does understand the policy now, and just by spending a little time listening to her, I'm happy to report that she is no longer seeking membership at another church."

Tonya met the senior pastor's glacial glare head on. He had absolutely no right to be upset. So she arrived at the staff meeting late. Big deal. It wasn't like they were balancing the federal budget or dissolving world hunger. Besides, whatever she missed she could read in the minutes.

"If my memory serves me correctly, Sister Debra is on Section 8. She's not even a tithing member of this congregation. Jane, how many times has she accessed the benevolence fund?"

Jane, the chief financial officer, paged through the stack of papers in front of her. "Twice, Pastor Maxwell in the last six months. Once for her gas bill, another time for her light bill."

Tonya mumbled something under her breath.

Ted leaned back in his chair and pinned her with his gaze. "Care to share it with the team?"

"I said, God forbid the woman have lights and heat." Tonya said, making it a point to enunciate each word.

"You seemed to have missed my point, Minister Malone. I simply brought that up to say that if she's not happy, she should attend another church."

"I disagree. She is the population this church opened its doors to serve," Tonya said.

"She's a drain on this ministry's assets," Ted countered.

Tom, one of the elders of the church, cleared his throat. "Why don't we just agree to disagree, folks."

Adrina, Tonya's friend and administrative assistant, clapped her hands. "Amen to that. Besides, we have something important to celebrate." She removed the cover from a cake plate to reveal a dozen beautifully decorated cupcakes.

"As many of you know. One of our very own is graduating with her PhD. What you probably didn't know is that she is the first licensed minister here at Now Faith International, female or otherwise, to hold a doctorate degree. Let's give it up for our future First Lady, Minister Tonya Malone."

Handclaps went up around the room.

"Thank you, everyone, but you didn't have to go through any trouble for me," Tonya said.

"Of course we did. We all love you," Jane said.

"Everyone please grab a cupcake on your way out," Ted said, effectively ending the meeting. "Tonya, can you hang back for a moment, please? I'd like to speak with you."

"Sure."

Tonya watched as the last of the staff filed out of the conference room. Ted walked to the other end of the conference room and took a seat on the edge of the table in front of her.

"What hat are we wearing?" Tonya asked.

"Work."

She nodded. "Fine."

"I don't like the way you challenged me just now in front of the team. I think it sends the wrong message. Don't you?"

"I think your implying that Timmy's mom is a less valued member of this church because she's not a tither sends the wrong message to the team."

Ted stood and straightened his tie. "I received your vacation request, and I'm denying it."

"You don't like that I challenged you in front of the team so you're denying my vacation request? Typical."

"I'm denying your vacation because you just put it in yesterday. The request falls on a Sunday that the children's choir is preforming. You are the director of that ministry in case you've forgotten."

"I am the director. Who has hand-picked and trained a very capable staff. The children's choir performs every third Sunday, are you suggesting that part of my duties as the director of the children's ministry is to be here every time an activity comes up out of children's ministry? Because if so, I don't remember that being in my contract.

Oh wait, that's right, I don't have a contract because this isn't a salaried position."

"Then you should quit because there are about twenty more sisters in line waiting to fill your shoes!"

Tonya nodded, "You'll have my resignation on your desk by Monday." She rose from her seat and strolled quickly to the door. She attempted to turn the knob but Ted had made it there first. His hand was pressed firmly against the door above her head.

"Move!"

"Stay."

Ted leaned in close. Close enough for Tonya to feel his breath on the back of her neck. "Please."

Tonya folded her arms across her chest and turned to face him.

"You'd walk away just like that? From everything we've built together?"

Silence.

"Look, I'm sorry, okay? I spoke out of turn. I don't want you to quit. This church doesn't work if you quit. Most importantly I don't think the two of us could continue to work if you quit."

"The church will be fine, Ted. Just call one of those other sisters waiting in line to take my spot," Tonya said, yanking hard on the doorknob.

The door opened, but Ted managed to close it back quickly.

"That's not what I meant. Baby, look at me. I'm sorry, alright. That's not what I meant. Work hat off. Okay?" Ted positioned his body against the door then lowered his frame so that he was peering directly into Tonya's eyes.

Tonya sighed hard. "Just say whatever it is you need to say, Ted. I have somewhere I need to be."

"Tonya, as a fellow staffer, you had every right to challenge me. You're probably the only one around here with the guts to do it. I love that about you professionally, baby, I really do. But as my fiancée, real talk, Tonya, sometimes you're a little hard on a brother's ego."

He flashed her his most charming smile. She wasn't charmed. He tried a different approach. "But something tells me that I'd better get used to it because the future Mrs. Theodore Maxwell isn't going to back down for me or anybody else. Will you accept my apology?"

"Apology accepted," Tonya said. Her tone was clipped, professional.

"Will you tell me where you're going and why you've requested the vacation time?"

Tonya stared at him blankly. "Why?"

"Work hat off, remember? I think I have a right to know where my lady is going on vacation, especially if she's going without me."

"I'm going home for a few days to see my mom."

"She'll be here in a few months for your graduation, correct?"

"What exactly is your point, Ted?"

"I'm not picking a fight with you, Tonya. I'm just trying to figure out why you have this sudden urge to go home, now."

Tonya shrugged. "I just have a press in my spirit that tells me I need to get there."

Ted studied her for a beat. "How can any god-fearing man argue with that?" He smiled down at her again. The second smile she didn't return. Ted lifted a tendril of Tonya's naturally curly hair which was pressed bone straight, just the way he liked it. He breathed in the scent of her shampoo as he held the lock of her hair up against his nose. "Tonya, I need my first lady right here beside me. She can't be jet-setting off to God knows where, whenever she feels . . . led. When we're married, I need to know that things will be different."

"Ted, if we are married—"

Ted pulled her into his arms. "When. When we are married. You already said yes. Just because your angry right now doesn't mean you get to take it back." He moved in for a kiss and Tonya stepped out of his embrace. "Like I said, if we are married, you'll be my number one priority."

CHAPTER 3

Mike rolled his car up to the checkpoint and nodded to the guard posted at the gate of the Home Court Advantage urban renewal site. The gates were put in place to make the residents feel safe. No one got through the gate unless they had business in Safe Harbor or family members who lived inside Safe Harbor. Unless of course they were the owners or perhaps members of the owners' family. That's exactly what Mike was banking on now.

"Good to see you, Mr. Dutton."

"Likewise, Mr. Joseph."

"Come on now. How many times I got to ask you to call me Joe. Just Joe."

Mike found himself smiling despite his somber mood. "I guess I'll remember to call you, Just Joe, when you remember to call me, Just Mike."

The older resident laughed. "Alright, Mike, will do."

"How long you been at the gate?"

Joe rubbed his greying beard. "Since two o'clock today. Milton was here before that. Why, we ain't had no problems today have we?"

"You remember my nephew, Jabari." Mike pulled up a picture of Jabari on his cell phone.

"Yeah, of course. Your brother's boy, right?"

"That's right. You seen him?"

"I let him in 'bout an hour ago. Got dropped off in a cab. Said he was headed over to the basketball courts."

11

❦ ❦ ❦

Mike drove through the Safe Harbor community scanning the basketball courts. When he got to the third court, he saw him. Jabari stood by a fence looking like a lost puppy watching the older boys play a game of pick-up. Mike picked up his phone and dialed his brother. Joshua answered on the first ring.

"I got him. I'mma take him to the ranch for a few days, give him a chance to cool off. Yeah. I know. I love you too, bro."

❦ ❦ ❦

Marcus picked up his ringing cell phone to hear the deep baritone voice of Michael Dutton, AKA the Man of Steel, on the other end. Marcus had been living with the legendary basketball star for almost six months and the whole experience was still mind blowing to him.

"I'mma take Jabari up to the ranch this weekend. You hanging with or hanging back? It's up to you."

"I think I'mma hang back. My mom wants to do that family thing tonight. I'mma chill out with her at Hope House for a little bit, maybe catch a movie."

"Yeah, what y'all watching?"

"Probably some chick flick."

Mike's rich laughter filled the phone. "Well, suck it up. Duty calls."

"Yeah, I know."

"I left some cash on the kitchen counter for you. Use the credit card I gave you for emergencies. If you need anything else, holler at my man, Jeeves, he'll take care of you. I'll see you Sunday."

CHAPTER 4

Jabari didn't know what to think when he saw his uncle Mike walking towards him. His first inclination was to run, but Jabari quickly squashed that impulse. His uncle had been the number one power forward in NBA history. He'd surely outrun him, and running, that is to say, running again, might make things worse. Was his father so mad that he sent his uncle, instead? Did he call his brother up and say, "Yo, Mike, man, you better go get Jabari, 'cause if I get my hands on him, I'mma kill him?" Uncle Mike never hit people on the court when they made him mad, but it was a known fact that he did not play. In a situation like this, Jabari didn't know who to be more afraid of, his uncle or his father. His uncle crossed over into the playground area, stepped onto the asphalt of the basketball courts, and stopped. A clear indication to Jabari that he was expected to walk the rest of the way. His uncle was wearing dark sunglasses, a dark colored suit, and a black trench coat. With his bald head glistening in the fading sunlight, he looked like a huge muscle-bound Shaft. Jabari felt his throat go dry and his hands turn clammy. He hadn't gotten many whippings in his lifetime. In fact, he could count them on one hand. One for running out in the middle of the street. The second for wandering away in the grocery store. Both of those had been at the hand of his mother. To his recollection, he had never been spanked by either his father or his uncle. But then again, running away had to at least be up there with wandering away in the grocery store. *I'm about to get a beat down for sure.* Jabari thought, as he willed his legs to walk towards his uncle. He fought against the voice inside of him, the one screaming in his head at him to turn around and run the other way. Then he tried to make his face the unreadable mask of stone he had seen Marcus and other young black boys erect against the world. When Jabari was finally standing in front of him, Uncle Mike removed his sunglasses. What Jabari saw in his uncle's eyes surprised him. *Was that fear? Nah, impossible. Love?* Yes. And something else, concern.

"You alright?"

Jabari nodded his head. The thunder that had built up in his chest from the moment he had spoken to his mother threatened to erupt again. But this time he didn't want to spit curses, all he wanted to do was cry. When his uncle pulled him tightly to his chest, he did just that. Jabari cried body-quaking tears. His uncle held him until his sobs quieted, and then he paid him the greatest respect that one man could give another. As they walked back to the waiting car, Uncle Mike ignored him. They drove in silence for a few miles, until Jabari saw the expressway taking them out of the city.

"Ain't you gon' take me back?"

"Nope. I figured you needed sometime to wrap your head around all of this."

After that, Uncle Mike remained silent for the rest of the journey.

CHAPTER 5

Joshua hung up the phone and exhaled. It had been exactly one hour and forty-three minutes from the moment he discovered Jabari had gone missing. One hour and forty-three agonizing minutes before his brother had called to say, "I found him." When Mike's number popped up on his screen, Joshua had taken the phone call out in the hallway out of pure instinct, a need to protect Bella. Because the very next time she looked into his eyes and asked him where Jabari was, he needed to be able to tell her that he was safe. Joshua opened the door to the master bedroom to tell Bella the news, but she wasn't on the bed where he had left her. She wasn't in the master bathroom either. After a quick search of the entire master suite, Joshua found Bella curled up into a tight ball on the floor of their bedroom closet. He would have thought her asleep if it had not been for the rocking. Her eyes were like hard beads of glass, focused on some point that only she could see. Joshua dropped to the floor and cocooned Bella in his arms. "It's okay," he crooned softly into her ear. "Mike's got him, he's okay. Jabari's safe, Bella. He's safe. Come back to me. I got you, baby. Just come back to me."

⚹ ⚹ ⚹

Bella heard his voice. Somewhere on a distant shore of her mind she could hear Joshua's voice. He was calling her back to sanity. He was warning her away from the jagged cliffs of the past. She could feel his powerful arms lock around her like a prayer, securing her, pulling her back from the jaws of death. But the memories were like strong wet winds washing over her, huge tidal waves that threatened to choke her as they sandblasted her soul. The only thing that kept her from completely going under, from drowning, was Joshua's strong arms wrapped tightly around her, and the sound of another voice. A sweet, quiet, gentle voice telling her: ***If you soar to the highest heights, I'll go with you. And if you make your bed in hell, I'll be there too.***"

New Orleans
Summer
1987

CHAPTER 6

T he wheels on the bus go . . . round and round! Round and Round! Round and round! The doors on the bus go open and shut all through the town!"

Forty campers from Southern Baptist Pastor's Children Camp sang all the way from Baton Rouge, to New Orleans at the top of their lungs. A chorus of hoots and hollers exploded when the bus finally pulled into the church parking lot. Camp was over, summer was ended, and they were finally home. Eight-year-old Bella pressed her face to the window, looking for her parents, in the waiting crowd. She saw her mama, who she mostly tolerated, blowing kisses up to her and her daddy, whom she absolutely adored, standing proudly next to her mama waving up at her. Bella saw her best friend Timmy's parents next. They were smiling and waving too. But despite their smiles, they both looked tired and sad. Too sad, like Bella almost couldn't stand to look at them sad. So Bella prayed and asked Jesus to turn on her other eyes. Sometimes if she prayed and asked Jesus to open her heavenly eyes she could see exactly what the problem was and she would know how to pray. She didn't see monsters riding on top of Timmy's parents, but she did see slime. Lots and lots of monster slime. Maybe she should pray and ask Jesus to send an angel with a giant water hose. As Bella was considering this, the monster who always rode her mother, peeked over from behind her mother's shoulder and stuck its giant, green, bumpy tongue out at Bella.

It mocked her, made faces at her, and screeched at her so loudly that Bella could hardly hear herself think. Right now the monster was saying, "Let me see you try and jump bad with me, while you're on that bus!" The one attached to her mother carried a great big Bible and wore a huge Sunday-go-to-meeting hat. Bella knew him all too well. She had done battle with this one plenty of times. He kept up a constant stream of bickering between Bella and her mother. But what concerned her right now was what she saw on her daddy's back. She had never seen a monster riding her daddy before. The demon attached to her father was even more dignified then the one attached to her mother. He wore priestly garments, and a funny little, pointed hat with an upside down cross on it. Her mama's monster was small, about the size of a monkey. Her daddy's monster was big, way too big to have sprung up overnight. Even too big to have sprung up in the time she had been away at camp. Where had he come from, and why hadn't she seen him before?

"Go ahead, try it! Stab me now! If you bad!" the monkey monster screamed as it hopped up and down on her mother's shoulder. "Let me see you try and stab me while you on that bus!"

Bella closed her eyes and prayed. It was her first day back from camp, and she did not want to get into a fight with her mother. She asked the Lord to send an angel with a sword to poke the annoying, little monkey spirit. Suddenly the monkey let loose a piercing howl, he jumped off her mother's back, and ran from the church parking lot. Bella laughed. Then she sent the angel to attack the strange looking creature sitting on her father's back too. The angel sheathed his sword, then pulled out a cutlass and prepared to attack. The monster held one huge hairy paw up in surrender. With the other he reached into his garment pocket and pulled out a strange looking document. He and the angel exchanged a few words.

Then he climbed down quietly, cast Bella a withering stare, and stalked off.

The doors to the bus opened with a swoosh and kids began to tumble out. Bella didn't run off the bus with the other children. She stayed back with her wheelchair bound friend, Timmy, who would have to be unloaded from the bus.

⁂ ⁂ ⁂

"Bella Rose, so tell us how was camp?" her mother asked once they had settled themselves into the car.

"Great."

Her father smiled at her through the rearview mirror. "Lead any revivals this year, sweetheart?"

"Yes, I did, and God came and healed Timmy. Now he's not going to die."

Bella's mother and father exchanged a look between them. "Bella, honey, did Timmy tell you that he was dying?"

"Uh huh, he said this was his last summer at camp. But we had church and Jesus came and He healed him."

"Bella, I know you really like Timmy."

"He's my best friend, Daddy."

"Sometimes people die, baby. Long before their time. It's just the nature of being human in a sin-sick world. Nothing we can do about it."

"Daddy, are you saying that there's nothing God can do for Timmy?"

"No, baby, I'm not saying that. I'm saying that God doesn't always heal when we want him to. I'm also saying that I'm glad you got to see Timmy one last time on this side of glory because it doesn't look good for him."

20

Sylvia shook her head. "I just keep thinking about that child's poor, poor, mother. His poor, poor, mother."

"God healed him, daddy."

"I hope so. For his parents' sake, I sure hope so. But healing Timmy at this point would be the equivalent of Jesus raising Lazarus from the dead."

"Well, I guess somebody needs to take his grave clothes off and let him go. 'Cause he is healed!" Bella declared.

"Lamech, this child is a natural born preacher."

"Don't go putting thoughts into the girl's head, Sylvia. You know I don't believe in women preachers."

"Well, you had better tell her that. And all her teddy bears that are slayed in the spirit up in her bedroom. 'Cause this child is gonna preach."

Lamech's huge baritone laugh filled the car. "She'll be a missionary then. Missionary Bella."

CHAPTER 7

Bella sat on the bed and watched her mother get ready. "Why can't I go?"

"Because it's a lady's tea."

Bella didn't know why she was pressing so hard. It wasn't like she enjoyed spending time with her mother, much less any of her mother's uppity friends. The only fun thing about the lady's tea at all was watching the Monsters' Ball—and even that wasn't so fun with her mama giving her the evil eye every single time Bella laughed. All of her mama's church friends would arrive laughing and talking with one another, giving each other air kisses and hugs while the monsters that rode in on their backs would begin to brawl. Monsters fought so fiercely that they fell from atop their human steeds, biting and clawing at one another, ripping hair away from roots, and smashing cake into each other's faces. New monsters were rare, in fact, Bella knew most of the monsters by name, and when she didn't know their names, she could always identify the monster by what they wore and how they behaved. For example, Sister Lela's monster used to wear a low-cut lace bodice blouse, until the lady's tea where she and Sister Merriweather got into a fight. Sister Merriweather called Sister Lela a man-stealing hussy and then Sister Merriweather's monster proceeded to rip the lace from Sister Lela's monster's blouse. Now whenever Sister Lela's monster rode in, it was with its large double D's proudly swinging all over the place. The fighting between the monsters would go on until somebody decided to open the luncheon with a hymn or a word of prayer.

One single angel would enter the room, and the monsters would jump down from their human host and run helter-skelter from the building, jumping from windows, and beating a path to the door.

Sylvia Leblanc turned from her position in the mirror to study her daughter.

"Bella Rose, you've never liked these things before. Why do you suddenly now want to go?"

"I like the Monsters' Ball."

"You like the what? Bella Rose, what in the world are you talking about?"

"Nothing."

Bella wished she could tell her mother the truth. That the monster she saw riding her daddy's back, the one who had sprung up seemingly overnight, he wasn't funny like the other ones. He scared her. Really scared her. And for the first time in her life, she didn't want to be left alone with her daddy.

"I'm bored, can I please go with you?"

Sylvia looked down at her daughter's overalls with thinly veiled disgust. Bella stared back unapologetically at her mother. Her daddy bought them, and they were pink.

"Bella Rose, you will have to wear a dress, a bonnet and gloves, if you are coming with me. Now, if you can manage to do all of that without complaining, then you are welcome to join me."

"Never mind," Bella said, sliding down from her parents' bed. She'd take her chances with the big, hairy monster.

CHAPTER 8

Call it a mother's intuition but the moment Sylvia Leblanc crossed the threshold into her house that afternoon, she knew something was terribly wrong. She'd left one child that morning and returned to find another one. In the mere span of the two hours that she had been gone, something inside her child had died. The knowing came first. Then she saw. Blood stains on the bed. Crumpled little girl panties on the floor. She heard the sound of her daughter whimpering from somewhere inside the bedroom closet, and from her position in the doorway of Bella's bedroom, she could hear the sound of the shower running in the master bathroom as her husband washed himself in the middle of the day. A horrible scene she had not been privy to began to play over and over again inside of Sylvia's mind.

"No. This isn't happening," Sylvia hissed to the walls. It couldn't, not twice in one lifetime. Lightning never struck twice.

"Lamech!!!" Sylvia barged into the bathroom, whipped back the shower curtain, and began to beat him with her fists. "What did you do! What did you do, you bastard! What did you do to my baby!"

Lamech was a big man with a voice that filled up Sylvia's world, but when he spoke in that moment, his voice was very small. He stood there naked and shriveled as she beat him, cowering underneath the blows delivered to him at the hands of her small fists.

"I-I don't know. I don't know what happened."

That's when Sylvia knew. Lightning could and had struck her life twice. Later that evening after he had regained his voice, Lamech tried to enter Bella's bedroom. "Sweetheart, it's me, Daddy. I—"

Bella let out a high-pitched scream, and Sylvia pushed him from the room with a strength she didn't even know she owned.

Bella stayed in bed for three days. She didn't speak, she wouldn't eat. A little chicken broth was all Sylvia could manage to force down her throat. In her bones Sylvia knew what she had to do. What she was supposed to do. But as she camped out in Bella's room with Lamech sleeping on a makeshift pallet outside the door, she wondered if she had the courage to leave. Where would she conjure this courage from, and what did it look like? Her mother certainly hadn't had it. Even if she were to muster it up, how would she raise a child alone? She'd have to return to Flatbush, Tennessee, a town so small you couldn't even find it on a map. To her mother's house. To her mother and that man. Then they'd both be victims. And if Sylvia was a victim, how in the world could she possibly protect her daughter? How, with no money, no education, and no social standing to speak of? As it stood, her only standing in their community at all was that she was Mrs. Reverend Lamech Leblanc. If she left, he'd remarry in a heartbeat, and she could forget about alimony or child support.

Right now, Sylvia was only poor in spirit. A body could limp through life with a broken spirit, but if she left, she would be broke indeed. No good could come out of raising her child in poverty.

"There has to be another way." Sylvia knelt on the floor beside her daughter's bed and whispered weakly to the walls. "Maybe we can still get through this, without letting it destroy our family."

"Why we most certainly can," the monkey monster cooed, as he stroked Sylvia's hair and caught her words as they bounced off the walls. "All we need is a little bit of prayer and a whole lot of pretense. Why, that's exactly what the Bible calls it. Isn't it? Calling those things as not as though they were."

Sylvia nodded her head in silent assent. The thought took strength, and Sylvia Leblanc began to rebuild her house. She told herself she was building on a strong foundation of prayer and faith, like that of the apostles and the prophets. That Jesus himself was the chief cornerstone.

Hadn't her mother done the same thing for her? Given Sylvia a new story. A black woman couldn't make it in the world unless someone rewrote her story. And so, in that moment it was decided. Sylvia would give her daughter what had been bequeathed to her, the gift of a new existence.

Each night for three days, Lamech returned home from the church and took up his own vigil outside of Bella's door. He would knock once then quietly plead for Sylvia to open the door. But Bella didn't want to talk to or even so much as look at the daddy whom she had once adored. She hated him now. Hated him as much as Sylvia hated her own daddy. Sylvia's relationship with her own mother had always been combative, and as a result, she didn't know how to have any other type of relationship with her own child. But she tried, Lord knows she tried. Up until now, Sylvia had been grateful and proud to say that at least her daughter had Lamech, and that he was one of the good daddies. Now Sylvia's heart broke at the thought of her Bella not having anyone at all. *Maybe it's my turn. Maybe now she can choose me,* Sylvia thought, as she climbed up onto the bed with Bella and held her daughter, touched the child for the first time since everything had happened.

"Mama's here now, baby, and you don't have to say a word 'cause I already know. I know what happened. You just go on ahead and you cry. You let this out of you one good time."

She'd at least give her that. The child would go crazy if she tried to bottle this up inside.

Bella broke. The first signs of life in three days. She clung to Sylvia as if she were a rescue craft and released a deep, heavy sob. Just an eight-year-old child, but she wept like a woman who had been holding in a century's worth of pain. And Sylvia imagined that with her tears, Bella was making supplication for all the dark secrets held by so many little girls in their family. *Lord, please hear her prayer.*

"This is not the baton I wanted to hand to you." *I asked you Jesus. I begged you, didn't I?* Sylvia said as she cursed God silently inside her mind. Sylvia let her tears run down her face and comingle with her daughter's. "I'm so sorry, my sweet girl. But what I'm about to give you, it's the best mama has." Sylvia took a deep breath and began her tale. "Your father walked in on you while you were—while you started your monthly cycle. And it scared you. It's such a private moment in a young girl's life when she passes over from girlhood to adulthood that it scared you. And believe me, it's natural that you don't feel the same way about your daddy anymore."

Bella shook her head frantically as the tears ran down her checks.

"No, now Bella, it's okay. It's okay. The same thing happened to me. And God knows . . . I wish—I wish I would have been there to protect you, but from now on I will be here to protect you. I swear before God, Bella, I'm going to protect you the best way I know how. I'm going to show you how to make it through."

❧ ❧ ❧

Bella lay on her cotton candy pink canopy bed being held by her mother's monkey. Why were her parents suddenly turning into monsters? What had she done? Why wasn't God helping her? Didn't He see? Didn't He care? Suddenly, all around the room monsters began to multiply. New monsters filled the room. And they weren't afraid of her.

They didn't keep their distance. They walked right up to her and introduced themselves.

"Why hello there, Bella, my name is Shame. I do declare. If you ain't the spitting image of your great-grandmother, Elsie! I knew her very well and I can tell we're going to be fast friends too."

"Hi, my name is Subterfuge."

"I'm Insanity."

"They call me Little Lie, but it ain't true. I do big things. You hear me, Bella Rose, big things for my god! Shucks, one time, I brought down the mighty King David all by myself!"

They were surrounding her, filling every nook, cranny, corner, and crevice of her room. Bella couldn't breathe. They took away the light and blocked out the sun. Where was God? Why couldn't she breathe? Her father's monster was there. The big hairy one with the pointy hat and the funny robe was standing in the doorway. The other monsters were loud as they clamored around her room. But this one spoke in whispers.

"You asked for the fire. I heard you, little one." her father's monster said.

Bella suddenly had a memory of a visiting preacher who had spoken at their church saying you must suffer for the anointing. He said that if anyone wanted the kind of anointing that would change the world, they should ask for the fire. Seven-year-old Bella had walked up to the altar that day and asked for the fire that would change the world. Then again, in the woods, right before she laid hands on Timmy, Bella asked for the fire again.

"I DON'T WANT IT NO MORE! I DON'T WANT IT!" Bella screamed.

"I know you don't, baby," her mother's monster cooed as it rocked Bella in its' arms.

I don't want the fire anymore! It's too hot! Please, Jesus! This fire is gonna burn me up.

Present Day 2006

CHAPTER 9

It was after ten when Joshua heard the doorbell ring. He turned the television to the home security station and saw three women from Broken Vessels, the accountability circle he had required Bella to join since her return home to Houston. Joshua opened the front door. "Ladies, this really isn't the best time."

"We know and we're sorry to stop by so late and unannounced but we each got 911 texts from Bella this evening," Anna, the group's leader said.

"She reached out to you?"

After Bella had snapped out of her trance, Joshua had carried her back to bed. When he'd left her he'd thought she'd been sleeping, but apparently she was awake.

"That's right, so you might as well step out the way, Mr. Bad Boy 'cause we gon' see our sister tonight."

Joshua stared at the pint-sized spunky woman who currently had her finger trained on his chest.

Anna laid a calming hand on the woman's arm forcing the hand back down to her side. "What Sadie meant, Pastor Josh," Anna said, emphasizing the word pastor, "is that we all compared notes on the way over here tonight in the car. Bella has been heavy in each of our spirits even before she sent her text. We're glad she decided to reach out to us."

"Sister Bella is married to the pastor?" Sadie asked, looking back and forth between Jilly and Anna.

Jilly nodded. "One of them, yes."

"But this is Bad Boy Joshua Keys. You saying he's a pastor?"

"Yes. That's right, Sadie," Jilly said.

Sadie sucked her teeth. "Well, I guess there's hope for me yet, 'cause as much hell as you used to raise—"

"Sadie!" Anna gasped. "Please forgive her, Pastor Josh. She's a new convert."

Sadie nodded. "Yes, please forgive me, Pastor Josh. Sister Anna is right, I've only been saved for real for about a week. I backslid, cussed my supervisor out last week and walked off my job. Had to go back up to the altar and recommit my life to Christ again this past Sunday. So much sin inside of me, I guess Jesus didn't really take a firm hold—"

Jilly and Anna both cleared their throats.

"All I'm trying to say is that I'm sorry. When I saw Sister Bella's 911 text, that old man rose up on the inside of me. I came to your house tonight ready to bust some heads. Yours just happened to be the first I seen."

"She means in the spirit, Pastor," Jilly, added. "Busting the devil's head, figuratively . . . in the spirit." Jilly's voice trailed off.

Joshua stared down at the three woman standing on his front porch. If the situation with Bella hadn't been so serious, this exchange would have actually been comical. Bella had already regaled him with the antics of the newest member of her accountability group. According to Bella, the group had met Sadie on a ministry outreach field trip last month. Sadie had accepted Christ, joined the church and the Broken Vessels accountability group all in one day. Bella had spoken fondly of the woman, and Joshua could tell that although Bella had come to love all the members of her group, Sadie held a special place in her heart. The woman was definitely rough around the edges, but Bella was a keen discerner of character. The fact that Bella had reached out to Sadie when she was hurting spoke volumes to Joshua about the type of person Sadie really was.

Joshua let his gaze fall on the woman called Sadie. A tiny smile tugged at the corners of his mouth. "You're right, I was a hell-raiser. If God can change me, He can change anybody. Come on inside. Bella can use some friends like you."

CHAPTER 10

Bella began to cry when she saw the women from her accountability group walk through the door of the master bedroom. The three women rushed to her, flanking the large king-size bed. Bella felt the arms of many mothers holding her.

"I don't know if my child will ever speak to me again," Bella sobbed.

"Bella, you've been walking with us for quite a while now. We know you, we know your story, the beginning part at least," Anna said.

"That's right, because this is nowhere near the end. The end is going to be so much better than this, sweetie. I can promise you that," Jilly said.

"It's time, Sister Bella," Sadie said.

"Time for what?" Bella asked.

"Time for you to turn your life over to Christ and come all the way back home," Sadie said.

"I think I would really like to do that. But the only thing I can concentrate on in this moment is my son."

"Yes, but Brother Michael found him, right?" Anna asked gently. "That's what your text message said."

"Looks like God's already moving on your behalf. He answered one very important prayer today. Jabari's not lost. So let's go ahead and put first things first," Jilly said.

"Bella, are you ready to recommit your life back to Christ?" Anna asked.

Bella was quiet as she considered this for a moment. Finally, in a small voice she whispered, "I am."

CHAPTER 11

Pearl stood in the kitchen doorway at Hope House and watched her daughter prancing around the kitchen, to some hippity-hop song playing on the radio as she popped corn for her and Marcus's so-called movie marathon. Pearl knew Belinda was up to no good. The girl never paid Marcus two cents worth of attention unless she wanted something. Some days, Lord help her, Pearl wished Belinda had never been born. But then she would think about Marcus and remember that with her grandson, God had given her beauty for ashes. Out of the rubble of Belinda's life had come something wonderful and sweet. *Father, don't let Marcus be the only thing this child ever do right. Make her latter days better than her former days. Make it so, Lord. Even if I don't live to see it.*

Belinda had sent Marcus to the store and Pearl figured that now was as good of a time as any to have a confrontation.

"Marcus doesn't have any money, Belinda," Pearl said, startling Belinda as she spoke to her back.

Belinda turned to face her mother. She quickly composed herself. "Well, damn, Pearl. Can't I spend some quality time with my son without you thinking anything wrong with it?"

Pearl saw hurt reflected back in Belinda's eyes. Genuine hurt. As if the fool child didn't know what she had already made up in her mind to do. It reminded Pearl of the time that she had caught Belinda at ten years old outside letting that boy . . . *what was his name?* Terrence Richardson, dry hump her against the side of an old abandoned building. Belinda had been outraged, just like she had the nerve to be right now. Even caught in the act Belinda swore that she and Terrence wasn't doing anything wrong.

Pearl shook her head. "Sometimes I just don't understand you. If they was to look up plum fool in the dictionary there would be a picture of you sitting right there just as big as day. And it don't have to be that way either. You're a smart girl, Belinda. I don't know where I went wrong with you."

"I ain't tryin' to hear all this today, Pearl." Belinda said tapping her foot agitatedly against the linoleum as she waited for the butter she was heating in the microwave to melt.

"I took you to church every Sunday. I ate right when I was pregnant with you. I didn't drop you." Pearl had tried her best to introduce her daughter to all the finer things in life. Operas, plays, and music lessons on credit. That was about as fine as she could manage, raising her child in the Lower Ninth Ward. But no matter what Pearl did to make the grass greener for her daughter, to introduce Belinda to a better grade, a higher class, Belinda gravitated towards the gutter. She wanted concrete instead of grass.

Pearl tried a different approach. "You've been clean since we got here. Why don't you go see the counselor Nurse Monica was telling you about?"

"That's right, I have been clean. Haven't I, Pearl. So get off my back. All I want to do is spend some quality time with my son," Belinda said biting back angry tears. As always, seeing Belinda's tears both confused Pearl and caught her off guard.

"Okay, Belinda, we'll see," Pearl said quietly as she turned to leave.

"That's right, Pearl," Belinda shouted at her departing back. "We will see!"

CHAPTER 12

I can't tell you how much it means that the three of you would drop everything going on in your own lives to come over here to see about me."

"Girl please. Thanks for trusting us." Jilly had kicked off her shoes the moment she had entered the bedroom and was flanking Bella's left on the huge four-poster bed. Sadie flanked Bella's right, and Anna sat cross legged at the foot of the bed.

"How are you feeling now?" Sadie asked.

"I feel great. But truthfully, I'm still worried about Jabari. You all prayed so powerfully for me, could you please pray for my son? I know Mike found him. He's taking him to the ranch this weekend so he'll be surrounded by family and love." Unbidden tears slipped down Bella's face. "But I want to pray for his heart to stay tender. I was just a little younger than Jabari when my heart grew cold because my daddy became a monster to me. Jabari has in Joshua what I will never have, a real daddy. I don't want him to lose that because of me."

Anna gently patted Bella's feet at the bottom of the bed. "Bella, I hear you, but I have to take issue with one thing you just said. You have a daddy. A daddy who loves and hears you. I'm so sorry for the torture that you went through at the hands of the man who helped bring you into this world. I really am. But you have a Father in heaven and He is fiercely in love with you."

A new round of tears sprang forth as Bella broke down and wept.

"Anna's right, sweetie. This was not His plan for you," Jilly said. "And now that you have broken agreement with the Kingdom of Darkness, your Father is ready and waiting to recompense and resource you."

Sadie reached into her purse and pulled out a small notebook and a pen. "Now look a here sisters, y'all know I only been saved for real for about a week. So y'all gon' have to break that down for me. Recompense? What exactly is that? Is that like back pay for pain and suffering?"

"That's exactly what it is, Sadie. For every day that the enemy illegally held on to our sister's freedom she is entitled to compensation. That's why the scripture says, He'll make our latter days better than our former days and that He will restore everything the locusts and the canker worms ate away," Anna said.

"When I say, He wants to resource her, I mean that God wants to equip her with everything she needs to fight and win the battle ahead," Jilly added.

"And why would he do that?" Bella asked.

"So you can take back everything that was ever stolen from you," Jilly said.

"And so you can become a terror to the enemy who tormented and terrorized you," Anna added.

Sadie made a note in her notebook and stuck it back inside her bag. "Well, I say that for every single night you weren't safe as a child, it's time to rise up my sister and bust this devil's head till the white meat show."

All four women fell back onto the bed in a fit of giggles.

"That's a hilarious visual, but Sadie's right, Bella. It's time," Anna said, wiping tears of mirth from her eyes. "No one, and I do mean no one, has more authority over Jabari in the realm of the spirit than his parents. We will agree with you, Bella, but you have to pray."

"Me?"

"Yes you. Heaven needs to hear your sound."

CHAPTER 13

Belinda sat on the couch in the community room of Hope House stealing sidelong glances at her son. He was a good-looking kid. Just like his daddy, the finest dopeman on the block. He was one of the good ones too. Never allowed Belinda to smoke when she was pregnant with Marcus. And they lived well, until he got sent away for life. Marcus never asked about his daddy, and Belinda never saw fit to bring him up. As she stared at him, she noticed the long, now scabbed over scar on his neck, the one she'd put there the day he'd pulled her out of a crack house in New Orleans. The day they had escaped Katrina. She wouldn't even be alive if it wasn't for this boy, this son. As she studied the trajectory of the jagged scar on his neck, Belinda felt what she always felt concerning Marcus: a deep, abiding sensation of guilt. And she wished as she had a thousand times before, that the sensation would make her do right. She wished, even as she knew it wouldn't. She loved her son, but the monkey inside of her needed to be fed. That need drowned out all other feelings for Belinda. Love, fear, hunger, grief. When the monkey needed to be fed it had to be fed. Otherwise it would claw its way up out of her chest and she would die. It was as simple as that. So to hell with her mother. Pearl had no idea what it was like to be a junky.

CHAPTER 14

Bella prayed that evening with a power that was not entirely her own. Bible verses she had memorized as a child, verses she didn't even remember as an adult, poured up out of her belly and exploded off the tip of her tongue. And after the scripture came the unknown tongues. A new language surged up from her belly, one that Bella didn't even know she had. This too was something she could remember experiencing as a child. Yet somehow it was more developed, more seasoned now. It was almost like her Spirit man had picked up at age eight, where she had left off. Only she was wiser now. Stronger. This Bella had endured fire, wind, and rain. This Bella had been tested, and she'd weathered the storm.

Her eyes were open, just as they had been when she was a child. She saw herself standing before the Father. Naked but not alone. As she prayed the Father lifted His scepter and the angels came and brought her a robe. They placed it on her, and Bella felt her prayers take on new strength.

Words tumbled out of her mouth with force, speed, and authority. The angels were there again, this time giving her a crown. Now, beneath the robe, she wore polished armor as well.

The atmosphere in the room shifted as the prayers of the other women took on strength. Now Bella stood before an armory in Heaven. Two gigantic doors swung open for her, and she saw rows and rows of spiritual artillery. Bella ran down the aisles, strapping on the supernatural guns. She picked up a bow with a sheath of arrows, hand grenades, rifles, a bazooka, and a few handguns—all things she knew instinctually would help her break the curse of fatherlessness off her life.

Bella made an oath that evening. Her son was coming home. Every curse would be broken off her family lineage. They would no longer eat their seed, offer their children to Molech, or forfeit the call of God on their lives. Bella was back, and Jabari was coming home.

"My portion will not be your portion, Jabari," Bella declared solemnly. "I walked through the fire, so that you could stand on solid ground."

CHAPTER 15

Mike and Jabari pulled up to the ranch a little after ten o'clock that evening. Jabari's grandmother, Melissa Kennedy, a thin white woman with blue eyes and blond hair came running out the house first. His grandfather, Jack Kennedy, a tall thicker man, with equally pale skin and silver hair, followed closely behind her. His grandma swooped down on him like a bird of prey as soon as he got out of the car.

"Jabari, what were you thinking running off like that? You had us all worried sick," Melissa said.

"Scared shitless is what he had us," Jack exclaimed. Melissa threw Jack a look.

"It's true, my bowels haven't moved all night."

"Your grandpa does get cranky when he's constipated. Jack how many times do I have to tell you, not to talk like that in front of the children?"

"What children, Melissa? You're standing in front of two grown men. That's what my daddy would call somebody who left home on his own accord and stayed gone all night."

"Well it's late now," Melissa said, steering Jabari inside the house. "We can talk about all of this running away business in the morning."

❧ ❧ ❧

"So them rich ball players really give you a million dollars?"

Marcus looked up from the television and stared at Belinda. "What?"

"You a millionaire for real?"

"I guess."

"When you gon' break your mama off, Marcus. I ain't had no money in my hand since I got here. You around here pushing Lamborghinis and I ain't got nothing."

Marcus stared at his mother hard.

"I ain't gon' smoke it, I swear. I left that life behind in New Orleans. I've been clean ever since I got here. You know it too. That's why my behind is getting fat."

Marcus turned his attention back to the television. "You ain't fat."

"I am too. They got me in these old lady clothes. I want some fresh gear like the kind you got. But you just done went on with your life and forgot about your mama."

"Chill with that, alright? That money is in a trust. I can't touch it until I turn 21." Marcus rose to leave. "And you ain't got to worry about nothing, 'cause I'mma always take care of you."

Belinda stood too. "Wait w-w-where you going?"

"It's getting late and you ain't watching this movie no way."

"You can't go yet." Belinda pulled a DVD out of a bag on the side table. "Look what I found. Yeah, boy! I saved the best for last."

Marcus laughed. "Where'd you get this?"

The video store at the mall. I used one of the gift cards they gave us on the first day to get it. 'Cause this usta be your favorite remember?"

"Yeah. I remember."

"The way I see it, you might as well stay the night, 'cause we gon' be up all night long watching it."

CHAPTER 16

Jabari awoke in his father's childhood bedroom. Everything about the room reminded Jabari of his dad. It even smelled like his dad. Strangely, considering all the trouble Jabari was in, this was a comfort to him. He hadn't spoken to either one of his parents since he'd all-of-a-sudden up and left the house yesterday. But he figured that if his grandparents knew he'd run away, then his mom and dad had to know that he had been found.

Jabari chose a pair of jeans and a t-shirt from the pile of new clothes his uncle had left for him on the desk. He added a pair of socks, found his dad's old slippers, and padded into the kitchen. Melissa greeted him with a smile.

"You're up pretty early."

"Couldn't sleep." Jabari took a seat at the kitchen counter and rested his head on his arms.

"Nope, this is a no moping zone, buddy. I've got a better idea. Why don't you help me with breakfast?"

"What do you want me to do?"

"You can set the table."

Jabari grabbed a stack of plates out of the kitchen cabinet and begin setting the table. "Just four?"

"Just you, your uncle, Grandpa Jack and me. Why? Who else did you think was here?"

"I don't know. That guy, Stuart maybe."

"Oh, gosh, no. We haven't seen him since your mother punched his lights out and your grandpa threatened to shoot him with the shotgun."

Right after they'd come back from New Orleans

they'd come to the ranch for the weekend. Stuart had agreed to give his mom some jewelry making lessons. Some kind of way, Stuart had convinced his mom to get on Lady, his dad's old horse. Lady bolted, and his dad had to go and rescue his mom. That day Jabari thought for sure his mom was gone and that his world had changed. He thought back to the words his dad has said to him in his office yesterday. *Jabari your world has not changed.* But it had changed. If he wasn't Joshua Keys's son, then who was he? Everything he knew was a lie.

"Now I know why she punched him out. Did you know my mom's pregnant?"

"Your uncle Mikey told us."

"Did you know the baby's not my dad's?"

"Yes, Mikey told us that too."

"Did you know that I'm not my dad's?"

Melissa stared at him for a second, then asked a question of her own. "Did I ever tell you the story of how your dad came to live with us?"

"No."

"I had just buried my son, Jack Jr. He was three years old when I left the back gate open. He was a very curious boy. One day I was distracted, I thought he was taking a nap but he wasn't. He had climbed out of his playpen and made his way out into the yard. He ran out into the street and was mowed down by a truck. It took me a very long time to forgive myself. I blamed myself for a long time and then God sent me your daddy, Joshua Keys." Melissa smiled and wiped a small tear from her eye. "Your grandpa thought I needed to get out of the house. So, I started going up to the local hospital and holding the babies in the NICU ward. That's where I met your father. And boy, let me tell you. I held that little butter-colored baby boy in my arms and something inside of me just unlocked. And in that moment, I realized that what happened to Jack was a horrible, horrible, horrible, thing, but that it was not my fault. What was happening to me was so wonderful I drug your grandpa Jack up to that hospital, to hold that special little boy. He fell in love too and a few weeks later, we adopted him. Try not to hate your mother. We mothers do the best we can. My guess is she hates herself enough for the both of you. Nobody's perfect."

"Marcus said the same thing."

"That Marcus is a wise young man."

"I yelled at my dad."

Melissa waved Jabari away with her hand. "Your dad's a former hothead. He, of all people, knows you didn't mean it."

"I just don't understand why they didn't tell me."

"I think they've been thinking about how to tell you for a very long time."

Jabari shook his head. "I hear everything you're saying, Grandma Mel, but this is different. What you said about Jack, that wasn't your fault, but my mom—"

"Hey, you think it's your mother's fault that her slime bag father abused her when she was a child? Listen up, I got her back, buddy."

Jabari couldn't help but smile at his grandmother's uncharacteristic use of slang.

"I almost lost your dad, the day he told us he was going to marry your mom. You know what your mom did? She helped your dad to see the light. The women in this family stick together. We have to, there's only two of us."

CHAPTER 17

Marcus awoke fully expecting to see Belinda sleeping beside him on the couch, but she wasn't there. She was gone. Something about the silence in the community room told Marcus that she was gone, gone. Not, in the bathroom gone. Or in another part of the house gone, but gone, gone. He reached for his wallet and keys, both gone. And he knew. The first time she had left him alone he had been four.

"I'll be right back," she said. "When the big hand gets on the six. Stay right here and look at the clock. As soon as it gets on the six I'll be back."

"But where are you going?"

"I'm sick, mama needs medicine."

That was the last time she kept a promise to him. She came home just as she had said, when the big hand got to the six, but she went into the bathroom and never came out. The telephone rang and rang, and she didn't even come out to answer it. So, when their upstairs neighbor knocked on the door to say that Pearl was trying to call, Marcus picked up the phone and told his grandma that he was afraid. Then his grandpa came over and busted the bathroom door in. After that Belinda never did drugs in the house. She'd go out for an hour, which stretched into three hours, which turned into a whole day and then a week.

"Don't answer the door, and don't answer the phone."

"What if it's Grandma?"

"Then you really bet not answer the door. Don't let that woman in my house under any circumstance. You hear me?"

Marcus had lived alone in the house for a whole week before his grandparents knew his mama was strung out on drugs.

"I told you I was coming back! I told you, Marcus! Why'd you have to go and tell? See what you did!" Belinda screamed at him from across the courtroom.

Four-year-old Marcus had slid down to the floor and grabbed a hold of his grandpa's pants leg. His grandpa had patted the seat beside him. "I want you to sit back up here in this seat like a big boy. Look straight ahead and don't you pay that no mind. You did the right thing. So don't you pay that no mind." When Marcus did muster up the courage to climb up off the floor and back up into his seat, his grandpa had smiled down at him and patted his cheek.

While he was alive his grandfather had taught Marcus how to be a black man, how to live in a world that constantly robbed you of dignity, with some respect. "Don't worry about that. Don't you pay that no mind," was his favorite phrase.

And as long as the older man was alive, Marcus didn't worry too much about anything. But his grandpa was gone. Michael Dutton was here, and Marcus's crack head mama had just stolen his credit card and the keys to his car. Marcus knew he should call Jeeves or at least tell his grandmother so that they could report the car stolen, but it had been ingrained into Marcus to wait. *Don't call, don't cry for help unless things really get bad.* Right now his mama still had a chance to do the right thing. Marcus hoped and prayed that Belinda would do the right thing. So he waited.

CHAPTER 18

Mike rose from the kitchen table, and kissed his mother's forehead. "As always, Mom, the food was delicious."

Melissa smiled at Mike, then Jabari. "This is such a rare treat for us isn't it, Jack? To have our family home."

Jack grunted and grabbed another slice of bacon. "Would be better if I didn't have to wear pants."

Mike looked over at Jabari and addressed him for the first time that morning. "Speaking of pants, I see you found the clothes I left you."

"Thank you."

"You're welcome. Go put on the Timberlands and meet me outside."

"Where are you two off to so early?" Melissa asked.

"Aunt Barb's. Jabari and I are going to repair that north fence."

Jack frowned. "Coyote get at one of her calves again?"

"Two in one month. Apparently, he keeps getting in the same way. Jabari and I are gonna go check it out."

❧ ❧ ❧

Barbara squealed in delight when she opened the front door. Mike lifted the pretty petite woman off her feet into a bear hug and thought for the millionth time, how in another twenty or so years this is exactly how the love of his life would look.

Barbara cupped Jabari's face in her small hands. "Oh my, look who you brought to see me. Jabari, I know you don't remember me, baby. But I remember you. You sure have grown into a handsome young man. I'm your Aunt Barbara, your Auntie Tonya's mama."

Barbara looked at Mike. "What am I talking about? He's been gone for so long, he probably doesn't remember Tonya either. Come in off this porch and have a seat. She was mostly living overseas a lot when you were a baby."

Jabari smiled. "Actually, I do remember, Auntie Tonya, but mostly from her letters."

"What letters, baby?"

"Auntie Tonya wrote us letters while we were living in New Orleans."

Mike and Barbara exchanged a look.

"She told me lots of stories about her, my dad and Unc growing up."

"What kind of stories?" Barbara asked.

"Well, she told me that you and Grandma Mel are best friends and Grandpa Jack and her dad where best friends. That you moved to Texas to help Grandma Mel and Grandpa Jack raise my dad and Unc when you found out they had adopted two black boys. I also know that you're my dad's godmother but not Unc's, because when Unc was my age he told you and Auntie Tonya's dad that he was going to marry Auntie Tonya one day and that would be way too weird."

Barbara threw her head back and laughed. "He certainly did. Kicked us to the curb with the quickness. Jabari, your uncle sat us down and told us very respectfully that he wanted a divorce. Said he loved us, but that he couldn't see any other way around it. Jabari, I wish you could have seen our faces. Harold and I were both trying to talk him out of it, telling him that he and your auntie had a long way to go before they were marrying age and how he might as well keep us around as his godparents in the meanwhile. But he was resolute."

Katie walked into the living room and Mike rose from the couch to greet her. "Aunt Katie. When did you get back?"

"Two weeks ago. Who's this?" She asked pointing to Jabari.

Barbara patted Jabari's hand, "This is Jabari, Josh and Bella's son. Jabari, meet my sister-in-law, Katie."

Katie raised an eyebrow. "So you the one who ran away, huh?"

Jabari's face colored with embarrassment. "Yes, ma'am."

"What'd they do to you? Beat you or put you on punishment?"

"Nothing yet."

"I'll tell you one thing. In my day, kids didn't get a weekend in the country after they ran away. They got a strap to their hind quarters."

"Yes, well thankfully, Katie, times have changed," Barbara said.

Katie sucked her teeth. "They certainly have."

Mike leaned over and kissed Katie's cheek. "Jabari, Aunt Katie is your Aunt Tonya's favorite aunt, mine too."

Katie rolled her eyes. "I'm the only aunt."

"Katie, I thought you were back there playing your video games," Barbara asked.

"I beat the computer. I need fresh meat."

"You play video games?" Jabari asked.

"What's it to you?"

"Nothing, I just think it's cool."

Katie looked Jabari up and down. "What you play? Xbox or Sony."

"What you got?"

Katie winked at Mike. "Thanks to your uncle and your dad. I got everything they ever made."

"Word? That's cool."

"Say, by the way, Jabari, you don't cry do you?"

"Why would I cry?"

"Come on back, you'll see."

"Unc, can I?"

"Yeah man, for a little bit. But don't forget why we came over here in the first place."

"I know, I know, to fix the fence. This'll be quick. I'm mean seriously, Unc, how hard can it be?"

Katie cackled. "Oh, I like it when they talk tough. Barbara, where's my camera?"

"On the bookshelf where you left it."

Katie shuffled over to the shelf and picked up her camera. "I'm going to beat you so bad, Jabari. And then I'm going to take your picture for my Wall of Shame."

"Unc, am I even allowed to beat her?"

"Jabari, if I were you, I'd give it everything I've got."

Jabari walked off with Katie.

"Thanks for the history lesson. He needed that."

"Honey, please. No need to thank me. That's what family is for. Come on in this kitchen. Mel told me you were coming last night so I made a pound cake."

Michael followed Barbara into the kitchen where she cut a giant piece of cake and set it in front of him.

"Thank you."

"Michael, now you know I'm always happy whenever you stop by, but you do not have to mend that fence. We have a team of capable ranch hands to run this place, let one of them do that."

Mike shook his head.

"No, you don't think one of the ranch hands should handle this?"

"No, I can't believe all this time she knew where they were."

Barbara took a seat in the chair beside Mike and laid her hand on top of his. "Michael, you know my child better than anyone. There has to be a reasonable explanation for all of this."

"Yeah, but for five years?"

"We have to remember that Tonya's not the only one around here keeping secrets. She still has no idea about our little business arrangement."

"That's totally different and you know it."

"I do, but if she knew you were the one who kept this family afloat all of these years, that Harold's life insurance policy never paid out, she'd be angry about it just the same."

"It's that fiancé."

Barbara jumped at the sound of her sister-in-law's voice.

"He's the one got her keeping secrets. They told you she's engaged, right?"

"Yeah. I heard." Mike said dryly.

Barbara rolled her eyes and laughed nervously. "Katie, I thought you were back there playing video games with Jabari. Why you out here bringing up old stuff? That's old news, Michael knows all about that."

"Turns out my fresh meat is stale. I beat him already. He's back there studying up on his game. It's the jack-legged preacher. Got her walking around on eggshells. Now he's got her hiding stuff from the family. You know he's beating her right?"

Michael stood abruptly from the kitchen table. Knocking his chair over in the process. "What?"

"Michael, that's not true!"

"Then where is this coming from?"

"Katie, take it back!" Barbara demanded. "You know it's not true!"

"I will not! I lived with the girl for a month. I'm telling you she's in an abusive relationship."

Mike rubbed his large hands over his head and began to pace the length of the kitchen floor.

"Katie Marie Elizabeth, you don't like that boy so now you're trying to get him killed. You ain't right. Michael, sweetheart, listen to me. I've talked to Tonya, myself. I am confident that she is not in a physically abusive relationship."

Katie slapped her hand down hard on the table. "Ah ha! So you do admit that the man is abusive."

"I don't particularly care for the way he talks to her. He can be somewhat controlling, and he doesn't seem to be very supportive of her career goals, but Katie whether we like it or not, this is Tonya's choice."

"Barb, the man is downright insulting! Mark my words, if he's talking underneath her clothes today, he'll be snatching them off in public one day real soon."

"Everybody calm down, alright? Let's all just take a deep breath and relax." Barbara picked up the overturned chair off the kitchen floor. "Michael, sit back down here and eat this cake. Katie, you stop causing trouble. Tonya is fine. The day that boy tries to lay a hand on my daughter is the day— you know what, I'm not even going to put that mess in the atmosphere. You just trust and believe Harold and I did not raise a fool."

CHAPTER 19

This ain't your fault. You did the right thing. I only wish you would have told me sooner."

It was 3:00 AM the next morning when Marcus finally decided to wake his grandmother and tell her about the car. Marcus sat on the couch next to his grandma with his head tucked between his hands. This was like freaking de ja vu. This is the exact same thing she told him when she found him in their apartment alone after seven days, eating frozen peas. *You should have called me.* He was four then, he was sixteen now. How come he still didn't know any better?

"What we need to do now is contact Mr. Dutton."

"I can't face him, Grandma. What am I supposed to say?"

"Marcus, listen to me. This is gonna work out for your good. We gonna go to church this morning and give God the praise. But before we do that, I'm gonna call Mr. Dutton myself."

"Grandma, I ain't got nothing to sing about. I really messed things up bad."

Pearl stood and laid a soothing hand on her grandson's shoulder. "As long as you got breath in your body, Marcus, you got something to sing about. Besides, like I said, this ain't your fault. And it's high time you realized that your mother's problems aren't yours. It's time we both put Belinda in God's hands."

※ ※ ※

It was 4:00 AM Sunday morning, the sun wasn't even up yet, and Jabari and his uncle Mike were walking back to the car, headed back to Houston. His grandmother had rose early and made them a breakfast, and now the two of them were about to get on the road. Jabari had been bracing himself for the lecture from his uncle all weekend but it hadn't come. They'd gone fishing. No lecture. They'd repaired the fence in the north meadow together, no lecture. When he, Uncle Mike, and Grandpa Jack sat on the porch together after dinner last night, Grandpa Jack gave Jabari a big lecture, but Uncle Mike had remained quiet. Over and over again his grandpa drilled into him, doesn't matter how you got here, what matters now is that you're here. Grandpa Jack wasn't all soft touch about it either. Not like Grandma Mel had been with her story about Jack Jr. With Grandma Mel safely out of earshot next door at Auntie Barbara's house, Grandpa Jack had used every single curse word in the book and some new ones Jabari suspected he had made up on the fly.

"You think I love your dad and your uncle Mikey any less 'cause they're adopted? What kind of stupid *bleep* is that? They're my sons *bleep- bleep!* I love them, end of *bleeping* story. Just like your dad *bleeping* loves you. So what you're just finding out? Big *bleeping* deal. The way I see it, things happen the way they're supposed to happen. You're a man now. So I'm gonna tell it to ya straight. Just like my daddy would have told me. Get over it!"

Jabari and his uncle had settled themselves into the car but Uncle Mike didn't start the engine up and drive, as Jabari had hoped he would. He just sat there and stared at Jabari for a long time, until thankfully Uncle Mike's cellphone started to ring.

"Hey, Granny P, What's up?"

Jabari strained to hear the conversation on the other end. He couldn't hear a word.

"Is Marcus okay?"

Again Jabari strained to hear the response. Nothing.

"I don't really care about any of that right now Granny P. All I want to know is if Marcus is okay? Alright, then we're good. Call my guy, Jeeves. He'll handle everything. Thanks for letting me know."

Uncle Mike pushed end on the call and turned his attention back to Jabari.

"Unc, is Marcus okay?"

"He's fine, man. What about you? You have a good talk with your grandma?"

"Yeah, I did."

"I want you to know, you get a free pass this time but don't you ever do anything like this again, you understand me?"

"Yes, sir."

"I love you very much, Jabari. I hope this weekend showed you that you got a whole family full of people who love you very much."

"It did."

"Good 'cause it's time to get back. Your daddy's preaching this morning."

Jabari raised his eyebrow. "My dad, AKA, Bad Boy Joshua Keys?"

"Yep, and you don't want to miss it. It's something to see."

CHAPTER 20

Tonya stared open mouthed at the three elders seated before her. "I cannot believe that all of this has happened and no one in this family thought to call me."

Jack picked up the remote and turned off the television. "What I can't believe is how in the heck you haven't seen this. It's the hottest trending thing on social media right now. Seventy-nine million viewers around the world watched your godbrother carry Bella from the Astrodome. Not to mention that Katrina is the storm of the century."

"Jack's right, honey, we're not what you call social media buffs but even we know that. Why don't you?" Barbara said.

"I'm a dissertator, Mom. I don't follow social media. I don't have time to keep up with hurricane footage. I go to school and work, that's it. How could you guys not tell me about this?"

"Well, it has been a long time since you've been home," Melissa said.

"Three years," Jack said.

Tonya shook her head. "That's not true. I was just here for Josh's ordination."

"Which was three years ago," Barbara said. "We talk to your answering machine more than we talk to you."

"And let's face it, sweetheart, this ain't exactly the type of news you leave on an answering machine," Jack said.

"You guys call me when a cow gives birth," Tonya

sputtered.

Melissa shrugged. "Well, the birth of a calf, that you can leave on an answering machine."

Jack and Barbara both nodded in agreement.

"My godson is back, my best friend is back and not one person in this entire family thought enough about me to inform me."

Barbara rolled her eyes. "Oh, Tonya, don't be so melodramatic."

"Every time we call you're always on your way out to church or school," Melissa said.

"We were going to let it be a surprise for Christmas, but then you didn't come home," Jack said.

"One month slipped into the next," Barbara added, "and the next thing you know six months had gone by."

"Actually, Bella's about to have the baby so it's been almost nine months," Melissa corrected.

Tonya dropped down onto the couch. "There's a baby?" she whispered reverently.

"Yeah, but were not supposed to talk about that either," Jack said.

"And then there was the whole mess with Jabari running away this past weekend," Melissa said.

Tonya bolted up from the couch. "Jabari's missing?"

Jack waved her away with his hand. "He was only missing for about hour and a half before Mikey found him."

"If it had turned out to be anything more serious than that I'm sure we would have called you," Melissa added quickly.

"Mikey left for Houston this morning. You just missed them by a nose hair," Jack said.

Tonya shook her head. "This still doesn't add up. Even if none of you thought to tell me, Michael would never leave me in the dark."

Tonya watched as all three elders averted their eyes away from her at once. "Auntie Mel, why didn't Michael call me?"

"Mikey didn't take the news of your engagement so well," Melissa said.

Tonya closed her eyes while her stomach took a nose dive off a cliff. "Michael knows about my engagement? You told him?"

Melissa bit her lip nervously. "It came up in conversation."

Jack ran his hands through his hair. "Hell, we didn't know it was a secret. And we sure as hell didn't know he'd take the news the way he did. He's probably even more pissed that you didn't tell him yourself."

"Uh, you think?" Tonya said.

"Mikey took the news so hard that we decided that we wouldn't be the ones to share information between you young people anymore," Melissa said.

Barbara nodded. "Michael's been much more transparent with his feelings since he's given his life to Christ. We're not used to that. Seeing him hurting like this has been very painful for all of us."

"Yeah, so we don't talk about it. End of story," Jack said gruffly.

"Painful for you? Wow. Wow, Mom. I told you that in confidence. I can't believe you would just go blab something this sacred to, Auntie Mel. I can safely assume that's how it happened, right? You told Auntie Mel, she told Uncle Jack, and he made some glib comment about my engagement to Michael," Tonya said biting back tears.

"Now just hold on a minute, young lady," Jack said.

"No, Jack let me," Barbara said. "Tonya, first of all, you never said it was a secret, and second of all, I don't appreciate the accusation or your tone of voice. If you're grown enough to get engaged, young lady, then you ought to be grown enough to stand up under it. But no, you want to waltz in here and tell us how we should have reacted to something you didn't do right in the first place."

"What didn't I do right!"

"Honey, all of this heartache could have been avoided if you would have brought this man home and properly introduced him to your family. Your aunt Mel was there when you lost your first tooth. And when you went tinkle on the pot for the first time. So tell me, why shouldn't she know? Why shouldn't we all know? We don't know a thing about this man."

"Mom, you've met Ted! It's not like—"

"We haven't spent any time with him. I don't know a thing about his character. All we have to go by is what Katie has to say and trust me, baby, that ain't pretty."

"Katie told Mikey this guy was beating you." Jack chuckled at the panicked expression on Tonya's face. "Relax, sweetheart, your boyfriend's still alive."

"Jack, how could you be so cavalier about a topic as serious as our goddaughter's safety?" Melissa snapped.

"'Cause it's not true, Mel. If that joker was hitting her do you think Joshie would be the one trending on social media right now? Nobody would be watching, 'Joshua Keys's Passionate Plea for His Family's Return.' We'd all be watching, 'Pastor Hits Girlfriend and Draws Back a Nub.'"

You got that right, Tonya smirked. She blew out a breath. "I'm sorry. For my tone of voice and for reacting the way I did a second ago. Of course you're right, Mom. My family has every right to know about my engagement."

Barbara laid her hand on top of Tonya's. "You're making a lifelong commitment to this man, so the real question is why didn't you want the family to know?"

"You're not having cold feet are ya?" Jack asked.

More like frozen.

"It's quite alright if you are dear," Melissa added quickly. "Have you considered that this fellow may not be the one?"

Yeah, more times than I can count.

Tonya shook her head. "This has nothing to do with Ted, Auntie Mel. I just wanted . . . well what I didn't want was for Michael to find out this way. The last thing I'd ever want to do is to hurt him."

Melissa patted Tonya's hand. "Moving forward we've decided that's how we are going to deal with you kids from now on. You're all adults, so we've decided to leave it up to you to share with each other what's happening in your personal lives."

Jack and Barbara both nodded, as if the matter had been decided.

Now that you've effectively ruined my life. Great policy. Tonya was too emotionally drained to continue this conversation. "Is there anything else I should know?" Tonya asked wearily.

"Well, since we're laying everything out on the table, Mikey knows about the letters you wrote to Bella and Jabari."

"They actually got my letters?" Tonya's eyes swelled with tears again. "I think this is the first good news of the whole day."

"You didn't know?" Jack asked.

Tonya shook her head. "I got a postcard one day in the mail. It didn't have a name or return address, just a PO Box. So, I just hoped and prayed, and took a chance."

All three elders breathed a sigh of relief.

"Well," Jack said, "I'd say that's a whole lot better than the alternative."

CHAPTER 21

Joshua sat uncomfortably in his reserved spot in the pulpit. Usually he and the congregation alike looked forward to the Sundays when he would bring the message, but today was different. A little over 48 hours ago, his world had been turned upside down. Joshua listened to the choir sing from his position in the pulpit, a spot he hadn't sat in since Bella and Jabari had returned. He looked over at Bella now, and she gave him a reassuring smile. She hadn't spoken much around the house that weekend. Come to think of it, not at all since her little episode. He was actually surprised to find her dressed and ready for church this morning and drinking a cup of tea in the kitchen.

"I'm a big girl, Josh. I think I'm ready to stand up on my own." She had told him this confidently when they walked into the large auditorium that served as their church's sanctuary that morning. Much to their delight, Bella had taken her seat for the first time in the front row with the other pastors' wives, who had been eagerly awaiting her arrival.

As the worship team went forth, Joshua watched Bella singing and swaying to the music, her ease and comfortability evident. Somehow, along the way, the people of New Horizons had become something more than a group of strangers and a life that Joshua had thrusted upon her.

The First Wives Club as well as the women in Bella's accountability group, Broken Vessels, were largely responsible for the changes he saw in her and for that Joshua was grateful, but what concerned him now was Jabari.

He hadn't seen his brother or his son enter the sanctuary this morning. Of course that didn't mean they weren't there. With a membership of over two thousand people it would be almost impossible to pick them out from the crowd. The music ended and Joshua took his place at the podium and settled his notes. He felt a familiar tug in his spirit and realized that God was leading him to go a different way.

Release Jabari, Joshua. Give him to me.

It all seemed so unreal, to find his son, after five years of longing for him, only to lose him in a matter of minutes.

Release him, Joshua. Give him to me.

Joshua had heard those same words before. Only before it had been release *her*. Give *her* to me. It had taken every ounce of willpower inside of him to obey the voice that had been his constant companion since he was a child and to give up searching for his wife the last time she ran.

"Is that why you didn't come find me? Because I'm not yours?" Jabari's words from Friday night still hacked through Joshua's heart like a knife.

If I release him Lord, he could be lost to me for years again. Maybe this time forever.

Release him.

Joshua crumbled the paper that contain his sermon notes for the morning message and let it fall to the floor in an act of surrender.

⧉ ⧉ ⧉

"I had planned to come up here and talk to you this morning about service and how the service you perform for others is an act of worship to God. But there's a strong pressing in my spirit, and I feel God urging me to go a different way. So instead I'm going to talk to you today about a subject that's near and dear to both God's heart, and mine. That's adoption. If you've had the opportunity to meet my folks, you'd know, just by looking at them, that I am adopted. You see they're white, and my brother, Michael, and me are both black.

"That's exactly what Jesus did for us. He took those of us who were no kin and he made us kin. My earthly father would go to the mat for me and my brother. He even threatened to punch a reporter on my behalf once."

A half smile played across Joshua's face as he rubbed the back of his neck. "I'm sure many of you in here watched that little family drama play out live on national television."

The crowd chuckled. Many of them nodded their heads, yes, they had.

"When you adopt someone you take them in, you give them your name, you cover them, and they become yours. And in turn, you become theirs. In fact, everything you have becomes theirs. All the rights and privileges that are afforded to you, you afford those same rights and privileges to your child, your adopted. And here's the thing that I didn't know folks, the thing that it took me a long time to understand, to be adopted, means to be chosen."

Joshua paused for a second allowing his words to sink in. "I don't know about you, but I'm so glad I'm adopted. Every last one of us who makes Jesus our Lord and savior can say that. We're all adopted."

All over the sanctuary, church members stood to their feet, shouting their agreement and clapping their hands.

Joshua paused again, allowing the crowd to take a moment to settle down. "Adopted kids often struggle with abandonment issues and rejection. They battle with feelings of unworthiness, feelings of bitterness, self-loathing and rage. I know because I was adopted into a good, loving, Christian home just days after my birth and still, for the majority of my life, I struggled with many of these same things. I had been adopted, but I still didn't know that I had been chosen. The battle raging inside of me made me want to fight. All throughout grade school, high school, and college I fought. If anyone got in my face, if they said or did something that I didn't like, I'd fight. Then I became a point guard in the NBA. Success didn't strip away the desire to fight, it only gave me more opportunities and a bigger platform to fight on. Most of you know that after my retirement from professional ball, they retired my jersey and I was inducted into the Hall of Fame."

Houston Rockets fans all over the sanctuary stood and hooted for their newest associate pastor. Bishop Micah Ford and the other associate pastors seated behind Joshua in the pulpit stood to their feet as well. Bishop Ford, Pastor Darren, and Pastor Keith pumped their fists excitedly in the air, while Pastors Carlos and Dave began to do a dance that looked to be a cross between a church shouting dance and the funky chicken. The musicians began to play back up as the two pastors danced and the congregation roared with laughter.

Joshua turned and spoke to the pastors behind him. "Alright, alright, sit back down you clowns."

The music stopped in a flourish, and the crowd laughed some more.

"We got the Houston Rockets Power Dancers up here, y'all. Pastor Carlos, Pastor Dave, I'm going to remember that the next time you two preach. Pastor Dave, if my memory serves me correctly, next week is Youth Sunday and you'll be preaching."

All the young people in the audience shouted and clapped.

Joshua nodded. "That's right give it up for your youth pastor, Pastor Dave. But I know one thing. He'd better grow some eyes in the back of his head between now and next Sunday, 'cause I'm telling you, it's on."

The crowd roared with laughter.

Joshua chuckled. "What was I saying before the halftime show began?"

"They retired your jersey!" someone called.

"You were the youngest player to ever be inducted into the Hall of Fame!" someone else called.

Joshua nodded. "That's right, most people know that. But what they don't know is that I also have more fines and lawsuits than anyone else in the history of the NBA. My brother, Michael Dutton, AKA, the Man of Steel, and fellow hall of famer himself—"

More hoots went up from the crowd as they cheered for Mike. The camera operator located Mike in the huge auditorium and flashed his picture up on the big screen. Mike, who had been engrossed in the sermon, gave a nod and a wave toward the audience as the congregation turned their attention towards him.

"My brother, Michael Dutton, negotiated countless settlement agreements on my behalf," Joshua continued. "He paid millions of dollars in legal fees, and even went so far as to establish a legal defense fund on my behalf, which my family jokingly referred to as the punch fund." Joshua shook his head. "And I can't even stand up here and say that this was pre-salvation y'all. I had accepted Jesus Christ into my heart as a child. But I was still living like the world long after I came into the Kingdom because I was adopted, but I didn't know I had been chosen. I'd like to make two altar calls this morning. The first call I'd like to make is to those who have never made a personal commitment to

Jesus Christ. Perhaps you're tired of doing this thing called life alone, and you want to be adopted into the family of God. My next call is to those of you who have already made a personal commitment to him, the already adopted. Maybe some of you out there are living like I was. You know you've been adopted, know you've been bought with a price, but you still haven't wrapped your mind around the fact that to be adopted means to be chosen. Maybe you're still fighting, still trying to prove yourself, still trying to measure up. If that's you, I'd like you to come to the altar this morning and embrace your chosen identity. Myself and the other pastors and ministers here are waiting to pray for you. If my call is for you today, please come."

One by one people started coming down the aisles, responding to Joshua's call. Some making a commitment to Christ. Others embracing their chosen identity as the adopted. Joshua and the ministerial staff of New Horizons Christian Training Center prayed for and spoke into the lives of every single one.

"Joshua, look." Dave, who was standing beside Joshua at the altar, motioned toward Jabari making his way down the center aisle. "Praise you, God. Thank you, Jesus!" Dave exclaimed.

Jabari came and stood directly in front of the two men. "Dad, Pastor Dave? Can I have prayer for both? I need to accept Jesus and the fact that I'm adopted."

Both men stared at Jabari with tears in their eyes. "You certainly can, son. You certainly can," Joshua said as he pulled Jabari into a tight hug. Bella stood when she saw Jabari up at the altar. Joshua motioned for her to come forward and join the circle as Dave lead Jabari in the sinner's prayer. Afterwards, Joshua prayed over Jabari that he would accept his chosen identity as the adopted. "That took so much courage, man. I'm proud of you," Joshua said as he hugged Jabari one last time.

Jabari hugged Bella next, squeezing her around her waist. "I'm sorry for running away and for all those things I said to you."

"Hush, now, it's okay," Bella said through her own tears.

Joshua took his place back up at the podium and addressed the congregation. "Today is one of the happiest days of my life. Many of you know that for five long years my son and wife were lost to me. Many people right here in this room, fasted and prayed with me for their safe return. You were there to celebrate with me when God brought my wife and my son safely out of Hurricane Katrina. I think it's only fitting that you celebrate with me now. My son just gave his life to Christ."

The crowd was up on their feet clapping and praising.

"I'm having a banquet at my home today, to celebrate Jabari's coming into the Kingdom, and you're all invited."

CHAPTER 22

Keith clasped Joshua on the shoulder when he took his seat in the pulpit with the other pastors. "Well it's been real nice knowing ya, buddy."

Joshua smiled. "What are you talking about?"

Dave threw his head back and laughed. "Is he serious?"

"Man, you just invited the whole church to your house this afternoon for dinner. All 2000 of them, bro," Darren said.

"Correction. He invited them to her house," Keith said and nodded towards Bella seated in the front row.

"I mean I know you're loaded, Josh, but I'm pretty sure that even rich guys have to give their wives advance notice before they invite that many people to their home," Carlos said.

"Yeah, like two years' notice," Dave scoffed.

"Bella's going to kill you," Carlos said.

Bella. Truthfully Joshua hadn't considered Bella and how she would feel with having such a large number of people in her house. Church family or not. Joshua took in the facial expressions of the other pastors in the pulpit. Even Micah, the picture of optimism, looked worried.

"Don't look now, buddy, but Dee's throwing daggers your way and it's not even her house," Keith said.

Nope, definitely don't look in the wives' direction. Joshua would play it cool and deal with Bella after service.

"You know, Joshua, it's not too late to change the venue. We could have Jabari's party here in the Fellowship Center," Micah said.

Joshua shook his head, "Naw, I got this, but thanks. Are we going to throw a party for every single person who gives their lives to Christ? Because that's what we'd have to do if we did this on church grounds. It'll be fine. I've got a big enough backyard for something like this. The weather's been nice, we'll have it outside. We can handle it."

"Famous last words," Carlos said.

Joshua felt his cell phone buzzing in his inside jacket pocket. He took it out and read the text.

"Let me guess, that's Bella. It says, 'sleep with one eye open tonight.' Right?"

Joshua grinned at Keith. "It's my secretary, Selena. She's just texting me to let me know we got this."

After the offering, Bishop Micah Ford stood at the podium to do the benediction.

"Normally, I don't do the benediction when it's not my Sunday to preach, but I was just so struck by Pastor Keys's generous offer. I want to talk to us for a minute because we're family. Pastor Keys and his wife have just very generously opened up their home for a party after church. Now I want us to be family, but let's not forget that we are also the Church. Let's behave with the upmost decency and decorum at our brother and sister's home. Not like fans. Amen."

Handclaps of agreement went up from the entire congregation.

"Now if you are planning to attend, the information for the party, as well as ticket badges, will be available at the Information Center. Where is the information for the party?"

In one unified voice the church called back, "At the Information Center."

"Don't ask Pastor Keys any details about the party, do not ask Sister Bella Keys any details about the party. Go to the Information Center after service. You must go to the Information Center if you are planning to attend the party.

Don't Google Pastor Keys's address and show up because you will not get in. There's a whole process in place to make sure this event runs decently and in order. Let's do this right, people of God. We want to be invited back. We love our newest pastor and his beautiful family, don't we?"

Many of the members stood to their feet and clapped. Micah waited for them to settle before he continued.

"The life of a professional athlete is tough. Especially for one that is constantly in the limelight. It takes a toll on you. So the last thing we want to do is to go over there and act like star-struck fans. As my dear friend and brother in Christ, Michael Dutton, once aptly explained it to me, it's like living your life in a fishbowl. After a while people forget that you are human and entitled to a life of privacy. Thankfully the weather has been unseasonably warm for this time a year. I am told that this is an outdoor party and that everything we need, including some very high-end portable bathroom facilities will be outside.

❦ ❦ ❦

Joshua stepped out of the pulpit. He greeted a few parishioners then made his way over to Bella. He ignored the glares of the other wives and pulled Bella up from her seat into his embrace. "I missed sitting beside you in service today."

"Did you really now? You looked so comfortable up there I hadn't noticed," Bella said, fiddling with his tie. "This suits you, Josh. You did a great job. I just have one question for you."

"What's that, Beautiful?"

"Did you *really* just invite the whole church to our home?"

Joshua chuckled and pulled her in closer. "I'm sorry. I should have checked with you first. I just got so hyped when Jabari gave his life to Christ. You won't have

71

to do a thing. We're having it catered. Selena's already on it. She sent me a text a few minutes ago. A company is delivering grills to the house as we speak."

The smile slid off Bella's face and a sour taste seeped into her mouth as the understanding dawned on her, that his impromptu invitation to the church extended also to Selena.

"Bella, are you mad at me?"

You mean mad that you're clueless enough to have that shady secretary of yours do anything, in, around, or within the general vicinity of our house? A whole afternoon with Selena, yeah, you bet, I'm mad. Under normal circumstances she would have told him exactly what she was thinking, but a peace had come over her since she'd prayed with the ladies from her accountability group on Friday. And Bella was not about to waste that peace on Selena Mason. So instead she replied with, "Your heart was in the right place, Josh, besides, I can't stay mad at you."

He grinned a beautiful lopsided grin down at her and Bella found herself blushing at the heat of his gaze.

Bella cleared her throat. "Just tell me how I can help?"

"By staying off your feet as much as possible this afternoon and letting Selena run with this."

CHAPTER 23

Man you were right, your secretary handled everything. I even had to sign a waiver saying I wouldn't upload any pictures from this event to any social media sites," Carlos said as he, Joshua and the other pastors from New Horizons stood outside in Joshua's backyard talking by the pool.

"Everyone seems to be having a grand time and behaving themselves," Micah said.

Keith raised his glass in salute to Joshua, "You're still alive so I guess that means Bella didn't totally blow her lid."

"Bella was real cool about it." *Almost too cool*, Joshua thought. "But you're right Los, Selena did go above and beyond on this. I'mma have to give her a raise."

A brunette server in her mid twenties approached the men. "Gentlemen, can I take your plates?"

"Please do," Miach said handing the woman his empty plate.

"Is there anything else I can get you? Shall I refresh your drinks?"

"I'll take my drink refreshed if you don't mind," Carlos said.

The woman took Carlos's glass and walked away.

"Thanks, Sarah," Joshua called to the woman's back.

She smiled over her shoulder. "My pleasure, Mr. Keys."

Keith rolled his eyes at Carlos. "You'll take your drink refreshed?"

"Her words man not mine. I know how to act. When I'm in Rome I do like the Romans do, okay?"

All the men laughed.

"So Josh, what's it like having all these people wait on you every day hand and foot?" Dave asked.

Joshua shook his head. "I wouldn't know. I don't have staff. I got a cleaning lady who cooks."

"So where did all these uniformed people come from?" Carlos asked motioning to the staff moving throughout the party. "And the one who just left, I didn't see a name tag but you knew her name."

"Selena couldn't find a catering company who could staff this type of gathering on short notice so Mike's house manager sent over his people."

"Hey, I met that guy. He's like a black, Englishman or something. Name's Geoffrey, right?" Dave said.

"Jeeves," Joshua corrected. "And he's Moroccan. Mike's propety is much bigger than mine and requires a lot more maintenance. Jeeves keeps everything on point and makes sure that happens."

"At least we got to keep our cameras at your place. At your brother's house the first thing the security team did was confiscate our cell phones," Keith said.

Joshua nodded. "That's why you've never seen pictures of the inside of my brother's house splashed across the pages of some magazine or any place else for that matter. Jeeves makes sure that won't ever happen."

Micah lifted his glass of root beer in the air. "Thank God for Jeeves."

ᴥ ᴥ ᴥ

Mike led Pearl into the large covered tent that had been erected on Joshua's property and pulled a seat out for her.

"I take it you haven't seen Marcus since you've been back, have you?" Pearl asked.

"No ma'am, I haven't."

"I suspect he may be avoiding you. Marcus is really broken up about the car. He can hardly face you. I know that grandson of mine well enough to know that he's angry with himself. He knows he should have told you right away. When he first found out that the car was missing—"

"But he thought she was coming back. Or at least he hoped she was."

Pearl stared at Mike like she was looking into his soul. "What you know about this?"

"Unfortunately, Granny P, my birth mother is an addict so I know a whole lot about it."

"Humpf, I know a whole lot 'bout it too, so I hope you don't think any less of me when I tell you that you should press charges."

Mike stared at her. "She stole a twenty-seven-million-dollar car. Trust me, I'm pressing charges. But I'd much rather see her in somebody's rehab program as opposed to prison."

"Sometimes hitting rock bottom is the only way up," Pearl said.

"Listen, Granny P, I'm not blaming Marcus or you for any of this. In fact, I want to talk to you about something I've been thinking about for a while now. Today's message just confirmed it in my spirit."

Pearl clapped her hands together. "That was a beautiful message, wasn't it?"

Mike grinned. "Every single time my little brother brings it."

Pearl reached across the table and grabbed Mike's hand. "Your brother's a good man, Michael. So are you."

"That does my heart good to know you think well of me. Especially in light of what I want to ask you. With your blessing, and permission, I'd like very much to adopt Marcus and raise him as my son."

Pearl sat back quietly in her chair. Then the tears began to fall.

"I don't know if these are good tears or bad tears. Talk to me, Granny P," Mike said quietly.

"These are happy tears, Michael. That's the best piece of news these ears have heard in a long time. I've been praying and asking God who will love my child when I'm dead and gone from this Earth."

Mike's dark, handsome face broke out into a smile. "Two things, Granny P. Number one, you gon' be on the Earth, as you put it, for a long time. You might outlive us all. And number two, I'm glad you feeling this whole adoption thing because the truth is, I've never had a grandmother and I'd like to adopt you too."

CHAPTER 24

Bella opened the front door and let out an ear-piercing scream. Joshua and Jabari, who were both out back talking with guests, stopped their conversations mid-sentence and ran inside the house. They found Bella in the foyer, she and Tonya wrapped tightly in each other's embrace. Both women were crying softly.

"Surprise," Melissa said, opening up her arms wide for Jabari.

Jabari ran to his grandmother and gave her a hug. "This is a surprise. I just saw you this morning."

"I know, sweetie. But when I heard that you gave your life to Christ, well, I just had to be here to celebrate with you."

"Let me guess, Dad live-streamed the service this morning?" Joshua said as he closed the front door that had been left ajar. "Let's take this somewhere private. You two can walk and hug," Joshua said as he ushered the small group into the private parlor directly across from the foyer.

"We always live-stream when you preach. Your father loves it. He says it's the only time he gets to go to church in his underwear."

Melissa sat down on the love seat in the parlor and motioned for Jabari to sit down beside her. "Jabari, your grandpa and I are so proud of you. He wanted to be here too but, wouldn't you know it a horse went into labor."

"Which one?"

"Missy Ann."

"Cool."

Melissa rose from the couch and greeted her son.

"Mom, always good to see you," Joshua said enfolding his mother into his arms. His eyes flew over to Tonya and Bella still wrapped tightly together. "This is quite the surprise."

Melissa's bright cornflower blue eyes sparkled as she looked into her son's eyes.

"I think I've been praying for Tonya's return about as hard as I have been for Bella's. And out of the blue, she just shows up at Barb's this morning, saying that she felt a strong press in her spirit telling her to get home. Now would you believe that's exactly what I asked God to do? Put a press in her spirit that she couldn't ignore. Isn't it wonderful, Joshie? God is restoring to this family everything that the locust and the cankerworm have eaten away."

Joshua studied his mother, "It is wonderful. I just hope you're not interfering."

Melissa brushed a wisp of hair out of her face, "I have no idea what you mean. Tonya is Jabari's godmother, besides, it's no crime for me to want to see both of my boys happy."

Joshua turned his attention to Tonya and Bella. "Alright you two, break it up. That's got to be the longest hug in the world. Tonya get over here and show me some love."

Tonya and Bella both laughed as they released each other and wiped away tears.

Joshua pulled Tonya close and kissed the top of her hair. "Welcome home, stranger."

"Feels good to be back."

Joshua held Tonya at arm's length and studied her carefully.

"Isn't she stunning, Joshie?" Melissa asked.

"Girlfriend, I am loving this new look," Bella said. "It's like you stepped right out of the pages of Cosmo magazine."

Tonya was stunning. But this was not the type of beauty Joshua was used to seeing on his God sister. Her natural curls had been pressed bone straight and hung loose around her nut-brown face. Her clothes were stylish and appropriate for a young Christian woman, but the soft material followed the path of her shapely frame.

As a child, Tonya had been a remarkable beauty. The kind that made grown men stare and young men lose their minds. On several occasions, Joshua's fist had been introduced to many of these faces—young and old. The only saving grace back then was that Tonya wasn't self-aware. Not in the way that this very confident, cosmopolitan woman standing before him now was. Joshua suspected that if his god sister had known then what she clearly knew about herself now, growing up, he might have caught a case. "Were it not for the grace of God, there go I," Joshua muttered.

"Josh, it's okay, you can tell me if you hate it."

"I don't. You're gorgeous. You've always been gorgeous. I'm just wondering how much of this is you, or somebody else's idea of you."

Tonya laughed. "Josh, it's me. This is just New York me."

"Okay, New York. Just try and remember that I'm a man of the cloth now. Don't make me have to hurt nobody while your home."

Bella looped her arm through Tonya's. "He's kidding."

"I'm not." Joshua said quickly. He motioned to Jabari who was sitting beside his mom on the couch. "Jabari, I want to re-introduce you to someone very dear to me."

"Auntie Tonya. I know who you are," Jabari said standing to hug Tonya.

Tonya squeezed Jabari tightly. "You were such a little guy when I last saw you. I can hardly believe that you remember me." Tonya's eyes filled with a fresh set of tears.

"Uncle Mike showed me pictures, but I remember you most from your letters."

Joshua's eyes flew to Bella.

Later, she mouthed.

Now, his mouth formed back.

Joshua grabbed Bella's hand and pulled her into the adjacent dining room.

"Mel, Tonya, excuse us for a quick second," Bella called over her shoulder.

Joshua folded his arms across his chest. The expression on his face clearly said talk.

"Okay, so the last time I ran I got a PO box," Bella said quietly so that the others in the next room couldn't hear her. "I took a chance and sent the address to Tonya, only I never told her that it was from me. I checked it every three months or so. I never wrote back, but whenever I checked the box there was always a letter in there from Tonya to Jabari and me."

Joshua was silent for what seemed like an eternity while Bella held her breath.

"Anybody else in my family know about this secret PO box?" he finally asked.

"No."

"Why not?"

"I couldn't trust anybody else not to tell you. Joshua, please don't be mad at Tonya."

"I'm not mad at Tonya."

Bella dropped her eyes sheepishly to the floor. "Are you mad at me?"

"Yes."

Joshua lifted her chin carefully causing her eyes to meet his. "But I forgive you. I think your heart was in the right place when you reached out to Tonya. His fingers slowly traced the outline of her lips. "Besides, it's pretty hard for me to stay angry with you." He was leaning in to kiss her when the door opened.

"There you are. I was running around checking on things when I heard the commotion. Someone mentioned that you were having some type of reunion out here."

"It's a family reunion." Bella turned to face Selena. "My sister-in-law just arrived into town."

Joshua leaned into Bella and whispered in her ear. "Be nice."

"Is Tonya not your sister?"

"The only one I got." Joshua said smiling at Tonya over Bella's shoulders.

Selena's eyes followed Joshua's line of vision. She walked into the adjacent parlor.

"Melissa, it's good to see you again."

Melissa shook Selena's hand politely. "Hello, Selena."

"Someone fill me in. I thought it was just the two of you. I didn't know you had any more siblings." Selena's eyes moved from Tonya to Joshua, then back to Tonya, "Are you an orphan too?"

Bella spoke up. "Tonya is Mike's—"

"Old news," Tonya said extending her hand to Selena. "Tonya Malone."

Selena hesitated. Tonya's hand hung awkwardly in the air several moments before Selena shook it weakly.

Tonya seemed to take the snub in stride. "Where is Michael?"

"I don't think he's arrived yet actually," Selena said, flipping her waist-length hair over her shoulder. "He went to get Jabari a gift."

Tonya scrunched up her nose. "Who gives gifts for coming to Christ?"

Bella and Tonya looked at each other and spoke in unison. "Rich people."

"Jabari, I didn't bring gifts this time, sweetie, just my love."

"You are the gift, Auntie Tonya."

"Oh, aren't you sweet," Selena murmured.

"Unc is going to be so happy to see you."

Tonya lifted her eyebrows. "We'll just have to wait and see about that."

"Any particular reason why he'd be happy to see you?" Selena asked.

Tonya slowly took Selena in as if seeing her for the first time. "I'm sorry I didn't catch your name."

"I'm Selena Mason."

"Selena is Joshua's secretary," Bella said.

"Who is also with Mike," Selena added firmly.

"Well you can put your claws up girlfriend. As I said, I'm old news."

There was a knock on the door. Melissa's face lit up when she noticed Marcus standing in the doorway.

"Marcus, sweetie come in," Melissa said, rushing to embrace the young man. "Tonya, this is the amazing young man I was telling you about."

"Hi everybody. I didn't mean to interrupt."

"Naw, you good, man," Joshua said. "Did you eat?"

"No, sir, not yet. I was hoping I could talk to you privately about something first."

"Yeah, sure. Let's take a walk down to my office." Joshua paused for a moment to look first at Selena, then Bella, then Tonya. "Uh, Mom—"

"We'll be fine, sweetie," Melissa said smoothly.

Bella flashed him a wicked grin as he walked past her. "That's right, sweetie, we got this."

CHAPTER 25

Marcus took a seat on the wine-colored leather sofa in Joshua's office while Joshua perched himself on the edge of his desk. "What's up, Marcus, what can I do for you?"

Marcus studied his hands for a long time before he spoke. "I'm in trouble. I need the money in the trust. The one million dollars y'all offered me."

"Why would you need that kind of money?"

"It's for my mom. I mean the car. The Steelmobile. I hung out with my mom Friday night. She stole the keys, I haven't seen her since."

Joshua watched the youth brace himself for his reaction. No doubt he was expecting something classically Bad Boy. It had taken a lot for Marcus to come to him, Joshua knew, and he would do his best to put the young man at ease. Joshua opened the door to the mini refrigerator, retrieved two bottles of root beer, and handed one to Marcus.

Marcus mumbled his thanks.

"I don't know if I ever told you this, but I appreciate everything you did to get my family out of New Orleans safely. In my book that makes us family. So, I want you to know you can always come to me, no matter what. Just shoot straight with me."

Marcus stared up at him. "So, you gon' give me the money?"

"I think you need to have a conversation with my brother first."

"If it's all the same to you, I'd like to have the money in my hand when I do."

"The money is locked away in a trust until you turn twenty-one. Mike is the executor of that trust. Either way you slice it, you gotta go through him."

"You could loan me the money," Marcus pleaded. "I'd pay it back when the trust paid out. I swear."

"I could, but I won't. Besides, the money you're asking for couldn't even begin to pay for that car. Like I said, you need to have a conversation with Mike."

"What am I supposed to say? Your car is gone. My crackhead mama had it chopped up for drugs."

Joshua popped the top on the root beer and took a long drink. The reality was that Belinda would be hard pressed to find a criminal in the tri-state area that would be willing to chop up the Man of Steel's car. Mike had fans everywhere and they all knew the Steelmobile. Once the car was reported stolen, and Joshua was sure that Jeeves had already reported it stolen, it would only be a matter of time before it would be returned, unmolested. And if Belinda was found anywhere in the vicinity of the car when it was found, she'd be taken into custody too. But Joshua saw no need in telling the already distraught youth this.

"He loves that car," Marcus said.

"Marcus, he likes the car. A lot. But the fact that he's let you drive it since you've come to Houston tells me more about how he feels about you. Real talk, man, he don't even let me drive it."

Marcus looked momentarily shocked. "For real?"

Joshua grinned. "For real. I can ride in it. But I ain't trying to be the Man of Steel's trusty side kick, you feel me?"

Marcus smiled. "Yeah, I feel you."

"Marcus, I can tell you've had to be responsible for a whole lot of things for the majority of your life. This is a bind. It's a terrible situation to be in, but it's not your fault. And since it's not your fault, it's not your responsibility to fix it."

Joshua pulled his buzzing cell phone from his back pocket and looked down at the screen. It was a text from his brother.

Where you at?

In my office. Talking to Marcus. Joshua typed back quickly. Joshua grinned at his brother's response.

Tell him I'll be down in a minute. I'mma go ahead and adopt Marcus. You ready to be a Godfather?

You know it, baby! Joshua typed back. *Besides, it's about time you made me an uncle.*

"What if he thinks I had something to do with this? The last thing I want is for him to think that I set him up. I mean it's like ever since I came to Houston, he's been like a father to me. I would never do that. Know what I mean?"

Joshua sat his phone down on his desk and turned his attention back to the conversation at hand. "I believe you. And if you give it to him straight just like you did here with me, my brother will believe you too. That was him on the phone, so I want you to take a minute and get yourself together. He's on his way."

❧ ❧ ❧

Joshua was leaning up against the wall outside his office waiting when his brother walked up. "We got a situation."

"Granny P already told me about the car. It's cool."

"I ain't talkin' about the car, man. Tonya's here."

Mike raised an eyebrow. "Tonya who?"

"Tonya, Tonya."

"Where?"

"She was in the parlor with Mom and Bella a few minutes ago, about to go toe-to-toe with Selena."

"Thanks for the heads up."

Joshua slapped his brother's back. "You took the news about the car better."

"It's cool. I'm the Man of Steel, right?"

"You know it, baby. You got this."

Mike lifted his chin in the direction of Joshua's office door. "He scared?"

"Terrified."

"'Member that time you crashed dad's truck?"

Joshua nodded. "I thought they were gon' send me back for sure."

"That was the day you learned that family is for life. Now it's Marcus's turn. Do me a favor. Find the women and run a little interference for me."

CHAPTER 26

Marcus stood when the door to Joshua's study opened. The imposing figure of his idol, Michael Dutton, AKA, the Man of Steel, loomed in the doorway. Marcus took in his face. It was always hard to gauge where the famous, former, ball player was. The only thing you had to go on were his words. Most days Marcus liked that about him. With Mike, life wasn't complicated. He didn't say one thing and mean another. He didn't say, "I'll be back when the big hand gets on the six," and never show up at all. He didn't try and butter you up with some corny movie and tired line about wanting to spend time with you and then take off with your wallet and keys. Mike wasn't smiling. But then again, he wasn't frowning either. If Marcus had to guess, he would say that the former ball player looked relaxed. Which made absolutely no sense considering the situation at hand. He certainly didn't look like a person who knew that their twenty-seven-million-dollar car had been jacked. *She must not have told him.* Marcus knew it was a coward's way out, but he had hoped that his grandma would have told him about the car when she called. Apparently, she hadn't. 'Cause given the circumstances, even for the Man of Steel, this was just too damn cool. Mike walked into the room and shut the door behind him. The first words out his mouth almost knocked Marcus off his feet.

"It's cool, Marcus. Granny P already told me about the car."

"Ain't nothing about this cool. You love that car."

Mike shook his head. "Marcus, I like the car, but I

don't love it. I learned a long time ago not to fall in love with things. Things can be replaced. People are a different story. When Granny P called this morning, the only concern I had was for you. How I would feel if I lost you. What I would do to the person who'd ever be foolish enough to harm you over that dumb car. The car is replaceable, Marcus. You aren't. So I want you to know, when it comes down to it, I don't give a damn about the car. You're like a son to me. Do you understand that? You are irreplaceable to me. That's why I spoke to Granny P a few minutes ago about making this living situation thing we got going permanent."

Marcus finally found the courage to meet Mike's eyes.

"I'd really like to be your dad, if you'll have me."

Marcus felt the wetness on his cheeks before he realized that he was crying. He couldn't remember the last time he cried. He didn't really know why he was crying now. Not really. Except that every single prayer he had never dared to pray had just been answered in this moment. Mike's words felt like a giant crowbar lifting a huge weight Marcus didn't even know he'd had from his chest. As the weight lifted from him, Marcus realized that he'd been holding his breath. Not just during this conversation but for the last sixteen years of his life.

Mike studied the young man standing in front of him. "Talk to me, Marcus. Where are you?"

"I never met my father. He went to prison before I was born. Never wrote, called, nothing. My grandpa told me that guys in lockdown do that to survive, close off the outside world." Marcus shrugged. "He told me not to sweat it, and I didn't. Not for a long time 'cause when I was a kid, I used to pretend that you were my real dad. I even got a little play at my old high school 'cause the girls thought I could ball and that I looked like you." Marcus's voice broke as the sob he had been holding back threatened to break forth from his chest.

"Come here," Mike said quietly as he reached out and pulled Marcus into his embrace. "I know you were looking forward to spending time with your mom. I'm sorry she disappointed you."

The sob broke free, forcing itself from Marcus's chest and out of his throat. Mike held on to him, anchoring him while he cried.

"No shame in that. Go ahead. Let it out."

The noisy sobs racked Marcus's body, and Mike held on. "Let it out," he crooned softly. "Let it out."

So he did and this time when he cried, Marcus understood why. He cried for the little boy who never had a father. The one who had lost his grandpa way too soon, the one who had been left alone for seven days straight, the one who couldn't tell anyone about it because it was his job to protect. Marcus thought about all of this as he cried.

"I need you to do me a favor and let this go." Mike spoke quietly into his ear, "It's not yours. Not anymore. I'm here now and you've got a new story. So you let this go."

At Mike's command, Marcus did. He let it all go, and for the first time in his life Marcus felt . . . free. Mike held on long after the tears had subsided. The tears had left Marcus weak, spent, like a wrung-out dishrag, but Mike held on to him until strength and peace returned to his bones.

"You good?" Mike asked studying the young man's face when he finally pulled away.

Marcus ran his hands over his face and cleared his throat. "Yeah, I'm straight."

Marcus watched the corners of Mike's lips turn up into a slight smile.

"What?"

"Naw, I was just thinking that you do kind of look like me."

Marcus beamed with pride. "I know I do."

Mike palmed Marcus's head playfully.

"Yeah, but don't get it twisted, son. You got a long way to go before you look this fly."

CHAPTER 27

Tonya followed Bella up the long winding staircase that lead to the house's third floor.

"Oh my gosh, Bella, this room is amazing," Tonya said when she stepped inside Bella's art studio.

"This was Joshua's Christmas present to me."

Tonya stared down at the stained wood floor. Each plank was stained a different pastel color. "I love these colors."

"I knew you would. I remembered how you decorated your cottage."

Tonya groaned. "I miss my colorful cottage." The two women curled up on the lime green leather sofa.

"We have so much catching up to do I don't even know where to begin. I guess I should start with thank you, for the letters. They really helped Jabari know that no matter where we were in the world he had a family who loved him."

"Girl, please, those letters helped me. When you left, those letters were a part of my faith walk. As long as I could write them I could hope and trust that the two of you would be alright."

Bella squeezed her eyes shut. "Stop. No more tears, okay? I don't think I can take it. Tell me about New York."

"Well in a few more months, I'll be graduating with my PhD."

Bella squealed with delight. "What are your plans? Tell me what are you going to do!"

"Well, for right now I'm going to continue working at my church. I'm the director of the children's ministry. My fiancé, Ted, who is also the senior pastor, doesn't agree with my professional goals. He doesn't see why I need a doctorate to run the children's ministry at our church."

"It's what you've wanted since I met you. I'm glad you didn't let anything, or anyone stop you from reaching your goals."

Tonya raised her eyebrows at Bella. "You've certainly mellowed out over these last five years. The Bella I know would have told me to drop the zero and find myself a hero." Tonya snapped her fingers to illustrate her point.

Bella shook her head. "Honey, I am in no condition to give relationship advice these days. Not that I ever was. Tonya, you should know that Joshua and my situation is temporary. This is not Joshua's baby. I found out I was pregnant shortly after I returned from New Orleans. He has agreed to let me stay here until the baby is born but he's made it very clear, this time he wants a divorce."

"But Bella, he's still touching you. You've been gone for five years but it's like no time at all has passed between you. He can't keep his hands off of you."

"That's what our public life looks like now. In public we touch. We pretend to be happy. In private we become polar opposites. I've spoken to Mike already. No matter what happens between the two of us, he's agreed to be the baby's godfather. I was hoping you'd agree to be god mommy."

Tonya reached over and hugged Bella tightly, "You don't even have to ask."

Jabari knocked on the open door and then peaked his head inside. "There you are, Auntie Tonya. Did you come to see me or to gab it up with my mom all day?"

"Listen to him. I came to see you, of course, sweetie."

"Good, 'cause I want to introduce you to some of my friends."

"And I want to meet them. So lead the way. Bella we'll have to pick this conversation up later. My god mommy duties call," Tonya said as she allowed Jabari to lead her out of the room.

❀ ❀ ❀

Joshua stood outside watching some of the children from his church laughing together as they played in the pool. Anna Parks walked up and stood beside him. "You know, I don't think I've ever seen you this happy."

Joshua smiled. "I've got a whole lot to be thankful for."

"Yes, you do, especially with Jabari and Bella both coming to Christ in the same weekend."

"What do you mean?"

"You didn't know? I just assumed Bella had told you. When we prayed with her Friday, she recommitted her life back to Christ."

"Excuse me, Anna. I think I need to go find my wife."

CHAPTER 28

Bella was sitting at her desk in her art studio when she heard footsteps approaching. She looked up just in time to see Selena strolling into the room.

"Selena, what are you doing? The second and third floors are our private residence. You can't be here."

Selena looked up at the soaring ceilings. "This house looks deceptively Colonial from downstairs, but this is more Victorian-like with a third floor. I saw Jabari and Tonya leave. I figured it shouldn't be a problem if I came up too."

"It is," Bella said flatly. "I just told you the residential quarters are for our family only."

"You just had to invite her, didn't you?"

"Excuse me?"

"I gave you Joshua."

Bella's forehead crinkled in confusion. "What did you just say to me?"

"You heard me. I gave him to you. Trust, if I *really* wanted Joshua, he would have been mine. But no, you just had to have both brothers. I guess that's just how whores roll. Isn't that right, Rosemary? I know all about you. Walking around here all high and mighty like you're the prefect pastor's wife when your nothing but a high-classed ho."

Bella willed herself to stay seated. She fought past every natural inclination inside of her that told her to beat the—

"Selena!"

Selena turned quickly at the sound of Joshua's voice.

"Joshua, I—"

"You're fired."

"Joshua, no! Y-y-you don't understand! I w-w-w-was defending myself! All I wanted was to help out with Jabari's party, but she just kept hurtling these ugly accusations at me all day long. I just got sick of it! I know it was wrong, but I had to fight back! I had to!" Selena stumbled towards him, sobbing.

Joshua sighed heavily and caught Selena in his arms. He did understand. He knew firsthand what it was like to find yourself in a situation with Bella where you completely lost control. Lord knows, his wife could make the most non-violent of pacifists lose control. Even still, Joshua had heard the tail end of Selena's rant, and he knew that if he and Bella had any chance at all of making things work, his secretary would have to go. *Dang, and I was just about to give her a raise too.*

Joshua pried Selena's arms from around his neck. He stared into her tear-streaked face as she continued to sob hysterically. "You need to calm down. I need you to breathe for me. Come on, in and out, Selena, breathe," Joshua said softly.

He waited until she had calmed herself considerably then he pulled a handkerchief from his back pocket and handed it to her. Selena blew her nose.

"Better?"

"Yeah, much. Thank you."

"Thank you for organizing the party for Jabari today. I really appreciate it, but I think you should go before this situation turns any uglier than it already is. Are you okay to drive home or should I have someone drop you?"

"I'm fine. I can drive."

"Take tomorrow off. You can clear out your desk on Tuesday. We'll set up an exit interview for the end of the week."

Shock washed over Selena face. "You mean I'm still fired?"

"Yes."

More tears filled her eyes, but she nodded her head and scurried away.

Joshua listened as Selena descended the stairs, then he turned to face Bella.

Bella remained seated in her chair. Her back was ramrod straight, and she was gripping the armrests so tightly that her knuckles had turned white.

"How about you, Bella, you alright?"

"I'm fine," she snapped.

"So, I guess that means what I just heard about you is true."

"Which part, Josh? The part about me just having to have both brothers because that's how whores roll?"

Joshua walked over and took a seat on the edge of the desk in front of her.

"The part about you recommitting your life back to Christ. Anna told me a few minutes ago. I was on my way to come ask you about it when I walked in and figured that it had to be true. I mean there was a time when . . ."

Joshua ran his hand over his head and let his words trail off. A small smile tugged at the corners of his mouth.

Bella's eyes met his. "There was a time when what?"

"When I would have walked in on a scene like that to find you mopping the floor with her face."

"I was tempted. I'd like to think it was the Holy Spirit who kept my body in this chair, but in my heart of hearts, I think I just didn't want to get blood on my new floor." Bella stared down at her belly. "And I also can't afford to hurt my baby." Bella sighed. "Besides, what she said about me was true. Scripture says you should agree with your adversary quickly."

Joshua pulled Bella up from her chair and wrapped her in his arms. "Thank you."

"For what?"

"All the reasons why you didn't stomp her."

"You didn't have to fire her."

"Of course I did."

Bella's hand flew to her mouth.

"What?"

"You just fired Mike's girlfriend. He gon' get you."

Joshua frowned down at her. "Woman, please, I ain't scared of Mike."

CHAPTER 29

Looks like the whole gang is here," Jabari said as he and Tonya walked into the dining room. "Hey everybody, there's someone I want to introduce y'all to. This here is my aunt Tonya. Auntie, this is the New Orleans crew. We all came here together."

A tall dark skinned man who reminded Tonya of the actor Samuel L. Jackson, stood and shook Tonya's hand. "Walter Trendale, nice to meet you."

Maggie, his cinnamon toned pretty wife stood next. "I'm Maggie, and Rose has told me so much about you. I feel like I already know you. Would you mind terribly if I gave you a hug?"

"Maggie, I would love a hug," Tonya said.

Pearl an elder with pecan skin and kind eyes stood up next. "I'm Pearl, and I'll take a hug too. You sure are a pretty little thing."

"Thank you, ma'am," Tonya said smiling politely at the older woman.

"You married?" Pearl asked.

"No, ma'am," Tonya said.

"You like kids?"

"I do. I adore them."

"Well, everyone loves the babies, how do you feel about the older ones?"

"I'm the director of the children's ministry at my church. I love children—all ages, all sizes, all colors."

"Oh, that's good, sweetie. Now what's your credit score?"

Maggie laughed nervously. "Please excuse her.

She's not usually like this."

Walter frowned. "Yeah, Pearl, what's with the twenty questions?"

"I just think she'd be the perfect match for my new grandson that's all."

"It's too late, Granny P. I already asked her to marry me. She turned me down."

The five pairs of eyes in the room turned to stare at Mike. He had silently entered the room and his tall frame was leaning up against the wall.

Pearl grinned at Maggie. "See there? I knew I felt a love connection."

Walter cleared his throat. "Come on everybody, let's move this party back outside."

"That's a good idea," Maggie said. Under her breath she whispered, "Pearl, let's give these two some privacy." In a louder voice Maggie said, "And Jabari, when we get outside, I want you to show us all the latest dance moves."

Mike pinned Tonya with his gaze while Walter, Pearl, Maggie, and Jabari filed out of the dining room.

Tonya spoke first. Even though he had sucked all the oxygen out of the atmosphere with his arrival, and was, right now in this moment holding her hostage with his eyes. Tonya had meant for her voice to come out sounding non-affected and confident. The best she could manage was a croaky, "Hello," so taken aback was she by the scrutiny of his eyes.

His eyes took in every inch of her frame. They reacquainted themselves with the curve of her lips, the shape of her face, her collarbone, her earlobes, her neck. His hands stayed in his pockets the entire time, but his gaze pried her open, forcing Tonya to both simultaneously remember herself and to forget.

When his eyes fell on a small beauty mark that rested slightly to the left of her lower lip, a spot he had kissed a thousand times, Tonya felt her mouth go very dry.

She closed her eyes and sighed as he pried her open again, making her forget she was engaged to another man, making her recall the sensation of his kisses. *Lord, have mercy.*

"You look good, Blackbird," he finally said.

Tonya ignored the involuntary flip her stomach did at the sound of his pet name for her and tried one last ditch effort to regain control. "Why didn't you tell me Bella and Jabari were back?"

"Why didn't you tell me you were married?"

"I'm not," she spat out indignantly.

"Just engaged, right?" He stared at her empty ring finger. "What's the matter, brother couldn't afford a ring?"

"No, he did. I just don't always wear it."

Mike pushed himself off the wall and started towards the door.

"Michael, wait. Why didn't you tell me that Bella and Jabari were back?" She walked toward him closing the space between them. "We had an agreement remember?"

He turned to face her. "You're the one who's been in communication with them for the past five years. You should have known they were back."

"Okay, Michael, maybe I deserve that."

"Maybe?"

"Yes, you have every right to be angry with me about Ted. But not about this. It's not what you think."

"I'm listening."

"I got a postcard in the mail one day with a PO box address on it. No name, or anything. I wasn't even sure it was from them. I just wanted it to be. So I took a chance and I wrote them every single chance I got. I never got a response back, but I missed them so much and writing the letters gave me so much hope that—"

Mike reached out and lifted a lock of her hair from her shoulders.

Tonya's heart caught in her throat.

"You permed your hair."

"It's just blown out."

His hand fell back to his side. "I guess your preacher likes the straight look."

"Most men do."

He smiled sadly down at her. "Not all, Blackbird. Some men just want their women to be authentic."

Anger shot threw her belly. "I'm surprised to hear you

say that. I met your girlfriend a few minutes ago. She's got tracks all through her head. But every single strand of this is mine."

"She's not my girlfriend."

"Whatever, Michael." And before he could see the traitorous tears forming in her eyes, Tonya turned quickly to leave.

He caught her hand and pulled her into his arms. "When's your wedding?"

"Why, you coming?"

"And watch you walk down the aisle to another man? Not a chance. I just asked because I need to know one thing."

Her arms had a mind of their own. Without her permission they were wrapping themselves around his neck and embracing him right back. "What do you need to know?"

He pulled her closer to him. "How much longer I have to hold you like this." He rested his chin on the top of her head. She settled her head against his heart.

"I haven't set a date yet," she finally said. Tonya felt the quiet rumble low in his chest, a sound that told her what no other soul watching them could have detected. Michael was laughing.

"What's funny, Michael?"

"You are. You don't wear his ring, and you haven't set a date. This brother must be one hell of a catch."

CHAPTER 30

It was after dark when the last of the party guests had left. "You sure you two don't want to camp out here and drive back tomorrow?" Bella asked.

"Don't worry, Bella. I'm okay to drive," Tonya said.

"I know you are, I'm just not ready to say goodbye yet. I don't know when I'm going to see you again."

Melissa, who was digging through her oversized purse for her cell phone stopped for a moment to look up at Bella. "Tonya's back in our lives. You both are. This time for good. You'll be seeing plenty of her, starting with the baby shower."

Tonya heard the emotion rising in Melissa's voice. She took a seat on the couch beside her. "I'm sorry, Auntie Mel. I've been so focused on completing my dissertation and working at the church, that I haven't done a good job of keeping in touch. But from now on, I promise I will. I'm going to be more purposeful about staying in touch with the family." Tonya looked up at Bella. "I'm going to call the both of you every week. We'll schedule it before I return to New York. But I can't make any shower promises, Auntie Mel. I'm still pretty much a broke grad student. Assuming the shower is in Houston, I would not only have to get a plane ticket home, I also have to factor in the cost of a hotel room."

Bella rolled her eyes. "Girl, please, you know you don't need a hotel."

"Who needs a hotel?" Joshua asked as he and Mike walked into the living room.

"Tonya does. She's engaged now and her fiancé wouldn't approve of her staying in her old spot," Mike said.

Tonya smiled sweetly up at Joshua. "Actually, Josh, if anyone's relationship is the problem it's Michael's. You were there when I met his girlfriend, right? She definitely would not approve of me staying in my old spot."

"Josh, would you please school this woman. I keep telling her that Selena is your secretary."

"It's true she is," Joshua said.

Bella cleared her throat.

"I mean she was," Joshua amended. "Up until today. I fired her."

Melissa's and Mike's eyes both flew to Joshua.

"I'll tell you 'bout it later," Joshua said in answer to his brother's unspoken question. Mike looked at Tonya and shrugged. "See, she's fired, non-issue, now what's your excuse?"

Bella stifled a giggle. "Tonya, if you don't feel comfortable staying at Mike's you know we always have room for you here."

"Seriously, Bella, despite what some people in this room think, I'm not the least bit uncomfortable staying in my old spot. I love my cottage. And, as for the offer to stay here, I wouldn't dream of putting you guys out. I know how Josh likes his privacy."

Bella raised an eyebrow. "Girl, did you not see all these people here today? Since Joshua has become a pastor he's become a regular social butterfly."

Joshua grunted. "I don't know 'bout all that, but what I do know is that you aren't people," he said staring at Tonya pointedly. "As long as I got a spot to lay my head you got one too. Believe that."

Tonya stood and kissed Joshua's cheek. "Thank you, Josh."

"And I have your plane tickets," Melissa said. "That's me and your uncle Jack's graduation present. A year's worth of air travel. Anywhere in the world you want to go."

"Here's the deal," Mike began, "It's too late for the two of you to drive back alone tonight. So the way I see it you have two options. Option one, you spend the night at my place, that's assuming your preacher man doesn't object."

Tonya opened her mouth to speak but Mike cut her off.

"Option two, I can have one of my people drive you back to Dallas tonight."

"I like option one," Joshua said firmly. "I don't want you two on the road this late. I don't care who's driving."

Tonya folded her arms across her chest. "And what if I don't agree?"

"Doesn't matter," Joshua and Mike both said simultaneously.

Tonya's eyes grew big as saucers. "Excuse me?"

Joshua rolled his eyes. "Tonya, please, kill the outrage. You ain't been gone that long. You know how we do things around here."

Mike nodded. "That's right, Blackbird. My city. My court. My rules. Your preacher man might not have a problem with you gallivanting up and down the freeway at all times of the night, but I do."

"Word," Joshua said, giving Mike a fist bump.

"As long as you're in this city I'mma take care of you," Mike said.

"I'm trying to get out of this city," Tonya said glaring up at the brothers.

"Tonya, we could have a sleepover at the mansion," Bella said in a singsong voice, trying to coax her friend out of her foul mood. "If Mike doesn't mind, I mean."

"I don't," Mike said.

Bella looked up at Josh expectantly.

He shrugged. "Pack a bag, let's go."

Bella clapped her hands excitedly. "This is going to be so much fun. We could sleep late and wake up to a fabulous brunch."

"Ah, there you are!" Melissa cried triumphantly as she pulled her cell phone out of her purse and dialed home. "Hello, Jack, looks like we're staying the night. Yeah, we're sleeping over at Mikey's. How's Missy Ann and the foal?" Melissa said walking into the adjacent room to continue her conversation.

"Let me call Granny P and see if she wants to get in on some of this sleepover action," Mike said, pulling out his phone. "What about you, Blackbird? You need to make a call, okay this with your man?"

"No I don't. And you know why I don't have to do that, Michael?"

"Enlighten me."

"Because I'm a grown woman, who comes and goes as she pleases."

"That ain't what I heard," Joshua said. "I heard dude be checking for you hard."

Tonya rolled her eyes. "Who'd you hear that from, Josh, Aunt Katie?"

"Yep."

Both brothers laughed.

"Ignore them, Tonya," Bella said. "Come help me pack."

Tonya bit her bottom lip. "I guess I should call my mom though."

"I already talked to her," Mike said.

"When?"

"About an hour ago. She knows you're staying the night."

"How could she know that, Michael, when I just agreed to it?" Tonya threw her hands up in the air. "You know what? Never mind."

"Don't be mad, baby. It'll be just like old times," Mike called to her back as she followed Bella up the stairs.

"Except for one thing, Michael," Tonya tossed back over her shoulder. "I'll be sleeping in my own bed."

"Suit yourself." Mike's deep laughter followed her all the way up to the second floor.

CHAPTER 31

Mike's house steward was waiting to greet the family when they arrived at the mansion.

"Welcome home, sirs," Jeeves said, speaking to both Michael and Joshua. "And young sirs," Jeeves said next, greeting Marcus and Jabari. "Mr. Keys, I trust our staff served your guests with excellence today."

"Thanks for loaning them out, G. The staff was on point as usual," Joshua said.

Jeeves turned to greet the women and a new round of welcomes began. He took Bella's hand in between his. "Ms. Bella, it is always a pleasure." Then Melissa's. "Ms. Melissa, so very nice to see you again. Ms. Pearl always a great honor."

When Jeeves got to Tonya, she ignored his outstretched hand and ran into the older man's arms. Jeeves, who was always formal, did something Michael hadn't seen him do in all the years he worked for him. He twirled Tonya around and laughed.

"Mademoiselle Tonya, oh how I've missed you! Welcome home."

※ ※ ※

Jeeves nodded to the servants who opened the two large double doors that led into Michael's formal ballroom. "When Master Dutton informed me of your slumber party, I took the liberty of preparing a few things for the occasion."

There were four massage tables set up as well as four manicure and four pedicure stations. Smiling women stood ready at each station.

Pearl took a look around the room then at the A-frame sign advertising the salon. "Wow, I've seen you on TV, never knew y'all made house calls."

"We normally don't, ma'am," one of the massage therapists said, "but for an important client like Mr. Dutton our company was willing to make an exception."

Mike, Joshua, Jabari, and Marcus went off to shoot hoops while the women had manicures, pedicures, facials, and fully body massages.

"Who's up for a movie night?" Tonya asked three hours later after their spa services were finally concluded.

"I'm not," Pearl said. "Somebody needs to stick a fork in me 'cause I am d-o-n-e."

"Me too, Pearl," Melissa said. "I'm a wet noddle. I can't do another thing except fall into bed."

Bella's eyes sparkled playfully as she looked at Tonya. "I still have tons of energy. Let's go find the guys."

A few minutes later, Bella and Tonya found Joshua and Mike in the game room. Mike was leaning over his pool table about to make his shot while Joshua stood beside the massive table looking on.

Joshua looked up at the clock when he saw Bella and Tonya enter the room. "It's after midnight. You two still up?"

"We're getting ready to watch a movie. We came to see if the two of you wanted to join us," Bella said.

Joshua took in Tonya first. She was dressed head to toe in the same sleepwear she'd preferred as a kid, practical, albeit, hot, flannel. Then he looked at Bella. Bella was wearing a pair of sexy cut-off blue jean shorts, with a tight white tee. Her hair had been put up in an intentional, but made to look unintentional, messy bun, the kind he loved to pull down right before he—

Yep, movie night was a set up. Definitely Bella's idea. His god sister wasn't the type to play games, but his wife certainly was. And since he had almost slipped up and kissed this woman twice today, Joshua decided right then and there, that he'd better not take any more chances.

❧ ❧ ❧

Mike took in Tonya wearing her not-trying-to-be-sexy-for-you-or-anybody-else pajamas, standing with one leg tucked securely behind her back in a stretch that could only be classified as a dancer's pose. It was a stretch impossible for most athletes to accomplish, but one that meant Tonya was totally relaxed. She had allowed the steam from her shower that night to ruin her hair, now it hung wild and carefree just the way he liked, in soft wavy ringlets around her shoulders and back. He could smell the uncomplicated scent of the lavender and vanilla lotion she wore wafting from her skin. A fragrance she knew he loved because he had told her so a thousand times. Tonya was toying with him, that much to Mike was clear. He glanced over at Bella. With those barely there shorts, his sister-in-law was definitely trying to get under his brother's skin. But Tonya was another story. She wasn't really the type to play games, or at least she hadn't been before she left home. Mike called his shot and then watched the ball sail into the right corner pocket.

"What y'all 'bout to watch?" Mike asked, making sure to keep his voice smooth. Making sure she knew just how unaffected he was.

Tonya looked up at him sheepishly and then quickly adverted her eyes to the floor. "We were thinking, *The Notebook*," she said hopefully.

Okay, so she wasn't playing games, not entirely. She just wanted him to hold her. She just wanted the same thing he had wanted from the first moment he'd laid eyes on her that afternoon, to wrap her inside of his arms and to sit someplace quiet for a spell. But no matter how good she looked, or smelled, that wasn't going to happen. He was just about to tell her that she couldn't have it both ways. Was just about to make it clear to her, that now that she was engaged to another man, their cuddling days were over, when Joshua spoke. His brother hadn't taken his eyes off of Bella from the moment she'd walked into the game room.

"I think I'll pass," Joshua said. As simple as that.

Mike nodded. "Yeah, me too."

❧ ❧ ❧

About thirty minutes later, Joshua and Mike found Bella and Tonya snoring softly on the couch.

"Lightweights," Joshua mumbled. He leaned down and scooped Bella up, careful not to wake Tonya in the process. "I'll catch you in the AM," Joshua said as he headed upstairs to the guest bedroom he and Bella shared whenever they spent the night at Mike's house.

"Night," Mike called at his back.

Mike lifted Tonya up, carried her up the stairs and deposited her in the bedroom directly across the hall from his. He pulled the covers up over her and placed a soft kiss on her forehead before turning out the lights.

CHAPTER 32

Tonya awoke the next morning to find herself in one of the mansion's many guest bedrooms. She looked around the room that she had decorated. The one that was supposed to be hers, in the event that she ever needed to sleep over at the mansion. The one she'd never actually slept in until last night, because in the past, whenever she had slept over in the mansion, it had always been in Michael's bed. Per her edict, however, they would keep things tight—if not completely right. They would absolutely never engage in the following: no horizontal kissing, no fondling, and no matter what, whenever they slept together, they would do so with their clothes on. Tonya sighed now, thinking of the pure insanity of that arrangement. For him as a virile sexually active man and her as a Christian woman trying to live holy. What was even crazier than her past insanity was the fact that she wanted nothing more right now than to run across the hallway and climb up into bed with Michael. She wanted to drown out all sounds of reason and rationality behind the soundproof master bedroom's walls. She wanted to push pause on life for a moment, escape reality, and just be held in his arms. It's what she had wanted to do since the moment she'd crossed the state line into Texas and had entered his orbit. She wanted to find peace, comfort, and safety as she had so many other times before, in his arms.

Help me, Jesus, please help me.

Michael made Tonya break all of her rules. Who was she kidding? Michael was the reason she had so many rules. Michael was the reason why, much to her fiancé's chagrin, they mostly dated publicly, rarely privately. Michael was the reason why she never went to Ted's home, except those times when he had the whole ministry staff over for an event. And when Tonya did allow Ted over to her place, he was never allowed to stay past three o'clock in the afternoon. And on those rare occasions Ted was able to convince Tonya to stay inside with him and watch a movie, and Tonya so happened to fall asleep, she would nearly jump out of her skin the moment Ted attempted to touch her. She knew that her skittishness was a source of much contention between her and Ted, but Tonya had pretty much blown it off until now. Until she realized that Michael had carried her up the long spiral staircase last night, put her to bed, and that he had done so without breaking her sleep.

"I'm a man of the cloth, Tonya, okay? I can deal with my woman having a revelation of holiness. What I can't deal with is the woman I love, tensing up every time I have the impulse to touch her."

They were at Ted's house sitting on his sofa. He'd convinced Tonya to stay over after a ministry staff meeting to watch a romantic comedy with him.

"I don't know what you're talking about. We're touching right now. Aren't we?"

"You're consciously touching me."

Tonya stared up at him not fully grasping his meaning.

Ted sighed. "Tonya, most women like to spoon when they fall asleep but you pull away from me when you're unconscious."

"I'm a light sleeper."

This was somewhat of an untruth. Growing up in Texas Tonya had slept like a rock. Technically, she had only become a light sleeper when she moved to New York. Tonya used to sleep so deeply and so soundly when they were children, that Joshua referred to her REM state as truth serum. Joshua claimed that even if their parents couldn't detect it, he and Michael always knew when she was lying, and that they could always get the truth out of her if they questioned her while she was unconscious.

"You're such a liar," eight-year-old Joshua declared this about her once in front of the whole family. It was after Tonya had fingered him as the child-culprit who had broken, and then attempted to glue back together, her auntie Mel's prized crystal vase. "The only time you're honest is when you're asleep."

Tonya had wrapped her arms around Ted's neck and planted a playful peck on his cheek. "I'm also an only child remember? I've never had to share my personal space."

That was a bold-faced lie. There wasn't a memory from her childhood that didn't include both Michael and Joshua, and until they had all embarked on their teenage years, the three of them didn't even know there was such a thing called personal space.

Oh God, Ted is right. Tonya felt tears prick her eyes as she stared up at the ceiling and prayed. *Lord, I know I heard you tell me to marry your minister. I know I did. I want to be obedient but how is that supposed to happen when—*

Tonya didn't have the words to explain it, except to say that Ted's touch, which was always above board as far as Christian conduct was concerned, felt illegal, and Michael's touch, which teased and tested the boundaries of God's law, felt right. Tonya rolled over in the queen-sized bed. She squeezed her eyes shut to dry the tears. Then opened them again to read the note on the bedside table left by Jeeves. He'd sent one of the servants to the cottage to retrieve some of her old things. Tonya rose from the bed and walked over to the closet. There, hanging on the scented padded hangers she found one of her favorite white cotton dresses and a colorful shawl. Now that she was up and moving about she could detect the glorious smells of breakfast wafting up to the mansion's second floor. She removed her clothes from the closet and walked into the adjacent bathroom and got ready to face the day.

CHAPTER 33

Tonya walked into the kitchen to find Melissa, Pearl, and Bella sitting around the large kitchen island drinking tea, and Joshua and Michael sitting at the kitchen table talking sports. Tonya hugged Melissa first, then Bella, and then Pearl.

"There she is," Melissa said.

"Sleeping beauty finally awakes," Pearl said.

Bella smiled up at Tonya. "Jeeves made crepes this morning. He says they're your favorite."

"He's right. They are." Tonya walked around the large kitchen island to the stove and kissed Jeeves's cheek. "Thanks G."

"You're welcome, mademoiselle."

Mike stood from his position at the table to greet her. "How'd you sleep?" he asked, pulling her into his arms.

She thought about the internal tug of war that she'd barely won that morning, how it took everything in her to resist climbing out of her bed and running across the hall into his arms. "Like a baby, what about you?"

His eyes roamed lazily over her form, causing a blush to rise to the surface of her cheeks. "I've had better nights."

Joshua pulled Tonya into a tight hug next. Then he stood back and examined her at arm's length. "So, which you are you today?"

Tonya laughed. "Definitely not New York me. These are my old clothes and my old hairstyle. So I guess you could say this is just regular, plain me."

Joshua yanked one of her long springy curls and kissed her forehead. "I like regular you. And for the record, there is nothing plain about you."

Tonya looked around the kitchen. "Where's Marcus and Jabari?"

"The young masters were up to the wee hours of the morning playing video games, mademoiselle," Jeeves said. "I suspect we won't see them until sometime around midday."

The adults sat around the large kitchen table enjoying lively conversation long after the food was consumed.

"Auntie Mel, I hate to bring this up 'cause I'm really not ready to say goodbye yet, but we have a long drive ahead of us so we should probably get a move on it."

"You're good," Mike said. "Your flight doesn't leave for another couple of hours."

A look of surprise flew across Tonya's face. "You booked us a flight? What about the car?"

"Joseph drove the car back to Dallas last night, mademoiselle, and I booked your commuter flight this morning," Jeeves announced.

"You're only here till tomorrow night, right?" Mike said.

Tonya nodded.

"Then you should spend as much of that time as you can with your mom, and Aunt Katie. The family really misses you."

Two hours later, after a final round of hugs, kisses, tears, and promises to make frequent calls home from Tonya to both Joshua and Bella, Melissa and Tonya were ready to depart for the airport. Harrison, Michael's driver, held the rear passenger door for Melissa as she climbed into the back seat of the town car. Michael held the other rear passenger door open for Tonya.

"Thank you," Tonya said looking up at him.

Michael stared down at her. "For what?"

"Everything. Breakfast, the massages, the flight back to Dallas. I guess what I'm saying in a nutshell is, thank you for always being a soft place to land."

"That'll never change, Blackbird. Have a safe flight back to New York. Call me when you land."

CHAPTER 34

I t was Wednesday, not Tuesday, when Selena had finally finished licking her wounds long enough to crawl back into the office. She cleared out her desk and set up her exit interview per Joshua's instructions. She had just returned from taking the last box of her personal things to her car when she spotted the handwritten sticky note from Mother Berry attached to her monitor.

Please stop by the office. Michael would like to see you before you leave.

Selena turned off the computer and headed down the long corridor to the other end of the building affectionately dubbed by the Home Court staff as Duttonville. As she walked through the corridor, she mentally kicked herself as she realized her mistake. She should have chosen the hero. In fact, if she had applied to work at Duttonville in the first place, she'd be married by now. She was sure of it. But no, she had to set her sights on the bad boy. *Why?* Why did she always fall for the bad boy? The wrong type. Heck, even if her plan had worked, Joshua was a we-can-hang-if-I-can-fit-you-into-my-schedule-type of brother. A woman would always love him harder than he loved her. Mike, on the other hand, was a rescuer. He needed a damsel, and she could be that for him.

As she walked to the other end of the building, Selena considered her options. He was rich, handsome, generous, and although he was not in love with her, per se, he was certainly attracted to her.

In time I could make him love me.

She could. All she had to do was recalibrate.

CHAPTER 35

Selena waved timidly to Mother Berry, who motioned for her to enter. Selena stood at the threshold of Mike's office and knocked softly on the opened door.

"Mike, you wanted to see me?"

"Yeah, come on in and have a seat," Mike said, rising to close the door behind her.

Selena took a seat on the leather sectional sofa in front of the fireplace. Mike sat across from her.

"How you feelin'?"

Selena stared down at her hands. "Right now I'm feeling very embarrassed and ashamed of my behavior. Bella just came at me talking this nonsense about me wanting Joshua and . . . I know I had no right to say the things that I said, but I was just so furious." Selena's voice cracked. "I've been trying to find a new church but New Horizons is my home, and I don't even know where to begin."

Mike slid over on the couch beside her. "Hey, no. That's not necessary. It's not even like that, alright?"

Selena shook her head and a smattering of tears ran down her face on prefect cue. "Joshua hates me. Bella's always hated me. They don't want to see me anymore."

Mike handed her a handkerchief from his inside breast pocket. "You don't change churches over something like this. Trust me. I know my brother, alright? He wouldn't want you leaving New Horizons over this. Besides, I don't want you to either."

"The crazy thing is, I didn't mean for any of this to happen. I thought I was doing a good deed, volunteering on my day off to help with Jabari's party."

Mike sighed.

"I mean I thought we had settled all of this over Christmas break you know?" Selena stared up at Mike. "I thought I made it perfectly clear which brother I wanted. Obviously, that wasn't clear enough for Bella."

"Tell me something. What do you see yourself doing with the rest of your life?"

Selena blinked for a second, momentarily caught off guard by his question.

What, you mean besides marrying you?

"What, besides working for one of the best companies in the world, and the two best bosses ever?" is what she actually said.

"Yeah, besides all that. You're too smart for this, and it's clear to me that you're living below your potential here. So, if you had your choice to do anything in the world, be anything in the world, what would that be?"

He was right. She was smart, smart enough to know that saying the thing that she really wanted, the thing that was on the tip of her tongue, would not garner her the respect or approval she was searching for. So instead she pulled something out of the air.

"Well, it's always seemed like a long shot because I really didn't have the letters of recommendations or the money for that matter, but I've always wanted to go to law school."

Mike sat back, he extended his long arm over the back of the couch and smiled confidently at her. "Well, now you have all the resources you need. Pick a school, any school."

CHAPTER 36

Whoa! Did you see that?" Joshua said as he jumped up off the couch. The Keys family were stuck indoors due to flooding on a wet, stormy Houston night. They had decided to pass the time by playing board games. Joshua almost toppled the Monopoly board when he saw Bella's stomach move.

Bella gasped. "I didn't see it, but I felt it. Please be still in there little one."

"That had to be an elbow." Joshua put his hand on Bella's belly. "Hey there, little one."

The baby kicked.

"Hey there, little one," Joshua repeated.

The baby kicked again.

Joshua chuckled gleefully. "Ah, the force is strong in this one. She's feisty."

Jabari sat his Monopoly money on the coffee table and brought his face close to Bella's tummy. "Let me see if she'll talk to me. Hey there, little girl."

Bella rolled her eyes. "Why do you both keep calling her a girl?"

"Trust me, Bella, she's a girl," Joshua said.

"Hey there, little girl," Jabari repeated. He frowned. "She won't move for me."

"That's 'cause she's smart," Joshua said. "She already knows that you're her big brother and that it's her job to annoy you. Watch this. Hey pretty, girl."

Joshua and Jabari looked on in delight as Bella's stomach moved back and forth with tiny little foot kicks.

"Josh, could you please just stop talking for a while? This baby obviously responds to your voice. And while it may be fun to watch my stomach roll around like something on *The Exorcist*, it's not so fun to experience."

Thunder cracked through the sky and the power in the whole house went out. Joshua rose to go check the fuse box. A few minutes later he returned with three flashlights. He found Bella and Jabari huddled together on the couch.

"The good news is, it's not an internal problem. The power is out for the entire area. Electrical outages are pretty common with storms such as this. The power should be on in a few," Joshua said as he handed a flashlight to Bella and then to Jabari.

"Can I sleep with you tonight?" Jabari asked.

"With who?" Joshua asked incredulously.

"With you and mom."

Joshua shook his head. "Naw, man, you too old for that. Everybody's sleeping in their own beds. It's just a storm. You've never been afraid of storms before. Tell him, Bella. Back me up on this. There is no reason to be afraid now." Joshua shined the flashlight on Bella. She looked about as terrified as Jabari.

A bolt of thunder ripped through the sky and Bella nearly jumped clear out of her skin.

"Yeah, Jabari, whatever your dad just said," Bella muttered.

Joshua looked into the panic-stricken eyes of his wife and then his son. Apparently, they were both experiencing some post-Katrina anxiety.

Joshua sighed. "Alright, just for tonight." Relief flooded both Bella and Jabari's faces.

"Before we go upstairs let me pray with you both." Joshua took a seat on the edge of the coffee table and sat the flashlight down beside him. He locked hands with his Bella and Jabari.

"Father God, I thank you for my family. I thank you for bringing them back to me, safely out of the storm. Right now, I come against fear. I break anxiety over them as it relates to storms. Whenever the lightning strikes and the storm winds blow, from now on, let them think about your goodness, your mercy, and your love. Let them remember how you were there with them, how you were with all of us, during the greatest storm of our lives."

Joshua laid in bed that evening with Bella nestled beside him, and Jabari sleeping peacefully at his feet. In the moonlit night, he could feel the soft butterfly kicks of the baby growing inside Bella's womb. Joshua was suddenly overwhelmed with love for his family. Even still, he wondered, how, after the baby was born, he would be able to hold on to them. He also wondered how he was ever going to be able to let them go.

CHAPTER 37

D r. Cadwell closed the file and smiled at Bella and Joshua. "Mama Bear's got a clean bill of health. Your labs look prefect. I can't tell you how happy I am to come back from vacation and find this. Tell me what exactly did you do?"

"We took Dr. Bennett's suggestions to heart and we worked the plan she gave us," Joshua said. "More water, more rest. We started taking the iron with vitamin C and switched out the prenatal vitamins, which were making Bella sick, with a children's chewable instead."

"She threatened to put me in the hospital. I didn't really have a choice," Bella said.

Dr. Cadwell smiled down at Bella. "By she I take it you mean my partner, the tall, gorgeous, redhead, Dr. Bennett. Put the fear of God in you, did she? I'll admit she's the heavy." Dr. Cadwell winked at Joshua. "I call her when I need bad cop. Mama Bear, I'm glad you took her seriously. I would have hated to come back from vacation to find you in the hospital. Seriously folks, I am very proud of the both of you. This turnaround is nothing short of amazing. I take it you are being careful in the sexual arena?"

Bella smirked. "Boy are we ever."

Joshua's eyes flew quickly to Bella's.

"How careful?" Dr. Cadwell asked.

"I have no sex life what so ever," Bella said flatly.

Joshua cleared his throat.

"Well, mama, you're a very beautiful woman. I can assure you, it's not because papa doesn't want to. He just wants to be careful. Just remember a little hanky-panky is good. Helps mama and papa both to relax."

Dr. Cadwell looked down at his clipboard as he checked off his list. "Let's see, baby sounds happy. Mama looks happy. Except for the need of a little more hanky-panky in her life. We talked about the labor and delivery plan some time ago. You still want to do natural childbirth?"

Bella nodded.

"I recommended you sign up for Lamaze."

"Already done."

"Very good, Mama Bear. Lots of mothers think they are going to do this without drugs but when those pains hit, it's a whole 'nother story altogether."

❀ ❀ ❀

Bella was preoccupied for the entire drive home. So much so that she actually seemed startled when Joshua called her name.

"Huh?"

"When did you sign up for Lamaze?"

"The day I asked Jilly to be my partner. She told me that since she volunteered at the hospital, she could sign me up and she did."

Joshua fixed his eyes on the road up ahead of them. "I told you I'd go with you this time. I meant it."

Bella sighed heavily. She rested her hand lightly on his arm. "I appreciate that, Josh, but sooner or later, I gotta stop depending on you." She stared out the window then and was silent for the rest of the drive home. She was so lost in thought it hadn't even registered to her when they arrived home.

"Bella?"

"Huh?"

"We're here."

"Oh, yeah."

"Are you okay?"

"Yeah, I'm fine."

Joshua stared at her for a beat, trying to get a read on her distraction.

"I'm fine, Josh, really" Bella said. There was a smile pasted on her face, one that didn't quite reach her eyes.

"I'm going into the office. I should be home today around three."

"Any special request for dinner?" she asked with her pasted smile firmly in place.

"Whatever you decide is cool," Joshua said.

"I'll see you later then. When you get home." Bella opened the passenger door of his truck and walked quickly into the house.

CHAPTER 38

Joshua sat in a meeting with his brother Mike and the executive staff members of their company, Home Court Advantage, consumed with thoughts of Bella. He ran the tape from that morning back over again in his mind. Bella complaining about their sex life to Dr. Cadwell. Bella signing up for Lamaze classes without him, without even mentioning it to him. Her distraction in the car. While the financial advisors threw out the preliminary specs for Home Court's upcoming projects, Joshua recalled the few words Bella had spoken this morning and the order she had spoken them in.

I'm fine.

I'm fine, really.

Anything special you want for dinner?

Sooner or later I gotta stop depending on you— and what the heck did she mean by that? Then Joshua recalled the last thing she had said.

I'll see you later, when you get home.

"She's getting ready to run."

Thirty pairs of eyes turned to stare at Joshua, as he stood abruptly from his seat at the head of conference table. Mike, who was seated at the other end of the conference table, studied his brother. "Josh, you alright?"

"Yeah, I just need— I gotta go."

CHAPTER 39

S o you mean to tell me he's not coming, at all?" Tonya and her administrative assistant, Adrina sat at a little outdoor bistro having lunch. Tonya popped a grape tomato in her mouth and shrugged.

"Apparently, there are a lot of pre-Oscar parties that Tatiana needs him to accompany her to."

"I don't care what you say, this is shady with a capital S. First, he shows absolutely no signs of supporting you in your career, now he's taking some wannabe-movie-star bimbo to the Oscars on your graduation day."

"No, not some wannabe-movie-star bimbo; she's our new sister in Christ, remember? She just got saved. Besides, he's already apologized a million times."

"Is he sorry enough to not go?"

Tonya stared at her friend pointedly. "Come on, Adrina, now you know your pastor. He ain't turning down the Oscars for nobody."

Adrina rolled her eyes. "That man is not my pastor. I keep telling you that. You're my pastor. If you ever left Now Faith, I'd quit in a heartbeat, and I'm willing to bet that at least half the congregation would walk out with me."

"Adrina, please don't say things like that."

"I only speak the truth. The man can preach. I'll give him that much, but he doesn't have a heart for people. And that crack he made about the Section 8 mother in the team meeting last week. Tonya, what the heck was that?"

Tonya sighed. "I'm sorry you had to hear that. Try to chalk it up to Ted's being human."

"You mean carnal."

"He just gets so one-track minded sometimes. With Ted, the needs of the church come first. But that's where we come in. We ministry leaders have to help him see that the church is only as strong as its' people."

"I can't help him do nothing. Besides, I'm still angry about this whole Oscars mess."

"Like I said, with Ted, the needs of the church come first, and he thinks the church needs this. But the good thing about all of this is that I can ask for anything I want right now, and the answer is, yes, yes, yes." Tonya's eyes twinkled. "I even got a forty percent budget increase for children's ministry."

Adrina sat back in her chair and stared at her friend. "Most women would have squeezed their guy for clothes or jewelry, but you're telling me you got a budget increase for the children's ministry?"

Tonya smiled. "What can I say? I do what I can for the children."

"That's because you, my friend, have a pastor's heart." Adrina's face grew serious. "Aren't you even a little concerned?"

"You mean about Tatiana, because she's gorgeous?"

Adrina shook her head. "No, she's not. That's makeup and wardrobe, Boo. All part of the illusion. What I mean is aren't you concerned because the woman oozes sex."

Tonya tried unsuccessfully to choke back a giggle.

Adrina laughed too. "Girl, I am so serious."

"I know you are. But I'm not concerned about her ooze for a few reasons. You want to hear them."

"Come on lay it on me."

"Well for one, after her very public break up with Big Baller, Tatiana just wants to lay low for a while. Bringing her handsome pastor to the Oscars is just the thing she needs to show the world that she's living saved now. Two, don't forget I've dated a public figure before."

Tonya watched Adrina's eyes light up as they often did at the mention of Michael.

"It's not like I don't know what it's like to have my man photographed with gorgeous, sex oozing celebrities. Three, and this is the most important reason why I'm not concerned, I'm graduating. I don't have time to be thinking about Ted. He's doing what he said God told him to do. My family will be here, and I'mma do them and me too."

"You think Michael will come?"

Tonya pasted a smile on her face and tried to look as nonchalant as possible. "He knows about my engagement now so I doubt it."

"Well, since everyone around here is doing what God told them to do. I think I'm going to go ahead and do what God is telling me to do, too."

"You're going to finally heed the word of the Lord and stop running down your pastor?"

"Actually, no. I'm going to heed the word of the Lord and throw my pastor a graduation party."

CHAPTER 40

The moment Joshua had dropped Bella off, she made a beeline into the house for the phone. Recently, she had run into the ex-wife of one of Joshua's former teammates at lunch. The woman, Carmella Jones, had given Bella the name of a very discrete celebrity realtor by the name of Margo Cantor. Margo had handled the sale and distribution of Carmella's and her ex's property during their divorce. Bella felt a huge sense of relief when upon calling Margo, the realtor told her she could stop by and show Bella some nearby listings that very afternoon.

Margo and Bella were in the dining room looking at the list of homes for sale in the area, when Joshua walked through the door.

Bella smiled up at him. "I didn't expect you home so early."

"Obviously."

"Margo, this is my husband, Joshua Keys." But given the scowl on his face at the moment, she almost said, 'Bad Boy Joshua Keys.'

"Joshua, this is Margo, she's a realtor."

Margo, who appeared in full control of her facilities just moments before Joshua arrived, did the thing Bella had been watching women do in the presence of her husband their entire lives. She lost her daggone mind. Margo's skin flushed a bright cherry red and she practically skipped, no, more like leaped across the dining room table to greet Joshua.

"It is such an incredible pleasure to finally meet you. I'm your biggest fan."

Bella watched Joshua, who was never rude to anyone lately, but especially not his fans, completely ignore Margo's outstretched hand. Joshua's hands were tucked deep inside the pockets of his dark blue, custom made suit, and he kept his eyes trained on Bella. When he spoke, his voice was calm, deadly calm, like the panic-inducing quiet before a hurricane calm.

Yep. This was bound to happen sooner or later. Hurricane Joshua was about to blow.

"Bella, may I have a word with you?"

Bella nodded and rose from the table. "Margo, could you give us a moment please?"

"No problem, you take all the time you need," the woman said cheerily, oblivious to the brewing storm.

Bella followed Joshua wordlessly into the adjacent parlor and closed the door behind them.

"Why is she here?"

"She's a realtor, Josh, and please lower your voice. I'm pretty sure she can hear you."

The look on his face was a classic bad boy, *I don't give a*—but to his credit, Joshua did lower his voice.

"When I said you could do anything you wanted with the house, that didn't include selling it."

"That's not why she's here, Josh. Margo's here to help me find a place of my own."

The scowl on his beautiful face deepened, and Bella found herself using more words in her attempt to explain.

"'Cause see, what had happened was, I ran into Carmella Jones, who told me about Margo. Margo handled Carmella and Mark's property sell after their divorce. According to Carmella, Margo is super private and really reliable. She works almost exclusively with famous people, and we don't have to worry about her blabbing our business in the street."

"I can't believe you're doing this to me again."

"What exactly am I doing to you, Joshua?"

"The same thing you always do when things get hard, Bella. You run."

Bella threw her hands up in frustration, "Are we having the same conversation?! Did you even hear one word of what I just said?"

"I heard you, every word."

Bella took in Joshua's demeanor, other than the scowl on his face there was no outward sign of aggression. His skin wasn't flushed, his pulse wasn't pounding, the slight hardening of his jaw muscle told her that he was restraining himself, possibly biting back a few choice words, but other than that, he appeared to be in complete control. Old Joshua would have broken something by now, at the very least dropped a few f-bombs. The hurricane would have put his fist through the wall.

The fact that he had come home in the middle of the day for the express purpose of picking a fight with her— the fact that he was the one standing here calmly now and that she was the one about to lose it—well that—that just made Bella's blood boil.

Hurricane Joshua might have been a no-show, but Hurricane Bella was definitely about to blow.

"Should I go?"

Bella looked up to see Margo standing in the now open doorway.

"Yeah, you should," Joshua said with his eyes still trained on Bella.

"No, you shouldn't." Bella bit each word out angrily.

Joshua smiled as he extended his hand to Margo, and Bella watched him turn on his signature panty-dropping charm.

"It's Margo, right? I apologize if I came across as rude earlier."

Bella rolled her eyes. *Boy, please you were downright rude and you know it.*

"Oh no, you weren't rude, Joshua," Margo gushed.

Yes, he was.

"It's quite alright. You don't have to apologize."

No it isn't! Snap out of it, Margo! Stop acting like that weak apology he just gave you is the equivalent to winning the freaking power ball!!

Joshua cupped Margo's hand in his. "I'm sorry you made the trip over here. I'm afraid this was a complete waste of your time."

Margo shivered. "Honestly, it was totally worth it for the opportunity to meet you."

Bella rolled her eyes. *Somebody gag me. Do it now, with a spoon.*

Margo removed a small camera from her handbag. "Would you mind if I got a pic—"

Bella froze the woman with an arctic glare.

Margo dropped the camera back into her handbag quickly. "Never mind, now is probably not the best time. Bella you have my information and I'll . . . I'll just see myself out."

Bella exploded once the front door closed. "Joshua, what is wrong with you?! Instead of treating me like you caught me in here with another man you should be thanking me!"

"I should thank you, for leaving me? Right, Bella. I'll try and remember that the next time you take off again."

"How about thanking me for being proactive about my move! And for caring enough to keep our business out the street in the process! You should be thanking the hell out of me!"

Joshua closed the distance between them, stalking towards her like a large predatory cat. The expression on his face forced Bella to take a step backwards, then another, until her body was pressed flat against the wall. Joshua placed his hands on the wall next to her, caging her in on both sides.

"You think I care what other people think?" Joshua's eyes roamed lazily up and down Bella's frame, tripping mini fire alarms inside of her body with his gaze. "In all the years you've known me, have I ever cared about what other people think?"

She averted her eyes.

"Answer me," he demanded.

"No."

He lifted her chin up to meet his gaze.

"So why are you running this time? What have I done now to make you unhappy?"

Didn't he know that she couldn't breathe when he was this close? "It's the middle of the day, Josh. Why are you here?" Bella asked weakly.

He dropped his hand away from her face. "I came home because you had that look. The same one you get every time you get ready to run."

"I was trying to do something right for a change. And—I am happy. Much too happy living here playing house with you. But I have two children to think about now, not just me. This baby will be here any day, and I've got to seriously get my act together. I have to think about how I'm going to take care of them and me." Bella had averted her eyes again, but this time it was so he couldn't see the tears building in them.

"So you're not running away this time?"

"No."

Joshua brushed his thumb lightly across her lips. "And you're happy here, with me?"

"Yes," she whispered hoarsely.

His sudden laughter made Bella finally dare to meet his eyes.

"Bella, your nesting."

"What?"

"Nesting. You went ballistic like this right before Jabari was born. You wanted to knock out walls and stuff. Remember? But your belly was so big, and you couldn't handle the paint fumes, so I had to get everything ready for him."

Bella bit her bottom lip and stared up at Joshua. "Maybe I am nesting. I do have this overwhelming urge to be settled in my own place. Jabari doesn't do so well with change. Come to think of it, I don't either. We've been here for almost nine months and I'm afraid we might both be getting too attached to our living arrangement. I asked Margo to pull some listings nearby, so that you could see Jabari whenever you like, but the houses around here aren't cheap. Even with the alimony and child support you've agreed to pay me I don't know if I'll be able to afford anything nearby."

Joshua took her hand in his and led her over to the couch. "I don't want you thinking about any of that right now."

He sat down on the opposite end of the couch and lifted Bella's legs up onto his lap. "You're making major strides with your group. I want you to continue to do that. I want you to focus on staying healthy and having a healthy baby. Okay? Can you do that for me?"

Joshua peeled her shoes from her feet and then began to massage one foot and then the other.

Bella swallowed. *Mercy.*

"Stay with me a little while longer, Beautiful Bella." Joshua pulled her left foot to his mouth. He kissed the slight hollow that formed the arch of her foot.

Lord. Have. Mercy.

"I can't stay forever, Josh," she croaked.

"I know. But I'm not ready to let you go yet. We'll turn one of the spare rooms into a nursery. I'll take care of it." Joshua removed her feet from his lap then and stood up. "I'll get dinner tonight. You rest."

CHAPTER 41

The office was buzzing with excitement when Tonya and Adrina returned from lunch. Martha, Ted's personal secretary, nearly tackled them both when they walked through the door. "Did you see your office?"

"Not since we left an hour ago. Why?" Tonya asked.

Martha's eyes danced with excitement. "I won't say a word, you'll just have to see it for yourself. But I will say this, Pastor feels awful about having to miss your graduation. He went all out this time and got you the most extravagant gift. He surprised us all. I usually do all the ordering, and I didn't know a thing about it. And given your profession, I think it will be very meaningful for you too."

Tonya raised an eyebrow. "Well, I guess I should go see this very meaningful, extravagant gift."

Tonya stepped inside her office to see a huge arrangement of yellow roses. She breathed in the scent of the fragrant petals as she read the card attached to the vase. *Congratulations, Blackbird, I always knew you'd do it.*

"Wow, they're beautiful. But why did he choose yellow? Isn't yellow supposed to signify friendship?" Adrina asked.

"Because he knows that yellow roses are my absolute favorite."

A black leather professional's couch with a red bow tied around it sat prominently in the corner of her office. Tonya took a seat on it. She ran her hands over the soft, exquisite, Italian leather and found herself remembering.

"How many fingers am I holding up?"

Nine-year-old Joshua stared impatiently up at Tonya from his position on the makeshift professional's couch in the barn. Tonya stood over him in her white lab coat and clipboard asking him a series of very important questions.

"Three."

"Interesting. How many fingers you see now?"

"Seven."

Tonya stared down into the grumpy face of her patient. "Sir, this will be so much easier for you if you just try to relax."

Joshua rolled his eyes. "Tonya, just tell me how to win this game so we can do something else."

"In my office I need you to remember that we aren't related. Please refer to me as Dr. Malone."

Joshua scoffed. "This ain't no office, Tonya. We're in Pepper's stall and I am laying in a pile of hay. I can't believe I agreed to this."

"I am Dr. Malone, and this is my office," Tonya said, pleased that given her godbrother's funky attitude, she was able to stay in character. "And to answer your question, there are no winners or losers in the game of life. In my office we get down to the root cause of your problems."

Joshua sat up. "Well, that's too bad 'cause I only play games where there are winners and losers."

Tonya stomped her foot. "Joshua, no fair! I played cowboys and Indians with you, and I let you tie me to that old railroad track!"

"Nobody made you do that. If you didn't want to you should have said no."

Michael, who was sitting in a chair reading a magazine in Tonya's makeshift waiting room outside Pepper's stall, peeked his head into her office. In that laid-back way of his, he tried to defuse the situation. "Josh, cool out. It's her turn to choose, so just play the game."

Joshua stood up. "No, this game is for losers."

Michael rose from his chair too. He stepped into Joshua's face. "I'm playing, little brother. You calling me a looser?"

"Gentlemen sit down! There will be no fighting in my office!"

Joshua pushed past Michael on his way out the barn. "Man, this game is wack and you just playin' 'cause you like her."

"Joshua Kennedy Keys you get back here this instant!" Tonya screamed, this time coming completely out of character.

"Let him go, Blackbird. I'll be your patient."

"So, I guess the couch and the flowers means Ted supports your career now?" Adrina asked, pulling Tonya away from the past.

"What?"

"Ted supports your career."

"The gifts are from Michael, Adrina."

Adrina's eyes bucked. "But Sister Mouth o' Mighty—you let her think they were from Ted. She's probably blabbed this to the whole church by now."

Tonya rose from the couch. She removed a yellow rose from the large crystal vase and inhaled deeply.

"I didn't let her think anything. Martha made some assumptions, and if she decides to report this to the entire church, I'll leave that for her and Ted to correct."

Adrina glanced down at her watch. "It's almost time for the Youth Core Workers meeting. We'd better get going."

"Why don't you head on down. I'll join you all shortly."

Adrina gathered her purse and walked towards the door. She smiled knowingly at Tonya, "Tell Michael I said hi."

CHAPTER 42

I take it this call means that you received your gift?"
Tonya smiled the moment she heard his voice come through the receiver. "I did, and I have to say, that hands down, this has got to be the second-best gift anyone has ever given me."

Michael's deep laughter filled the phone line. "Oh yeah, tell me about the first."

"Well, when I was ten this boy I knew gave me a unicorn."

"A real live unicorn, huh. How'd he manage to swing that?"

"He borrowed his dad's lathe to make the horn. He worked on it for weeks until it was prefect, until it looked just like the ones the horses on television wear. Then he tied it to my horse, Pepper, and from that day forward, Pepper became a unicorn. Have you ever heard of anything more amazing?"

"Whatever happened to that amazing kid?"

"He grew up to become an amazing man. The most thoughtful, amazing man I know."

CHAPTER 43

Mike and Mother Berry were sitting in his office reviewing Mike's schedule for the remainder of the week when Mike stood up and stretched.

"We been going at this for a while, Mother B. How 'bout we take a break and go grab something to eat? I heard about this a great new seafood place. Let me buy you lunch."

"Michael, I know you hate it when your calendar is jam-packed, but we just have two more agenda items to get through."

"Then we eat?"

"Yes, then we eat. There's a Francesca Milner who, for the last two months, has been trying to schedule a lunch date with you. She says that if you've forgotten who she is, I should simply say the word, Paris. Michael, do I even want to know what that means?"

"No, Mother B, you don't. Those were my pre-salvation years. Francesca now owns a wrecking firm. She wants Home Court to contract with her business. Tell her no to lunch. Business is business. Just 'cause we used to date back in the day, doesn't mean she has the inside track. She's going to have to go through the bidding process like everybody else."

Mother Berry spoke into a small hand held recorder. "Dear Ms. Milner, I regret to inform you that Mr. Dutton's schedule is full, and he will not be able to do lunch with you in the foreseeable future. He is however aware of your wrecking firm and would like to invite you to submit a proposal in the event that your company would like to gain a contract. I am including the information to Home Courts RFP process in the link below. Regards, Vernice Berry, Executive Assistant on behalf of Michael Dutton.”

“Great. Let's go.”

“Last thing. You got a call from a Ms. Adrina Dixon.”

“Name doesn't ring a bell. Is this someone else I used to date?”

“I'm thinking not, she says the two of you have a mutual friend, Tonya.”

CHAPTER 44

o what do you think?" Mike stood over the pool table in his game room while Joshua tapped the table with his cue stick indicating where he would send his next shot. "Ten right there." The ball soared into the hole. "I think there's not enough distance yet."

"What do you mean?"

"Well, I've learned that the key to not beating the hell out of someone is to put the proper amount of distance between them and you until you can calm down and deal with the situation rationally. Like that fool, Mattingham. Nine ball, side pocket."

Mike raised an eyebrow. "You telling me you haven't handled that yet?"

"I can't. Not without ending up on the five o'clock news. I don't have the proper distance yet. When I think about the fact that my family probably wouldn't have been caught up in Hurricane Katrina in the first place had he not stolen that money from Bella, I still see red." Joshua clipped the ball with the cue stick but missed. "When I get into the right head space, I'll be able to handle the situation in a way that brings honor to my God, my family, and me. I ain't there yet. So, for now, I gotta let it ride."

Joshua moved out of the way so that Mike could take his shot. "Just like you ain't there yet with Tonya's dude. Not to mention that this Oscars' stuff is on the heels of some foul mess Aunt Katie told you about the brother in the first place. What if he comes to his senses and shows up at her graduation?"

Mike leaned over the table and prepared to take his shot. "Three, left corner pocket. If he shows up, I look forward to meeting him."

Joshua pointed his pool stick in Mike's direction. "And that's the part I'm concerned about right there. 'Cause if it were me and this was the woman I loved, I'm not so sure I'd be able to keep my cool."

"That's you, Josh. Public displays of aggression aren't my style. Seven off the rails."

"Really? 'Cause I still remember the night Brady left here with four broken ribs, a broken jaw, and a dislocated collar."

"That ain't the same and you know it. This is about being there for Tonya."

"Look bro, with this high-risk pregnancy of Bella's, I can't travel. I'd feel a lot better about you being there if I could."

Mike grinned at his brother as he called the winning shot, "Eight ball corner pocket. I guess you gon' have to do what you always telling the rest of us."

"What's that?"

"Trust God, little brother."

CHAPTER 45

Martha knocked on Tonya's office door before entering. "Look who I found wandering the halls of the church office. If I had to guess, I'd say they were looking for the graduate."

Tonya stood to greet Barbara, Melissa, Katie, and Jack with a hug. "I would have met you guys at the airport."

"In that raggedy thing you call a car? No thank you," Katie said.

Barbara kissed her daughter. "Katie's kidding, dear. We're not concerned about the car."

Katie frowned. "I'm not kidding, I wouldn't be caught dead in that thing."

Jack kissed Tonya's cheek and wrapped her in a bear hug "It's your big day, kiddo. I told you we were coming to you."

"Thanks, Uncle Jack, but I hate the idea of you guys spending money on a New York city cab."

"No cabs this weekend dear. Mikey hired a private car to take us anywhere we want to go this weekend," Melissa said.

Tonya felt her stomach clench at the mention of Michael. She had no cause to think it, he certainly never told her he was coming when he spoke to her via phone last night, but she had hoped that he would be with them. It had been after midnight when her telephone rang.

"How did you know I was still up?"

"I could hear you worrying all the way out here. Why you stressing, Blackbird?"

"Just thinking about the future, what it will hold for me. If I'll be able to find a job in my field. If I'll make a difference."

"Do you realize that you single-handedly built a church that ministers to homeless kids in New York from the ground up? Blackbird, that amazes me. You already make a difference. And whatever you choose to do next, you're going to keep making a difference. Now go to sleep and stop worrying. I just wanted to be the first person to congratulate you on your big day tomorrow."

"Good night, Michael."

"Good night, Blackbird."

When Tonya hung up the phone, she thought about how often, over the years, since she had moved to New York, he had done that. Just knew when something was wrong or off. He would call, or send a note or flowers with a card that said something like, *Smile, Blackbird. Whatever it is, it ain't that bad.*

"Joshua and Bella send their love," Melissa said. "You know Bella could go into labor at any minute now so she can't travel."

"No. I wouldn't expect her to," Tonya said quickly.

"Jack's going to be shooting video this weekend on his fancy new camera for everyone who couldn't be here," Melissa said.

"That's right. Wave to the boys and girls back home, darling," Jack said.

Tonya smiled at the camera and waved. "Hi, everybody."

"We should open gifts now. So everybody back home can see your reaction."

"Barb, that's a fabulous idea," Melissa said, pulling a rectangular gift box from her purse. "This is from Bella."

Tonya removed the pretty satin bow from the box and lifted the lid. She pulled out a peridot and rhinestone necklace. "Oh, Bella, I love it. It's beautiful. Thank you!"

"The card is from Joshie."

Tonya opened the card. She read it quietly and smirked up into the camera. "Really, Josh?"

"Well, don't keep us in suspense, what does it say?" Katie asked.

"It says, and I quote, 'Tonya, take this money and don't you dare complain. You'd better use it too. Just a little something to help with school fees. Love always, Josh.' It's a check for $25,000. Thank you, Josh."

"This next present is from me and your aunt Katie both," Barbara said. She pulled a large scrapbook out and handed it to Tonya. "We made it together."

Tonya paged through the beautiful photo album. "So many beautiful memories. Mom, Aunt Katie, you couldn't have given me a better gift. I love it."

"Well, you out here with all these strange folks it's good to have a reminder of who your family really is." Katie said.

"This next present is from me and Jack," Melissa said.

Tonya tore the wrapping paper off the present and began hopping up and down. "Ow, ow! Dr. Seuss's *The Places You Will Go*. When I was a kid I absolutely adored this book. Thank you, Auntie Mel! Thank you, Uncle Jack!"

Jack chuckled. "Open it up and look inside." Tonya opened the book to find an envelope inside. She opened the envelope and read the contents. "One year's worth of airfare travel. You can go anywhere in the world you want, as many times as you want to go."

Tonya flew into Jack's arms. Almost knocking the camera from his hand in the process. "Thank you. Thank you both."

"Okay, explain to me why the jack-legged preacher isn't here?"

"Katie," Barbara scolded. "Jack's taping."

"Well, I want to know."

"It's fine, Mom. Aunt Katie, for your information, and that of the folks watching back home, one of our newest members is an actress. She's being nominated for an Oscar tonight and she has asked Ted to attend with her. He's not here because he's out doing work for the kingdom."

Katie rolled her eyes. "Okay, you just keep telling yourself that, girlfriend."

"I love all my gifts. But I want to direct your attention to the left side of my office. You'll see that the best gift of all was the one Michael sent me."

"Well, we can't compete with unicorn boy now can we?" Katie said.

Jack chuckled. "Katie, I don't think we ever could."

CHAPTER 46

When they called her name, Tonya Malone, he was there. Standing in the crowded auditorium of over three thousand people, he was there. She felt him, felt his smile of approval when she had received that long awaited piece of paper, the fulfillment of a lifelong dream. She could almost hear him whisper over the den of the clapping crowd, "You did it, Blackbird. You actually did it!" She hadn't asked him to come, hadn't dared to, because it would break her heart if he said no. The only thing she'd had the courage to do, was to slip an extra ticket in the envelope she had sent to his mother. Tonya walked off the stage feeling Michael's presence so strongly that she expected to be swept up into his arms for a hug. She expected him to be right there, no longer a part of the crowd, but waiting at the bottom of the stage for her. But when she descended the stage he wasn't there. That's when she knew that she had conjured the feeling. He had never actually been there. Tonya took her seat beside all the other graduates, accepted the pats on the back, and the we-did-its from her peers, and she bit back tears. *Of course he wouldn't come. I'm not his anymore.* When the ceremony was over Tonya posed for a couple of photos with some friends and then made her way over to the place in the auditorium where she had instructed her family to meet her after the ceremony. When she was about half way there, she saw him standing head and shoulders above the crowd. His hands were tucked casually in the pant pockets of the expensive tailored suit he wore. He was scanning the crowd looking for her. Tonya took off running like a bird in flight and leapt into his arms. The thought of him being there, then not being there, was all too much for her to bear. Now she was crying, weeping heavy tears of relief.

"Shhh, Blackbird? Why the tears on your special day?"

"You're here. You actually came."

"Where else would I be right now, baby? Huh? Tell me that. Where else would I be?" he crooned softly as he kissed her tears away.

Melissa and Barbara both stood off to the side, watching their children in delight. Each woman praying her own prayer secretly within her heart.

Jack caught the reunion on tape. "I definitely don't recall her greeting any of us like that," Jack said to Katie, and the two shared a laugh. When Mike and Tonya finally did break apart, Mike noticed the crowd of onlookers that had formed around them. They had abandoned their own celebrations to gaze at him and Tonya through the lens of cameras, cell phones, and various other recording devices.

"Come on. Let's get you out of here," he murmured. Mike led Tonya and their family out of the auditorium into the waiting car.

CHAPTER 47

Y ou're sure you don't mind?" Tonya asked for the umpteenth time. "It's going to be a dinky little house party in somebody's cramped New York City apartment. Nothing like what you're used to."

Mike sat across from Tonya in the back of the private car he had rented for the weekend. After her graduation ceremony, the family had all gone out to dinner. The driver had just dropped the elders back at the hotel and now the young folks were prepared to hang.

"What's the rule, Blackbird?"

"I know but—"

"What's the rule?"

"My city my rules, your city your rules," Tonya muttered.

"That's right, and whose turf are we on right now?"

"Mine."

"So you already know I'm cool with it. The question is are you? Sounds to me like you're the one who doesn't want to go to this party."

"Adrina put a lot of effort into this party. It would be rude for me not to make an appearance. But, I do have a guest from out of town, and this party is not going to be anything near the caliber of what you're used to so—"

Mike shook his head. "Nah, you're not about to put that on me."

"What?"

"You're having a meltdown right now and your projecting."

"I am not melting or projecting."

"Yeah you are. You've met your quota of outside people today, now all you want to do is go someplace and chill."

Tonya chewed her bottom lip. She'd been feeling like this a lot lately, especially when it came to scheduling quality time with Ted. Did that make the man she'd pledged to marry, outside people? Tonya pushed the thought out of her mind. "I was fine at dinner."

"Dinner with family, inside people."

"Maybe you're right."

"I'm definitely right. Nothing wrong with it. To thy own self be truth and all that jazz. Just don't go around projecting your feelings off on me." Mike stretched his long body out, and placed his hands behind his head. His handsome face broke into a sexy grin, "I'm an extrovert, baby. Crowds energize me. I can party in a penthouse or a shack. Makes no difference to me."

Tonya cut her eyes at him.

Mike pointed his finger at her. "See there. That's what I'm talking about. Rolling your eyes, sucking your teeth and thangs."

"I did not suck my teeth."

"In another two more hours you'll be downright rude."

"I'm never rude."

"Really? 'Cause you're about to be Bad Boy rude."

Tonya laughed. "I'd have to be falling down exhausted before I ever became like that."

The family had discovered during the brothers' professional careers, that Joshua, a classic introvert, should never do postgame interviews. One smart-aleck comment from a reporter was bound to unleash Joshua's dark side. The best course of action after a game was for Joshua to hit the showers and chill.

"Can you believe all those people at his house? Ever think in a million years that Joshua would throw a party and invite two thousand people?"

Michael's simple response caught Tonya off guard. "God has done an amazing work in my brother."

She smiled. "I need to suck it up and go to this party, huh?"

"Not my call, Blackbird, but for the sake of full disclosure I should let you know that your girl, called me."

"Adrina called you? Well, what did she say?"

Mike shrugged. "She started off talking smack. Said she played some college ball and thought she could take me in a game of one-on-one. Your girl got jokes, huh?"

She sure does. This time Tonya did suck her teeth. She loved Adrina dearly, loved her like a sister, but the whole *Love and Basketball* thing wasn't even about to happen. Not in this lifetime or the next would Adrina Dixon ever be playing Michael Dutton for his heart.

"She also said that she wanted to make sure that today was special for you. She was angry about your no-account-preacher not showing up."

"Michael, he's my fiancé. Can you at least try to be respectful?" Tonya said quietly.

"Her words, Blackbird, not mine."

"What else did she say?"

"That you should have someone here today who would always choose you."

"Is that the reason why you decided to come, because Adrina challenged you to a basketball game and asked you to?"

Tonya stared out the car window, she wouldn't dare in this moment meet his eyes.

Michael sighed. "I see my calculations were way off."

"Whatever," Tonya muttered.

"Blackbird."

"What?"

"Look at me and ask me that question again. I dare you."

CHAPTER 48

Wait!"

They were standing outside of Adrina's apartment. Mike's hand was at the door, posed to knock.

"We should have some sort of password or phrase we use when one of us is ready to go."

Mike shrugged. "How about this party is weak, let's bounce."

"No, I mean like if others are around. I don't want to offend anyone. Trust me, Michael. I know my friends. Once we walk through that door, they are going to want to keep us here all night. And as you so aptly pointed out in the car on the way over here, I have about two hours of sweet, kind, agreeable Tonya left."

"Less than that. I miscalculated."

"Okay, fine. All the more reason why we should come up with a password."

"I'll tell you what. You come up with the password, and I'll follow your lead."

As the evening progressed, Tonya found herself becoming increasingly possessive of the man she had introduced to her New York crew as, her oldest and dearest friend in the whole wide world. From the moment they had walked through the door all the women in the apartment had flocked to him. Married, single, it didn't matter. And why wouldn't they? Michael was handsome, charming, and extremely personable. He was everything you expected a celebrity not to be. Even when he could care less about a topic, Michael had a way of holding a person's gaze and leaning into the conversation, like who they were and what they were saying was the most important thing in the world. He made every single person he encountered at her party that night feel seen, heard, and special. Usually, this was a trait that Tonya admired about him. Usually, it was a trait she even tried to harness and emulate herself, especially when it came to ministry. But they had been at this party for forty long minutes and the fact that Michael's attention had been directed elsewhere for the entire time was causing Tonya to feel downright salty. This graduation party, thrown in her honor, was starting to wear on her last nerve.

Then they had to watch the Oscars, because someone thought it would be a good idea to see if their newest sister-in- Christ had won. As the nominations were being read, the camera panned across the faces in the audience, and settled on a very nervous looking Tatiana. Ted's fingers were interlaced with hers and he kissed the back of her hand when her name was read. Her fiancé looked every bit the part of somebody's else's supportive boyfriend.

The room of partygoers erupted in a sad, "Aw!" when the model turned actress didn't take the win. But Tonya caught a reflection of herself in Adrina's living room mirror. She was actually smiling. Michael caught it too. His eyes meet hers across the room over the head of a redheaded woman named Emma he was talking to. When he looked at her, he mouthed the words *ten minutes*. They had been at the party for an hour at this point, and she knew he was telling her she only had ten minutes left before kind, friendly Tonya left the building.

But then Adrina, her tall, beautiful, basketball-loving friend turned off the television and announced that it was time for a game of Spades, and that since this was her house, Michael would be her partner. Tonya cleared her throat and invoked the password.

"That's not going to happen. Because we actually have to get going. I promised my neighbor I would feed her dog."

"Aw, on your graduation night," one of the partygoers groaned.

"I'm afraid so," Tonya said with a fake smile.

Adrina's forehead crinkled in confusion. "I thought pets weren't allowed in your building."

"They're not, my neighbor has special needs. It's a service dog."

Mike kissed Adrina's cheek. "We will definitely have to get that game of Spades in another time." He said his goodbyes to the rest of her friends and led Tonya out the building with a hand pressed gently to the small of her back.

"By the way, you're banned for life from making up passwords," Michael said once they had settled themselves in the car.

Tonya rolled her eyes and stared out the window. "Please, that was a good one, and you know it."

"Really? 'Cause I'm wondering how your blind neighbor is navigating the mean streets of New York without her seeing eye dog?"

"I didn't say she was blind. I said she had special needs. She could be in the hospital right now."

"Sometimes the truth is just easier for people to swallow, Blackbird."

"And what's that, Michael?"

He nearly stole her breath with his full, dimpled smile. "That you're madly in love with me, and you want me all to yourself."

CHAPTER 49

As they walked up the path to Tonya's building, she pulled out the key to the large outer door.

"Where's the night doorman?"

"There is no doorman for this building. But it's super safe here, Michael. Everybody looks out for each other."

They rode the elevator to Tonya's floor, then walked down a narrow but well-lit corridor to Tonya's apartment. Tonya pulled out her keys again this time to open her front door. She stepped aside for Michael to enter. "Welcome to my humble abode."

He took a few moments to examine the flimsy lock on the front door but said nothing. Next, he eyed the old wooden bat Tonya kept by the front door. "What's that for?"

"Oh, that. A gift from Ted. Just in case there was ever an intruder. Not that there ever would be because it's super safe around here."

"Yeah, you said that already. Twice." Michael ran one large hand over his face and changed the subject. "What you want to do, Blackbird? I'm yours for the rest of the evening."

Tonya tried to stifle a yawn. "We could watch a movie."

"Or I could bid you goodnight and we could do breakfast in the morning."

Tonya leaned into his chest. "You said you were mine for the rest of the night."

"You're dead on your feet."

She shook her head. "You said you were mine for the rest of the night, and I'm not ready to say goodbye yet."

"Go get ready for bed. I'll stay and watch one movie with you, but the moment I hear snoring, I'm out."

Tonya squealed in delight and ran off to change clothes. At about 2:00 AM Mike lifted a sleeping Tonya off the couch and attempted to deposit her into her bed, but she wrapped her arms tightly around his neck and nestled her head into his chest.

"Tonya, let me go."

"I can't. I figured it out."

"Figured what out?"

"Why I've been out of sorts this whole evening. It's because you haven't held me. Not once. You sat across from me in the car. At dinner I had to share you with Aunt Katie, my mom, Auntie Mel, and Uncle Jack. At the party I had to share you with Emma and Adrina, and Mary, and Perry.

Mike chuckled. "Mary's husband?"

"Uh hum."

"You're delirious you know that?"

She yawned. "I know."

"Truth serum," Mike muttered. "Of course you do."

"I don't feel right when you're near and you're not holding me."

Mike sighed, absentmindedly running his hands up and down her back. "I'm just trying not to complicate things between us, baby, that's all. Trust me, when I'm near I always want to be holding you too."

"Prove it. Hold on to me for the rest of the night."

Mike kicked off his shoes and lifted her up onto the bed and Tonya fell back to sleep against the rhythm of his heart.

CHAPTER 50

Bella awoke to the sound of her cell phone buzzing on the nightstand beside her. She looked at the display screen to see a call coming through from Pamela Ford. Pamela was the head pastor's wife, and the unofficial president of their unofficial little group of pastors' wives at New Horizons Christian Training Center affectedly coined, the First Wives Club. A group Bella still hadn't quite reconciled herself fully to being a part of yet. Bella loved the women, yes. Each one of the five women had quickly won a place in her heart. But somedays it was still mind-numbing to think that her Joshua, her Bad-Boy-Rebel-Without-a-Cause, Joshua, was a pastor. Bella sat up in bed and answered the phone.

"Good Morning, Pam."

"Oh, Bella, I'm sorry, did I wake you?"

Bella looked at the clock for the first time. It was 11:34 AM. A normal productive person, one who'd gotten a full night's sleep the night before, would be up and at 'em by now, not still hugging the bed. Bella groaned. The further along Bella got in this pregnancy, she found herself sleeping more and more. Just the other day, she had asked Joshua to do one thing. One simple request. Please don't let her oversleep like this again. His response to her had been a flat-out no. No explanation, just, no.

Bella had been an early riser all her life. She'd even been an early riser when she was pregnant with Jabari. So she saw no reason why this pregnancy should be any different. Yesterday, she had set her alarm to go off at 9:00 AM, but somehow managed to sleep until one in the afternoon. Bella angrily rolled out of bed and stomped downstairs to find the culprit who had dared to unplug her alarm. She found Joshua and Jabari in the theatre room, their hands fiercely gripping video game controllers. Bella stood in front of the large movie screen blocking their view, causing them to have no other choice but to pause the game. "Yep, that's right. I'm standing in front of the screen, and I dare either one of you jokers to complain."

Joshua paused the game and stared patiently up at Bella. "Good morning."

Bella rolled her eyes at him and focused her attention on Jabari. "Jabari, from now on if I sleep past 9:30 I want you to come and wake me. I have a lot of things to do before this baby gets here, and I can't afford to sleep the entire day away."

"Sorry, Mom, I really wish I could help you out with that, but Dad said that under no circumstance am I ever to wake you. Even if the house is on fire."

Bella folded her arms across her chest and stared down at her husband and son. "Even if the house is on fire. Don't wake me up. Josh, are you kidding me? What kind of crazy mess is that?"

The corners of Joshua's lips turned up into a half smile. "Jabari, what are you supposed to do if your mother's sleeping, a fire breaks out, and I'm not here."

"Throw mom over my shoulders and fireman carry her out the house."

Joshua extended his arm to Jabari for a fist pound. "My guy." He turned his attention back to Bella. "I told you I'd get everything ready for the baby."

"Yes but—"

"But nothing, Bella. Don't I take care of you?"

Every once in a while, she saw it, the old spark in his eye that told her that the old Joshua might be subdued but he wasn't completely gone.

"Of course you do."

"I don't need you to bring home a check. I haven't

asked you to punch a clock. You got one job, Bella, and that's to bring the life."

"I know," Bella said defensively.

"If you know it, then bring it. I might check on you from time to time just to make sure you're still breathing, but other than that, I'mma get out your way and let you bring the life."

Bella rolled her eyes at the memory.

"No, it's fine, Pam," Bella said, adjusting herself in the bed. "I should have been up anyways. I hate it when Josh lets me sleep this late."

"I'm sure he just wants to make sure that you get your rest. Take it from the mother of three grown boys. Get all the sleep you can now my friend, because when that baby gets here, sleep will be a thing of a past. Anyways, I just called to see what you are wearing to the Pastors' Appreciation Banquet this evening. You guys are going, right?"

"Uh, I don't know. Hang on for a second, let me check." Bella could here water running in the bathroom. If Joshua was showering this late, it meant that he had gotten a full workout in already. Bella rapped on the master bathroom door. Joshua stood in the mirror, bare chested with a towel wrapped around his waist. He was shaving. He smiled down at Bella standing in the doorway. "Good morning."

"Or afternoon depending on how you look at it," Bella said.

Joshua walked toward her, closing the gap between them. Bella felt her stomach do a backflip when he leaned in close enough to kiss her. "One job, remember?"

"Yeah, yeah, I know, bring the life." Bella allowed her eyes to sweep lazily over his body one good time before she willed her eyes back up to his face.

"Hum, Josh, is there some sort of Pastors' Appreciation Banquet happening today?"

His eyes lit up at her question. "You coming with me, right?"

"Of course." Bella slipped out of the bathroom and returned to the phone. "Pam, we're going, but I don't have any idea what I'm wearing."

Pam laughed. "I guess that means we get to go shopping."

CHAPTER 51

Tonya awoke the next morning to find Michael gone. Other than the lingering scent of his aftershave on her pillow there was no proof that he had been there. Tonya slipped her feet into her fuzzy pink house slippers and padded into the kitchen biting back a sense of panic. A strong sense of relief washed over her when he looked over at her and smiled.

Lord, how am I ever going to be able to let this man go?

He was testing what appeared to be a brand-new lock on her front door. "Good morning, Blackbird."

"Good morning, when did you—"

"I called a 24-hour locksmith." Michael motioned for her to come near. "The deadbolt should hold, but in the event that it doesn't, an intruder will be stopped by the chain. So, no matter what time of day it is, always use the chain."

Tonya grinned and nodded her head obediently.

"I'm not playing, Tonya. If a two-hundred-and-fifty-pound man comes barreling through that door, a bat ain't gon' do you no good."

"Michael, I promise, I will always use the chain."

"Your new keys are on the kitchen table. Get your house keys and put them on your ring now."

Tonya walked over to her purse and fished out her keys. "My super is not going to be happy with this you know. We aren't supposed to make any structural changes whatsoever to the building."

"If the super has a problem with it, tell him to call me."

CHAPTER 52

Joshua set a cooler of meat down by Micah, who was grilling the food for the day's festivities, while the other pastors of New Horizons carried things in and out of his yard at their wives' command.

Joshua wiped his brow with the edge of his shirt and took a moment to survey his yard. His entire west lawn had been decked out in pale pink and seafoam green. "Ladies, thanks again for doing this. Everything looks prefect."

Carmen and Kim Lee, who were busy placing the tiny little lace bootie centerpieces on the tables, both stopped their work to smile at him.

"We love Bella, Joshua. There is no need to thank us," Kim Lee said.

"That's right. So don't thank us again. I already told you, Bella's our girl," Carmen said.

Joshua held his hands up in surrender. "I promise I won't."

Keith handed a box of party decorations off to Darren and came and stood beside his wife. Deanna was busy counting tables when Keith wrapped his arms around her waist. "Josh, is right, baby, you've done an amazing job."

"Thanks. This is only going to be the greatest garden party ever. Oh sweetie, that reminds me. Can you help Carlos and Dave move the ice sculpture? I'm afraid it's going to block the band."

Keith's eyes bucked. "Dee, you hired a band for a baby shower?"

Deanna nodded. "The Ga-Gas. They play children's music. Isn't that the coolest thing ever?"

"Babe, that sounds expensive. Did you clear that with, Josh?"

"I did, he gave me his gold card. He said he wanted this day to be special for Bella and that I should spare no expense."

⁂

Joshua kissed Melissa's cheek. "Hey, you made it. How was the drive?"

"Very peaceful, dear."

"Mrs. Kennedy, you might want to look through these, but I'm pretty sure we got everything," Keith said as he, Carlos, Darren, and Dave appeared with the presents they had retrieved from her car.

"Thank you, boys," Melissa said.

"It's no problem at all, ma'am," Dave said as the others echoed their agreement.

"I think we are gonna need another gift table though," Darren added.

Joshua looked from his friends loaded down with the colorfully wrapped packages then back again to his mother. "Mom this is . . . excessive."

"Well, it's not all mine, Joshie. Barbara and Katie couldn't make it. Two of those packages are from them."

"There's over twenty gifts here."

"Your dad and I got a few things."

Joshua raised his eyebrow. "A few?"

"Well, sweetie, we kind of started a little collection when Mikey first told us about the baby."

Joshua moved closer to her and lowered his voice. "You guys didn't have to do all of this, Mom. Despite the circumstances surrounding the birth, Bella is my responsibility. This child won't lack for anything."

Melissa patted her son's hand before she sat her

163

purse down and got to work. "Of course, she won't, dear."

🎇 🎇 🎇

Sharon checked her watch. "Pam should be arriving with Bella any minute now."

"Where did they go?"

"Shopping for an outfit to wear to the Pastors' Appreciation Banquet that Bella thinks is happening today," Carmen said.

Micah looked up from turning the meat on the grill. "Pam called this morning to ask Bella what she was going to wear. The two of them made a day of it."

Darren shook his head. "So basically, y'all got the First Lady of the church lying?"

"She didn't lie. There is a Pastors' Appreciation Banquet coming up, it's just not today," Sharon said.

🎇 🎇 🎇

"Surprise!!!"

Bella walked into the backyard and saw the former Dunbar Street crew, the ladies from her accountability circle, the women from the First Wives Club, along with their husbands, and her mother-in-law. Just about everybody she loved. She buried herself into Joshua's arms and began to cry.

"Josh, you—"

"I can't take the credit. This is all your girls. They wanted to do something special for you."

Joshua wrapped her tightly in his embrace and kissed the top of her head.

"Oh, Bella, please stop all that crying before you ruin your mascara," Pam said. "We got facials today." Pam spoke to the crowd.

"I'm sorry, it's just everything is so beautiful and . . . unexpected. I thought we were getting ready for the Pastors' Appreciation Banquet."

"Did I say Pastors' Appreciation Banquet? Well what I meant to say was, Bella's surprise baby shower." Pam said.

"I hope they massaged your fingers at that spa girlfriend, because you have a ton of presents to open," Deanna said.

CHAPTER 53

Bella pulled the baby quilt from between the folds of the soft tissue paper to the chorus of oohs, and ahs.

"Everybody did a square," Pearl explained. "Ms. Sally, the twins. Lola moved back to Louisiana last month, but she faithfully sent her finished square in the mail. Even that old crazy daughter of mine did her square before everything happened."

"Pearl and I both finished it with hand stitching," Maggie said.

"What a lovely heirloom for the baby," Carmen said.

"It's beautiful. I will cherish this forever," Bella said as she clutched the quilt to her chest.

Melissa fingered the intricate border. "I have always wanted to learn how to do this. Something creative with my hands."

"Oh it's, easy, Melissa. Pearl and I would be happy to show you a few stiches," Maggie said.

"Would you really?"

"Absolutely. We'll have you quilting in no time," Pearl said.

❧ ❧ ❧

"Attention everyone! We interrupt this party with a brief message from one of our very handsome sponsors," Deanna said. She pressed a button on the remote control for the large flat screen television she and Carmen had rolled out on a cart.

The screen settled on a living room with a red couch. Mike and Tonya both appeared in the frame and took a seat next to each other on the couch. Bella couldn't help but notice how Mike's arm hung causally around Tonya's shoulder and how Tonya leaned easily into him as if it were the most natural thing in the world.

"Hey, Bella baby, I'm sorry I couldn't be there to celebrate with you today. As you can see, I'm still in New York with the Blackbird."

Mike turned to Tonya. "Blackbird, you want to say something to the folks back home?"

Tonya waved. "Hi everybody. Hi, Bella. I love you, and I miss you so much. And I love, love, love the necklace you made me. It's so beautiful—"

"Baby, can the two of you talk about that later? We need to go ahead and finish this up," Mike said.

"Right, of course." Tonya winked at the camera. "Bella, girl, I'll call you later."

A sly grin spread across Bella's face. She spoke aloud to the TV screen even though she knew Tonya couldn't hear her, "You better call me!"

Mike spoke into the camera. "You're a talented artist, sis, and I'm proud of you. I figured with the restart of your business, you might need a little professional help around the house with the baby. So, you've got a nanny for as long as you need one, starting immediately, after the baby is born. Jeeves did the first round of interviews. Josh and I both conducted the second round."

"And since I can't have my little godson or goddaughter in the hands of some deranged psychopath, I created the psychological profile that served as the final cut," Tonya said.

"It's a girl," Mike said.

Tonya stared at him. "What?"

"You said godson or goddaughter. It's a girl."

"How do you know?"

Mike shrugged. "Josh, said it was a girl."

"And how does he know?" both Bella and Tonya said speaking into the monitor at the same time.

Mike smirked at Tonya and turned back to the camera. "Anyways, the five candidates you are about to see turned out to be our top picks. We'll leave the rest up to you. I know you're in the middle of your party. We gonna end this little intro. Later, when you feel up to it, you can put your feet up, read their resumes and watch the interviews. We got some sightseeing to do so, Blackbird, go ahead and say goodbye to the folks back home."

Tonya waved. "Bye, everyone."

❧ ❧ ❧

"Okay, so here's the deal. We got you something too 'cause, apparently, showers aren't just for women anymore. We figured you didn't want all the hoopla going on at the ladies tables so uh, here." Keith shoved the badly wrapped gift into Joshua's hand.

"Yo, Keith, what's up? I thought you were gonna wrap it, man," Darren said.

"It is wrapped."

"Who wrapped it, Ray Charles?" Carlos asked.

Micah and the other men laughed.

"Looks like his cat wrapped it," Dave said.

"Shut up. All of you," Keith snapped.

Joshua tore the tattered gift paper from the package. He removed a miniature Rockets jumpsuit from the box. Joshua smiled. "That is pretty fly. Even I gotta admit."

CHAPTER 54

Joshua's eyes snapped open immediately at the sound of Bella's muffled scream. He ran down the hall and burst into the master bedroom. "What's the matter?"

"My leg! It hurts!"

Joshua turned on the lamp on the bedside table. "Which one?"

Bella's eyes were wide with fear and sweat matted her hair to her face. "The left."

Joshua quickly examined the leg. "It's a charley horse. I know it's painful but I need you to relax for a second and try to breathe."

Joshua kneeled on the bed in front of her. He pulled Bella's leg toward him in a stretch.

"Josh, no, don't!"

"Just give me a second." He pressed the sole of her foot forward gently and elongated the stretch.

Bella sighed.

Joshua studied her face for signs of distress. "Better?"

Bella nodded. "This is so hard."

"I know, but you're doing great."

"Will you stay with me? Just until I fall back to sleep?"

Joshua wiped the sweat from her brow. "Yeah, I can do that." Joshua pulled the covers back. Bella climbed under the sheet and he climbed into bed next to her. Joshua reached over and turned off the lamp, then he pulled Bella into his arms and waited for her to fall back to sleep.

"Did you enjoy your shower today?"

"It was nice, especially having your mom there."

In the darkness, Joshua could hear the tears building in her throat.

"It made me miss her. My mom." Bella's voice hitched then, and Joshua knew she was crying.

"I tried calling the number the other day, it was disconnected. They've had the same number my whole life. Over the years I would call it, even when we weren't speaking. Just to hear her voice.

Joshua had figured that was the case. Shortly after they'd left New Orleans, Joshua would notice the random forty second calls to her parent's house showing up on the phone bill. He'd never mentioned it to her because he knew that despite everything that had happened between them, they were still her parents. It was only natural for her to want to hear their voices. This is what he told her now.

"They're still your parents, Bella. Nothing wrong with wanting to hear their voices."

"Not them, Joshua. Her," Bella said vehemently. "I needed to hear my mama's voice. For years, until I walked up to that altar and broke the soul ties, I heard my daddy's voice in my head. I called because I needed to hear hers."

"It's okay. I get it."

"What if I never hear her voice again? What if—" Her voice broke, and Bella began to sob.

Joshua pulled her close and planted a soft kiss at the base of her neck. "Either way it's going to be okay. We'll find them. Alright? I promise."

CHAPTER 55

Melissa walked into the kitchen while Joshua was making breakfast the next morning. She stood on her tiptoes and kissed her youngest son on the cheek. "Need any help?"

"Nope, but you can take a load off and keep me company. We haven't had a chance to catch up in a while. How was the graduation?"

"Oh, Joshie, it was—I don't know if I have the words for it. Your dad's got it all on tape. I brought it so we can watch later on."

Joshua smiled. "That's good. Especially if you don't have words."

"Tonya was a little out of sorts when we first got there."

"What do you mean?"

"Well with the preacher not showing up for her graduation and Harold being gone."

Joshua beat the bowl of eggs. "I hadn't considered that part."

"I think when she dreamed of this day, she always thought Harold would be there. But after she got her diploma and walked off that stage and saw your brother. She literally flew into his arms. Them holding on to each other like that, Joshie, I gotta tell you, it was the most beautiful symbol of hope these eyes of mind have seen in a long time. Kind of reminds me of you and Bella."

Joshua grunted. "Mom, what are you doing?"

"I'm sitting here talking to you, dear."

"No, your interfering. Tonya's engaged."

"I'm not. I'm just—Tonya is family. I would love for her to be my daughter-in-law, but I do understand that she is engaged. Until God says otherwise."

"Mom."

"What?"

"Stay out of this."

"As your aunt Barb would say, I won't say another mumbling word about it."

"Naw, that's Aunt Katie. Not another mumbling word."

"That's right. Barb would say—"

"I'mma take it to the Lord in prayer," Joshua finished for her.

"That's right. That's exactly what I'm going to do. But for the record, I've met this fiancé of hers and I am none too impressed."

"Maybe you can't be impressed because in your mind you still see Tonya and Mike together. They've both moved on."

"Is it a crime to want to see both my boys happy?"

"It's not a crime, Mom, but nothing good can come out of pushing him towards a woman who is already engaged to another man."

"If you're so concerned about your brother's happiness, why'd you fire his girlfriend?"

Joshua removed a pan of bacon from the oven. "Because she disrespected my wife. No matter how temporary Bella's and my situation is, she is still my wife. I can't have a person like that working for me."

Melissa stared at her son.

"What? I gave her a good severance package. Besides she shouldn't work for us if Mike is going to be seeing her anyways."

"Speaking of temporary. I saw this temporary nursery you're fixing up for Bella's baby."

"You obviously overlooked the keep out danger sign on the door, but other than that, how'd you get in? The door was locked."

Melissa dismissed her son with a wave of her hand. "Oh, that. I picked the lock. All those foster kids living in the house. One of the first things your father taught me how to do was pick a lock. That's why we never had any surprise attacks. We always went through their things. Of course, we never went through you and your brother's things though."

"Sure, of course not."

"Put yourself in our shoes. How else were we supposed to know what was going on? Some of those kids were dealing with some serious issues."

"I'm not judging, you did what you had to do."

"That's a mighty elaborate temporary nursery wouldn't you say?"

Joshua stared at her.

"You and Bella are good together."

"You think it was a good idea you and dad buying all that stuff?"

"What stuff, honey?"

"The 'I Love My Grandma' bibs. 'Grandpa's Little Angel' t-shirts. 'Cause Grandma Said So' onesies. Don't you think that could give this child the wrong impression?"

"Trust me it won't. I've made a decision about this baby. I'm keeping her."

"What do you mean, *you're keeping her?*"

"Joshie, you were right about Bella. Years ago, maybe after the third or fourth time she ran. I told you she was unsaveable. That you should just walk away. Do you remember what you said to me? You said, 'Mom, I'll never walk away. God gave her to me and I'm not going to give up on her.' You were right. I look at Bella now, and I can see what God has done. And I pray you don't give up on her now. But if you decided that you and Bella can't work things out. I'm keeping this baby. Mikey has agreed to be her godfather. I don't see why I can't be her grandma."

CHAPTER 56

When Joshua walked into the private eye's office the next day, the older woman with the cat eye glasses seated at the receptionist desk stared up at him with wonder and amazement. "Am I asleep or awake?"

Joshua smiled down at the woman. "I'm pretty sure you're awake."

"The gals at bingo are never going to believe this. Not in a million years. Say, could I get an autograph?"

Joshua read the nameplate on her desk. "Sure thing, Gertrude."

"It's Gertie. All my friends call me Gertie."

"Well, Gertie, I have a favor to ask you."

"Name it. Anything for you, Joshua."

Joshua took a seat on the edge of the older woman's desk, "Well here's the thing, Gertie. It'll probably get you fired."

CHAPTER 57

When Tonya walked into the restaurant the next day, all eyes seemed to be on her. Ted rose to greet her and pulled out her chair. "Good morning, beautiful," he said as he kissed her cheek.

"Morning to you too."

"When I saw you were running late, I took the liberty of ordering the sunrise omelet for you. I hope that's okay."

"No that's prefect, I'm starving."

Tonya glanced over at the people at the adjacent tables. Was it her imagination, or were these people really staring at her?

"They just want to get a closer look at Lois Lane," Ted whispered as he pushed her chair in. He took his seat across the table from her.

"Who?"

"You made the cover of *People*."

Tonya poured a glass of orange juice from the carafe sitting on the table. Ted removed the folded magazine from the inside pocket of his suit coat. He laid it down on the table.

Tonya looked down at the photo of her and Michael embracing at her graduation ceremony. The words: WHO IS LOIS LANE? were splashed across the magazine cover. Tonya calmly sipped her juice and said nothing.

"There's a really interesting article to go with this picture too. Shall I read it to you?" Ted's eyes met Tonya's in a challenge. He picked up the magazine, flipped to an earmarked page and read, "That's the Man of Steel but who is Lois Lane? Our sources identify her as Tonya Malone, the Man of Steel's long-time secret girlfriend. The only woman he has ever truly loved. According to one source, the Man of Steel has never been publicly photographed with her because he cares for her deeply and never wanted the media in their business. Given the way his brother, Bad Boy Joshua Keys's marriage suffered at the hands of the press, we can definitely see why the Man of Steel would want to keep his love life under wraps. We reached out to the Man of Steel and a representative from Mr. Dutton's camp had this to say on his behalf: 'Ms. Malone is a close, personal, friend of Mr. Dutton. The two are not romantically involved. Ms. Malone is actually engaged to another man. Mr. Dutton flew to New York to celebrate a special day with a dear friend and he asks that the media and his fans respect Ms. Malone's privacy. He also states that all inquiries regarding his love life should be forwarded to him.' That's his story folks and apparently, he's sticking to it. Still, we all know that a picture is worth a thousand words and this picture has this reporter for one asking, if Ms. Malone is engaged to be married, then where on earth is her engagement ring?'"

Ted slapped the magazine down on the table. "I'm actually wondering the same thing, myself. When you were hugged up with your celebrity ex-boyfriend, why weren't you wearing my ring? This makes me a laughing stock. You do know that, right? Everybody reads *People*."

The waiter approached the table. "Sunrise omelet."

"That's me," Tonya said.

The waiter set the plate down in front of Tonya and then another plate of corn beef and hash in front of Ted.

"Can I get you anything else?"

"No, thanks. We're good," Ted said, in a voice that told Tonya they were anything but good.

Tonya bowed her head and silently blessed her food. *Lord bless this food, bless the hands that prepared and served it. Help me to hold my tongue and not make a scene in this restaurant.*

Amen. Tonya lifted her head and took a bite of her omelet.

"Well, don't you have anything to say for yourself?"

🥀 🥀 🥀

Mattingham walked into his office to see Joshua sitting in his chair with his feet propped up on his desk reading one of his confidential files.

"What the f@%!

"You know, that's exactly what I've been trying to figure out for quite some time now," Joshua said as he slowly paged through the file in his hand. "What would make you think you could steal from me and get away with it?"

Mattingham's eyes skirted quickly towards the door. "How'd you get in here?"

Joshua rose from the desk and stalked towards Mattingham. "Gertie's a fan. Now try and keep up. You put three hundred dollars in my wife's hand and left her and my son to die in New Orleans."

"I'm calling the cops. You can't prove anything."

Joshua shook the file in Mattingham's face. "Wrong answer again. Don't you listen? Did I not tell you to keep up? I have access to all your files because Gertie is my biggest fan."

"Now, just hold on a second! I may have skimmed a little off the top, but I-I-I had no idea that storm was coming!"

"You call $21,500 skimming off the top? I'd hate to see what happens when you really steal from me."

Silence.

"I assume that was a loan. So how do you suggest we handle repayment?"

"I can't give you the money. It's long gone. Please don't hurt me." Mattingham dropped to the floor shielding his face with his hands.

Joshua stared at the cowering man in disgust. "Get up. I didn't come here for that."

Mattingham slowly rose to his feet, but he made sure to keep the large metal desk as a barrier between him and Joshua.

"I want my money, every dime of it, and since we can both agree to call it a loan, instead of the felony that it really is, I expect you to add my interest. Understood?"

"Mr. Keys I would love to pay you back, I really would, I just don't have access to that kind of cash."

Joshua cocked his head towards the open file drawer. "Is that right? 'Cause according to your records you do quite a bit of skimming from all your clients."

"You don't understand. Most of that money went to pay gambling debts. I'm an addict. I'm ashamed to say it, but it's true. I can't go to jail. I'm not— I'm not built for that." Mattingham's fat shoulders jiggled as he broke down and wept loudly.

"I'm going to allow you the opportunity to work off your debt with me," Joshua said quietly.

"Believe me, I am very grateful for the opportunity, sir."

Joshua reached inside his suit pocket. He removed an envelope and dropped it on the desk. "I need you to read and sign our new service agreement."

Mattingham looked warily up at Joshua. "That's it? That's all you want? You're not going to rat me out to the others?"

Silence.

In fact, the silence lasted so long to Mattingham it felt like an eternity.

Finally, Joshua spoke, "Get yourself into a twelve-step program, prove to me that you're attending the meetings, and those confidential files my number one fan just emailed me will never see the light of day."

ᕲ ᕲ ᕲ

"I saw a very interesting headline this morning too. That was one of the reasons why I missed my train. I stopped to buy it." Tonya opened her purse and pulled out a copy of a magazine and set it down on the table. The article title read: TATIANA HAS A NEW BOO.

Ted looked down at the photo of him with a skimpily clad Tatiana draped over his arm. Tatiana was kissing Ted's neck.

"Your picture didn't make the cover, but Tatiana isn't nearly as big of a name as the Man of Steel. But then again, who is, right? Still, page three isn't so shabby for a young rising star."

"Tonya, you know this picture isn't what it appears to be. This was just—"

"Oh, I know, you told me. Ministry. Lucky for you no one reads, *Vibe Star.*"

"Look, I'm—It's obvious that we've both been set up. These people are experts at making innocent moments look . . . salacious. Why don't we put this whole sorted affair behind us and enjoy the rest of our morning?"

Tonya sat back in her chair and took a drink of her orange juice. "Uh huh, I thought so."

ᕲ ᕲ ᕲ

Mattingham paced back and forth across his office like a caged bear for at least an hour after Joshua had left. He let out a string of curses before bellowing into the intercom on his desk.

"Gertie, get in here!"

"Don't bother firing me, Marty. I quit," Gertie called from the outer office.

Mattingham walked out into the outer office as fast as his stubby little legs would take him. He stood in front of Gertie's desk with his hands on his hips.

"Who said anything about firing ya? We have a mutually beneficial thing going here. You need this job to pay your husband's medical bills and I need you."

"Not anymore I don't, Marty. Joshua Keys retired Lonnie's medical debt and he offered me a job too. It seems he needs a new personal assistant and wouldn't you know it, I fit the bill. That, Joshua, I tell you, he knows a good thing when he sees it. He recognized my hard work and dedication right away."

"Come on, Gertie, don't do this to me, we're family."

"Family? Now we're family? You really are a schmuck you know that, Marty? A real schmuck. Don't talk to me about family."

"Gertie—"

"Is it because we're family that you've paid me below the minimum wage all these years?"

"Listen, I—"

"Were we family when I came to you for help when your own brother was in a car accident?"

"I gave you a job!"

"I gave you a job," Gertie repeated mockingly. "Job smob! You don't even pay a living wage! Effective immediately, Marty, I quit!"

CHAPTER 58

Two weeks later

Ted and Tonya walked into Tonya's apartment building to see a crew of workers and an "under construction" sign. The bustle going on inside the building was punctuated by random sounds of a jackhammer being used somewhere on the property.

"What's all of this?" Ted asked.

Tonya shrugged. "I have no idea. None of this was here when I left this morning."

Ted pointed to the uniformed man standing behind the makeshift desk. "You have a doorman now?"

The cheery looking man motioned toward them. "Step right this way please. Tell me your apartment number, and I will get your information packet."

"I'm in apartment 24B," Tonya said.

"Aw yes, you must be, Ms. Malone. I'm Ralph, your new doorman. Please excuse the dust, Ms. Malone. The building is under new management."

"As of when?" Ted asked.

The man smiled kindly and handed Tonya the information packet. "As of today, sir."

Tonya paged quickly through the folder. "But this can't be right. According to this, I have to be out of my apartment by the end of the week."

"Yes ma'am, just until the renovations are complete."

"This doesn't seem legal on such short notice, where is she supposed to go?" Ted asked.

"I assure you, sir. It's 100 percent legal. The management company is handling all relocation expenses for residents who live in the building." Ralph pointed to a phone number inside the packet. "When you're ready to vacate your apartment just call this number right here in your packet. Movers will come and pack up your things and put them into a secure storage facility and a car will take you to your hotel which will be . . ." Ralph scanned the materials in Tonya's packet. His eyes lit up. "Somebody upstairs must like you. You're going to Four Seasons."

"I guess I hit the jackpot, huh?" Tonya said.

Ralph released a hardy laugh. "Yes indeedy!"

"Ralph, you wouldn't happen to have any information on who purchased the building would you?" Tonya asked.

Ralph flashed Tonya a kind smile. "Well, if you're asking who signs my checks, little lady, it's a little company owned by a retired ball player in Houston, Texas."

Tonya and Ted shared a look. "Thank you, Ralph."

"My pleasure, Ms. Malone. Don't hesitate to let me know if I can be of service to you in any way."

Tonya flashed a tight smile at Ralph and then headed towards the bank of elevators with Ted following closely behind her. She almost collided with her neighbor who was exiting the elevator.

"Oh my gosh, Tonya, isn't it wonderful?" the older woman gushed.

"Mrs. Calloway."

"I've been on the super for years to make some changes to this dump and now we're getting a total remodel. I can't believe our luck."

"Yep, it's like a dream," Tonya said with feigned excitement.

"And the best part of all, no rent increase. Right? I tell you, I'm just over the moon with this new management company. They are a godsend whoever they are. I gotta go. We'll talk later. You're at the Holiday Inn, right? Everyone

I've talked to so far is at the Holiday Inn."

"I—"

"Don't worry, I'll find you. I gotta run."

Tonya waved goodbye to her neighbor and stepped into the elevator with Ted following behind her. She pushed the up button.

Ted stared at Tonya as the elevator climbed slowly towards her floor. "So let me get this straight. Your ex visits you one time. Doesn't like your building because he thinks it's 'unsafe' so he buys it. The whole building."

Tonya stared up at the ceiling. "Basically."

"This guy really is in love with you. How can any normal man ever compete with that? Do you know what kind of crazy money he had to throw the owners to get them to sell? These New York white folks don't sell, Tonya. Ever."

The elevator stopped on Tonya's floor and the two of them walked down the narrow corridor to Tonya's apartment. Tonya studied the carpet pattern beneath her feet and tried to think of the words that would help her explain Michael, to explain them.

"Buying the building doesn't mean Michael's in love with me, Ted. It's just—It's just him doing what he's always done, since we were kids. In that over the top, controlling way of his, he's trying to protect me." Tonya's eyebrows furrowed in frustration. "I'm sorry, but I'm not going to be able to hang out this afternoon after all."

"I completely understand." Ted drew Tonya into his arms and pecked her on the lips. Then he held her at arm's length and smiled down at her. "You're going to call him and read him the riot act once you're inside, aren't you?"

"You bet I am."

Ted chuckled. "Try not to be too hard on him. In fact, do me a favor and thank him for me, alright?"

Tonya stared at Ted.

"Don't get me wrong, I'm not happy with the idea of some man buying my future wife a building, but I'm not stupid either. He's got deep pockets, baby, and he is obviously a giver. A guy like that would be a real asset to our ministry."

CHAPTER 59

Tonya picked up the phone and dialed Michael's cell.

"Hey, baby, what's up?"

"Guess what I'm doing right now?"

"What?" Michael's fingers adroitly flew across the game pad causing his character to slam dunk on Joshua's character.

"Packing. Apparently, I'll be living at the Four Seasons, complements of the new owner of my apartment building while they do renovations on my place for the next month. Michael, a whole month!"

"At least they're putting you up in style. Four Seasons in New York ain't too shabby. And real talk, your spot needs a makeover. As far as I'm concerned this is answered prayer."

"You had no right to do this, Michael. What happened to, my city my rules, your city your rules?"

"What are you talking about?"

"Oh, please! Don't insult me. Ralph, the doorman, already confirmed that it was purchased by some rich ball player in Texas. My neighbors are thrilled about all the changes by the way. They love the new 24 -hour doorman. They especially love that despite all the upgrades their rent isn't going to increase. How humanitarian of you!"

Mike motioned to Joshua. "Man, pause the game for a minute. I didn't buy your building."

Joshua pressed the pause button. "Who dat?"

"Tonya." Mike removed the phone from his ear while she continued to fuss him out.

"What's her problem?"

"She thinks I bought her building."

"Put her on speaker phone."

"Blackbird, calm down."

"I will not calm down!"

"I'm putting you on speaker phone."

"What?"

"I said you're on speaker phone. Josh is here."

"I don't care about Joshua being there. Is that supposed to make me behave? Because I'm going to have my say, Michael, whether you like it or not!"

"Hey Tonya, how are you?"

"I'm pissed Josh, and you?"

Joshua chuckled. "Listen sis, did the doorman give you a copy of the new lease agreement."

"Yeah, it was in the information packet he gave me. Oh, and guess what else, thanks to your control freak of a brother, I don't have to pay rent anymore. I put up with this when we were dating, Michael! I shouldn't have to put up with this anymore!"

"I told you I didn't buy your building!"

"Yeah, okay, whatever. I got the lease agreement right here, Josh."

"Go ahead and read the fine print at the bottom of the page. What does it say?"

Tonya sighed heavily into the phone. "It says that this is a . . . Bad Boy Productions. But—"

"That's you?" Mike slapped hands with his brother, "Nicely played, bro."

"That's right. I bought the building. You're welcome," Joshua said.

"But you haven't even been here!" Tonya sputtered. "Why would you buy a piece of property sight unseen?"

"I saw my dad's video of your graduation. You live in a dump. He told me that he asked you nicely to move and that you refused."

"I can't afford to move!"

"He said he offered to help you."

"I don't want to be helped. I like my life the way it is." Tonya bit out angrily.

"He mentioned that too. So, since you were unresponsive to his very reasonable entreaties, I decided to purchase the building and upgrade it myself, end of story."

"I'm not going to move every time the men in my life have a problem with where I live! Do you know how absurd that sounds?"

Joshua looked at Mike. "Does she know how absurd she sounds?"

Mike shook his head. "She's on her I-am-woman-hear-me-roar soapbox right now, bro. She can't hear nothing else."

"Yeah, my building is old," Tonya was saying, totally oblivious to the brothers' side conversation, "But it has character and I like it! Do you hear me, Josh? My building has char-act-er and I like it! Furthermore, I live in a perfectly safe neighborhood!"

"Only people who live in unsafe neighborhoods make statements like that." Joshua said. "Relax, while they're repairing that decrepit thing and making it fit for human habitation, I'll make sure the work crew preserves your precious character."

"Gurrr! Joshua, you had no right to do this!"

"That's where you are wrong. I have every right," Joshua said smoothly. "It's a free country and I can buy whatever I can afford. Besides, Uncle Harold would approve."

"Yep, he would," Mike said.

Tonya rolled her eyes. *Uncle Harold would approve.* Every time Michael and Joshua wanted to micromanage her life they would throw out that statement as if invoking the name of her deceased father was some magic bullet. A cure all to everything. Never mind the fact that Tonya's father actually would approve. He would hate the idea of her living alone in New York city, much less in an unsecured apartment, but that was totally beside the point. Tonya was sick of it. She was absolutely sick to death of the men in her life. Between Ted not caring enough, and Jack, Joshua, and Michael all caring too much, it was altogether stifling.

"Well, I don't approve. I am an adult not a child."

"Then start acting like one," Joshua said.

"Excuse me?"

"The next words out your mouth should be, 'Sorry for the misunderstanding, Michael. Thank you for the upgrade, Joshua.' And if you can't find it in your heart to say, 'I'm sorry,' to actually admit that you were wrong, 'lots of love, hugs and kisses to you both,' or any other variation of goodbye will do," Joshua said.

"How 'bout this variation, Josh. I really, really hate you right now. Both of you!"

"That'll work too," Joshua said as he un-paused the game.

"We love you too, Blackbird," Mike said as he reached for his controller.

Tonya screamed and slammed down the phone.

CHAPTER 60

J oshua picked up the phone call his new secretary had patched through to his line. "This is Joshua."

"Hi, Pastor Keys. This is Jilly from Sister Bella's accountability group."

"Hello, Jilly, how are you?" Joshua said, greeting the woman warmly.

"I'm fine, Pastor. Thank you for asking. I do have a bit of a dilemma that I was hoping you could help me with. I told Sister Bella that I would be her Lamaze coach. The class starts this evening and runs for the next four weeks, but I totally forgot that I have a conflict tonight. In fact, I don't know what I was thinking when I signed us up for the class. I have a conflict every night. I'm not going to be able to do this, be her partner that is. I didn't want to leave her high and dry so I thought I'd do what I could to find her another coach. Can you fill in for me?"

"No problem, Jilly, I'm there. Just give me the class information."

When Joshua arrived home that evening, Bella was ready and waiting for Jilly. Joshua looked down at the maternity jumpsuit that she had put on for the occasion. "Jilly called. She can't make it to your Lamaze class tonight, or any of the nights actually."

Bella's face fell.

"She asked me to stand in her stead though. I hope that's alright with you?"

Bella smiled at him. "You know it is."

"Okay, let me go change, and we can bounce."

CHAPTER 61

"Hello everyone and welcome to Lamaze for Lovers." Seven pregnant women and their Lamaze coaches sat facing each other on the padded floor while the instructor, a large Kathy Bates looking woman stood at the chalkboard and wrote the words *Lamaze for Lovers* in bright pink neon chalk.

Joshua busied himself looking through the welcome basket the instructor had handed them upon arrival. A bottle of chocolate flavored massage oil, a tube of K-Y jelly, a back massager, a pair of furry handcuffs, and a pair of maternity-sized edible underwear. "So, you and Jilly . . . you signed up for this class together?"

Bella stared at each item as he pulled it from the basket. "Yeah, but . . ." Bella's voice trailed off in confusion.

Joshua's piercing brown eyes found hers. "Bella, is there anything else you need to tell me?"

Bella shook her head. "Joshua, I've been low, real low; just never on the down low."

"I guess it's a good thing Jilly couldn't make it then." Joshua held the whale size candy bloomers up for Bella to inspect. Joshua shuddered. "Just thinking about eating these off of you makes my teeth hurt."

Bella fell back onto the padded mat and cackled with laughter. Even when they had been together in that way, they'd never did the candy underwear thing. Bella learned early on in their marriage that Joshua wasn't a big sweet eater. He preferred spicy and savory dishes instead.

"Look into your lover's eyes and tell her, I adore you," the Kathy Bates look-alike was saying.

"I adore you," Joshua said.

"You know your lover better than anyone else. I want you to take a moment and find that pulse point. That point that makes them absolutely weak at the knees. I want you to rub that spot. It could be someplace sensual like your partner's breast or their buttocks, or it could be a totally non-sensual point like her elbow or her knee. For some people it's their knee." The instructor walked around the room as she spoke. "If you don't know your lover's spot just ask them."

"It's my knee. I go absolutely weak with desire when you touch my knee," Bella said grinning up from the mat at Joshua.

"Liar, it's the tip of your earlobe."

Bella pulled away from his touch. "Joshua don't."

"I thought this is what you wanted. You practically begged me to take a Lamaze class with you when you were pregnant with Jabari."

"You know what I mean. Don't start none, won't be none. I'm saved. I'm trying to live holy now."

Joshua leaned in close, chuckling softly into her ear. "Look around you, Bella. We're probably the only married couple up in here. Can't get no holier than holy matrimony."

Bella looked around the room at the other students in the class. There were three teenage couples, an odd trio of punk rockers, and two lesbian couples.

Bella looked at Joshua. "The marriage bed is undefiled."

Joshua nodded. "What God has joined together, let no man put asunder."

"For this cause shall a man leave his mother and father and cleave to his wife."

"And the two shall be one flesh," Joshua finished.

"Joshua?"

"Hum?"

"Jilly set us up."

"You think so?"

"Had to, she's the one who registered for the class."

Joshua reached out and gently stroked Bella's earlobe. "She did sound a little shady on the phone."

"Seriously, Josh, you need to stop. This is not a good idea."

"This is supposed to get your endorphins flowing."

"If you keep touching me, a whole lot more than that is going to be flowing."

CHAPTER 62

Thank you for being my partner tonight," Bella said, as Joshua walked her to the door of the master bedroom that evening.

Joshua smiled down at her. "It was fun."

"That was wild. I can't believe Jilly signed me up for that."

"What's wild is that the teacher assigns homework."

"I'm thinking we'd better forego the chocolate sauce."

"Maybe you're right. Next time you see Jilly thank her for me, alright?" Joshua cupped her face in his hands and kissed her. A slow passionate, mounting kiss.

When Bella did manage to come to herself and break away she was breathless. "No, Josh, that's not the assignment. We're supposed to answer the question first then kiss."

"Alright, what's the question?"

"What are you most afraid of in this pregnancy journey?"

"That's easy. Losing you."

CHAPTER 63

Bella was leaning against the counter drinking a mug of herbal tea when Joshua sauntered into the kitchen looking more handsome than the law allowed. The sheen glistening from his muscles told her he had just finished his morning routine. He smiled at her as he grabbed water from the refrigerator, and Bella felt her stomach do three cartwheels and a backflip.

Joshua's forearm lightly brushed against hers as he stood beside her at the counter and downed first one bottle of water and then the next. When their bodies touched in this small way, Bella felt a spark of electricity shoot up her spine. There was no doubt about it, she was craving this man. Like the deer panted for the water, like the desert craved the rain, she wanted Joshua. It had been hard enough as of late, living in the same house with him sleeping across the hall, but now that he was standing so close, he'd been doing that a lot lately—standing too close, and smelling too good. Bella though she might combust. Literally burst into flames.

He opened the refrigerator and took an apple from the fruit drawer. Bella closed her eyes as his clean crisp fragrance wafted past her again.

"Can I ask you a question?"

"What's up?"

"Why don't you stink right now?"

Joshua raised an eyebrow at her. "Do I usually stink?"

"No, it's just I can tell you've been working out, but you smell like . . ."

Joshua lifted the bottom of his t-shirt and wiped the sweat from his brow. The sight of tight ab muscles for days made all sound in her throat die.

"Like what?"

"Like vanilla, leather, and oakmoss."

Joshua grinned down at her. He took a bite of his apple, chewed deliberately, and swallowed. Joshua set the apple down on the counter and leaned his hands up against it caging her in on both sides. "I was just standing here thinking the very same thing about you. Shall I tell you what you smell like to me, Bella?"

Bella shook her head. "Nah, that's alright."

"Hey, Mom, hey Dad!"

Jabari bounded down the stairs into the kitchen wearing his Princetown Prep blazer with his book bag slung over one shoulder. Bella couldn't be more relieved. She and Joshua had been playing this game of cat and mouse for the last couple of weeks. With Bella trying not to have any private encounters with Joshua like this one, and Joshua pursuing her like he was a bill collector and she owed him money. Bella took this moment to break through the cage of Joshua's arms. She nearly ran to the other side of the room to greet Jabari. "Hey, sweetie."

"Can I spend the night over at Unc's?"

"Sure, why not?" Joshua said quickly.

"No, you can't." Bella said at the same time.

Jabari looked back and forth between his parents.

"He's going to wear out his welcome, Josh."

"He's just cooling with his new cousin, Bella. What's the big of a deal? When we were growing up me, Mike and Tonya constantly went back and forth between our two houses. We almost never slept in our own beds."

"Jabari, did you and Marcus even check with your uncle first to see if this was okay?"

"Mom, Unc said I don't have to ask if I can spend the night, ever. Dad told Marcus the same thing."

Bella shifted her attention back to Joshua who

winked mischievously at her before he took another bite of his apple. "He's right, I did."

"So why don't the two of you just hang out here," Bella said meeting Joshua's eyes with a challenge.

"Mom, no, we can't. We have plans."

A car honked out front.

"That's Marcus, I gotta go. So please, can I?"

Joshua reached across the island and gave Jabari a fist bump. "Have fun tonight."

"Thanks, Dad." Jabari kissed his mother's cheek and hurried out the front door.

"Jabari will be perfectly safe at my brother's house, Bella. You know, that right?"

Bella rolled her eyes. "Of course I do."

His eyes held that mischievous twinkle again, "Then what are you afraid of?"

"I'll tell you what I'm not afraid of Joshua. You." And before he could test that particular theory, Bella turned and hightailed it out of the kitchen.

CHAPTER 64

She had lied. She was terrified at the thought of being left alone with Joshua with no Jabari to serve as a buffer. So she called Maggie and begged her and Walter to change their plans for that evening and join them for dinner. After the couples had eaten, the men volunteered for dish duty and suggested the women go pick out a movie to watch in the home theatre.

Maggie bumped her shoulder playfully up against Bella's. "Can you believe it? My Walter and your Joshua doing dishes together. Honey, I don't care what nobody says, there is a God."

"Joshua's been doing little, thoughtful, romantic things all week," Bella said as she closed the double doors that lead into the home theatre. "It's driving me crazy. I'm so glad you two agreed to have dinner with us tonight." Bella bit down on her bottom lip and turned suddenly to face her friend. "You're a praying woman, Maggie. Will you say a prayer for me right now?"

"Of course, Rose. What would you like prayer for?"

"Can you come against a panty dropping spirit?"

"A what?"

"It's just I don't know if I'll be able to keep my vow of celibacy. Maggie, we're in this Lamaze for Lovers class together and this man is touching me so much that I feel him touching me even when he's not touching me. I can't afford to have sex with him."

"Rose, are we still talking about Joshua, your husband?"

"Of course we are, Maggie," Bella hissed. "Please try and keep up."

"Are you feeling alright?"

"No, I'm not, Maggie. He's breaking all the rules."

"Honestly, Rose, I don't see what the problem is. If Joshua is trying to have sex with you, it means he's not willing to let you go."

"How can I be so sure?"

"Easy, talk to him first."

The door to the theatre room opened and Joshua and Walter walked in. "Did you two decide what you want to watch tonight?" Joshua asked.

Maggie staged a yawn. "Actually, I was hoping we could skip the movie altogether. Walter, do you mind?"

Walter touched Maggie's shoulder. "You feeling alright, baby?"

"I'm fine. It's just with the girls at Pearl's for the rest of the evening I thought we could retire early." She flashed Walter a knowing smile.

Walter caught her meaning instantly. He planted a quick kiss on Maggie's cheek, "Girl, you ain't said nothing but a word. Let's go."

"Wonderful, I'll just grab my wrap and we can be on our way."

Walter turned to Joshua and extended his hand. "I hope we can get a raincheck on that movie, man."

"Oh, for sure, Walter."

"I can walk them out," Bella said.

"Maggie, what are you doing?" Bella whispered once they were out of earshot of the men.

"All of this sex talk has made me want some myself. I'm going home and make love to my husband. I suggest you have a conversation with your husband and do the same."

"Really, Maggie? Really? I come to you, a woman of God in my hour of need and ask you to pray for me and this is what I get. Abandonment."

Maggie hugged Bella tightly. "Oh Rose, my dear sweet sister. I'm praying for you right now. Go forth and drop those panties in Jesus' name." She kissed her cheek quickly. "Bye."

"Sell out," Bella called to Maggie's back as Walter hurried her down the front walkway a few minutes later.

Walter turned and looked at Bella over his shoulder. "Don't hate the player, Rose, hate the game."

When Bella walked back inside, she found Joshua in the family room instead of the home theatre. There was soft music playing, and Joshua had lit the fireplace. He was looking through a stack of movies when she walked in.

"You up for a romantic comedy tonight?"

Bella raised an eyebrow at him. "You're going to watch a romantic comedy with me?"

He smiled. "Why not?"

"Oh, boy." Bella faked a yawn. "Actually, it is kind of late. Maybe we should skip the movie all together."

Joshua walked towards her. Smelling outrageously good. "We can retire, Bella. I'm down with that."

Bella swallowed. *Lord be my strength.*

Joshua pulled her into his arms and kissed her and Bella found herself kissing him back. Then she remembered herself and pulled away.

"Joshua wait. I need to know where this is going."

"We've done this dance plenty of times. I think we both know where this is going."

"Yeah, but what if I don't want to go there with you?"

Joshua's hand caressed her neck and set her whole body ablaze. He stared at her with a cocky grin. "I'm pretty sure you want to."

Bella stepped away from him. "My body may want to, but I've set a resolve in my spirit. The next man I make love to will be my husband."

"Bella, I am your husband."

"The next man I make love to will be my husband for keeps."

Joshua rolled his eyes. "You want to talk about this, right now?"

"Yes, right now."

"Alright, so you want to know my intentions towards you. You want to know if I'm looking for something serious or if I just wanna bone."

Bella blushed. "You remember that?"

"The first words you ever spoke to me. Yeah, I do. I told you Bella, there's not much about us that I can forget. I don't want a divorce. I want my wife back. I want you right here, right now, in every way."

"Joshua, I think I'm ready."

"That's exactly what I want to hear cause I'm ready too."

"No, Josh, I mean my water just broke."

CHAPTER 65

Bella's water broke at 9:30 PM and Joshua arrived at the hospital, which was twenty-five minutes away from their home, at precisely 9:45 PM. He had filled out paperwork weeks ago, so Bella was taken directly to labor and delivery. There was a grueling, twelve-hour labor, but at 9:30 that next morning a baby girl emerged, butter colored, healthy, and howling.

Bella lay in the hospital bed asleep while Joshua sat in the chair beside her, thinking. A nurse knocked then opened the door. Joshua put his finger to his lips and followed the nurse into the hallway. He closed the door to Bella's hospital room.

"We were hoping that mom felt up to rooming in with the baby. She's not doing well in the nursery."

"What do you mean?" Joshua moved quickly towards the nursery with the woman falling in step beside him.

"Nothing's actually wrong with her. The doctor already examined her. She's just extremely fussy. She's been crying for over an hour. We've rocked her, and changed her, but we can't get her to settle down. She's practically started a riot with the other babies."

Joshua walked through the glass door of the nursery. He took one look at the now completely red-faced baby girl screaming in the nurse's arms.

"I will say this for her, she has a healthy set of lungs," the first nurse said.

Joshua walked over to the second nurse who was holding the baby. "May I?"

She quickly checked Joshua's hospital ID bracelet and matched it up to the one on the baby's leg. She laid the baby in Joshua's arms and the child stopped crying instantly. The tiny little girl peered up at Joshua with brown eyes identical to his own. The pout on her little face seemed to say, "I've been calling you. What took you so long?"

"Thank God," both nurses said at the same time. "We'll just get her bassinet and roll it right down to mom's room."

Joshua murmured and cooed to the baby as he walked her back down to Bella's room.

Bella awoke a half an hour later to find the baby sleeping peacefully on Joshua's chest. "You're going to spoil her."

"Nah, no such thing. How are you feeling?"

"Like a basketball just came out of me."

"The fam is blowing up my phone."

"Are Mel and Jack here?"

"They drove down this morning. I'm surprised they haven't stormed the hospital yet. Everyone wants to see you and the baby."

Bella looked over at the dark head of curls nestled against Joshua's chest, peeking out beneath the knit cap.

"Have you thought about a name for her?" Joshua asked, not meeting Bella's eyes.

"Have you?" she asked. Bella knew this man, knew him to his core. If Joshua was willing to name the child, it meant he was willing to claim her as well.

"Actually, I was thinking we should call her Serenity," he said. "Serenity Wildflower Keys."

CHAPTER 66

Your kid gets kicked out of the nursery and you name her Serenity," Carlos said.

"I guess you're calling those things that are not as though they were, huh, dude?" Dave said.

Joshua smirked at Dave. All the men laughed.

Visitors had been coming by the hospital all day in waves. First their family. Then there was the former Dunbar Street Apartments crew. Then the ladies from Bella's accountability group stopped by. Now the members of the pastoral staff of New Horizons and their wives had stopped by.

"Wow, Bella, she's so beautiful. She doesn't look a thing like you," Deanna said.

Bella's forehead wrinkled in confusion. "Uh, thanks. I think."

"Of course you're beautiful, sweetie. It's just that this baby is the spitting image of Joshua," Carmen said.

And there was nothing that Bella could say to that, because it was true. A child who shared Joshua's genetic make-up could not look more like him.

Micah held the baby up. "Is she smiling at me? Are you smiling at me, pretty girl? Look, baby, she likes me," Micah said to his wife, Pam.

"Honey, I think that's gas," Pam said.

"No, she likes me. I can tell. Look at those eyes, she's a wise soul. She already knows I'm her pastor," Micah said.

"I'm the youth pastor, so technically, I'm her pastor," Dave said. "If she's got a smile for anyone it's probably me."

Micah frowned at Dave. "I'm the head pastor of the church, and I'm the one holding her right now, so this smile is for me."

Everyone in the room heard it: the sound of a gurgle then a large splat.

Pamela laughed. "Well, I guess she just told the both of you."

"Here, I can take her, Micah," Bella said. She laid the baby down in the bassinet and removed the soiled diaper. Serenity began to scream at the top of her lungs.

"Boy, not only does she look like you, it seems that she's inherited your temper as well, Josh," Keith said.

"Bella, I think the wipes are too cold for her little bottom. Don't we have one of those warmer things?" Joshua asked.

Bella rolled her eyes in response to his query. "Babies have endured cold wipes for centuries, Josh. I think she'll be fine."

The women in the room all laughed. "Looks like this little girl has already got someone wrapped around her little finger," Sharon teased.

Bella completed the diaper change and lifted the crying baby up and handed her back to Joshua. Once again, Serenity settled down immediately in his arms.

Joshua smiled down at the child. "It doesn't matter what they think. Does it, Babygirl? You have peace here, don't you, Serenity?"

CHAPTER 67

Two days later, Bella and baby Serenity were both released from the hospital with a clean bill of health. When they arrived home, Joshua lead Bella into the nursery he had prepared for the baby.

Bella looked around the whimsically decorated room. Her eyes took in the name Serenity in big white scrolling letters and beautiful hand-painted wildflowers along the base boards of the sky blue colored walls.

"It's beautiful. When did you come up with the name?"

"The Lord actually gave it to me a few months ago. Right around the time He told me she was a girl."

"Thank you."

"For?"

"Loving my babies. I'm grateful. God knows this child and Jabari both need a father."

"So why do I hear a but?"

"Because this time I need something more."

Joshua walked towards her closing the gap between them. Which each step he took towards her, Bella felt as if her heart was about to pound out of her chest.

Father, if you see fit to one day bless me with another husband, please, please, let it be like this. Exactly like this.

"What is it that you need, Bella Rose?"

"I need to be loved for me. I know now that I deserve to be loved just for me."

"I wanted you before the baby came. We were about to go upstairs and consummate our union when your water broke. Remember that?"

"I remember things getting hot." *Very hot, like right now.* "And I know that sometimes in the heat of the moment things are said, promises are made, that can't be realistically kept in the light of day."

Joshua cocked his head to the side and grinned down at her. "So basically, you're giving me a way out, just in case I was horny."

A tiny smile crept onto Bella's face. "Basically, yeah."

"I wanted you the other night. I still want you now. Life doesn't work for me without you. I love you *and* I need you."

But it was the very next words out of his mouth that sealed Bella's fate.

"You're my air. I'm not complicated, Bella Rose. I can live without a lot of things, but I can't live without air."

That's when the tears came. Bella wept open tears of relief. Over the years, Joshua had told her this many times before, but she cried because this was the first time she actually believed him.

Her voice hitched. "So, we're really doing this, we're getting married?"

Joshua lifted her chin to meet his gaze. "Bella, we're already married. We can have a recommitment ceremony if you want, though. As grand as you please."

"How about a recommitment ceremony and baby dedication too?"

"Whatever you like."

He was kissing her now. At first his kisses were solely for the purpose of wiping her tears away. But then his lips began to travel to her neck, her shoulders, her collarbone, the tip of her left ear. The lower he got the fire intensified.

"Josh?"

"Yeah."

"I think we should hold off on you know. Just until after the ceremony."

"Why, are you sore?"

"No, not that, it's just that Jilly brought this article to the group last month about God's second time virgins, and I mean I thought. . ." She couldn't really think with him kissing her like this. "Don't you think it would be romantic to wait, until our wedding day?"

Joshua grunted. "I waited for you the first time."

Bella rolled her eyes. "We were engaged for three months."

Joshua smirked. "I still waited. And if you want to get technical about it, I've waited five years and nine months."

"Minus one night?"

"Yeah minus one incredible night. That's a whole lot of time to go without."

You telling me. Bella thought.

"I don't want to spend another night away from you. I want you now or just as soon as you heal up." He stepped away from her then. "But if you've made some type of vow to the Lord I won't—"

Bella shook her head empathically. "No, Joshua. It wasn't a vow. Just an interesting article."

"All I'm saying, Bella, is that if you want to wait until after the recommitment ceremony, I'm good. I'll respect that. Just know that if it gets too hard for you to wait, I'm right down the hall. Especially if there's no vow."

Bella shook her head adamantly. "Nope, no vow."

Joshua's dark brown eyes searched her face. "The public ceremony is just that, Bella Rose, for the public. Everything else between the two of us is private. You feel me?"

Was she feeling him? Heck yeah, she was feeling him. He wasn't even touching her anymore and the rich timber of his voice alone had turned her body into liquid fire.

He turned to leave. "I'll give you a minute to enjoy the room."

"Josh, wait! I'd be comfortable with appetizers. Just as long as we save the full course meal till after the ceremony."

Joshua paused for a moment to consider this.

"So, what do you think?" Bella asked coyly.

Joshua stroked his chin. "I'm pretty much an all or nothing type of guy, Bella Rose."

"I know. But the meal I plan on serving on our wedding night will be worth the wait. You know the Étouffée you love?"

His eyes lit up at the mention of his favorite creole dish. "Yeah."

"This will make that taste like lunch meat."

"How many servings we talkin'?"

"A four-course meal every night."

Joshua folded his arms across his chest. "In order for this to work I'mma need eight."

Bella's eyes bucked. "Eight, wait, Josh that's—"

"How much time will you need to plan the ceremony?"

Bella bit her bottom lip. "About three months."

Joshua turned and walked out the room. "Yep," he called over his shoulder, "at least eight."

CHAPTER 68

One Month Later

Tonya and Ted were hanging out together in the living room of Tonya's newly remodeled apartment, each working from their laptops. Their eyes meet for a moment, just briefly, and they both smiled.

"This is nice," Ted said.

Tonya nodded. "Yeah, nice."

"A great way to spend time together and be productive."

"What are you working on?"

"Sermon notes for tomorrow, you?"

"A job application."

The smile slid from Ted's face. "You already have a job."

"I know, but now that I have my doctorate, I figured I could probably do a little better than a job that was funded completely on church donations and love offerings."

Ted sighed wearily. "What hat are we wearing right now, Tonya? Work or personal?"

Tonya stood and walked into the kitchen. "Neither, we've been having a good day up until this point. Let's not ruin it."

Ted called to her back, "Can you get me another cup of joe?"

Tonya walked back into the living room to retrieve his mug.

"You know if you would go ahead and set a date, none of this would be a problem." Ted spoke loud enough for Tonya to hear him from the kitchen. "We'd live off my salary from the church, and I make more than enough to support the both of us. I mean I ain't pulling down the type of bucks that the Man of Steel is making, I can't afford to buy your building. But I do alright. Say, by the way, did you ever talk to him about donating to the ministry?"

Tonya walked back into the living room and set the mug of coffee down beside Ted. "Michael didn't buy my building, Ted. Joshua did."

"Your ex-boyfriend's brother, the bad boy turned pastor, bought your building. This just keeps getting better and better."

"My godbrother, who also happens to be a pastor, bought my building."

Ted scrubbed his hands over his face. "And why would he do this, Tonya?"

"He saw Uncle Jack's video of the graduation. Said I lived in a dump."

"I guess I can forget about him donating to the church then."

"Why would you say that? You don't even know him."

"He's a pastor, baby. Trust me, we take money. We don't give. Besides, ain't no brother trying to see another man's ministry built up like that."

"That's not Joshua's heart. He's about seeing the Kingdom of God built up."

Ted reached for her hand. "Baby, can we not talk about them anymore? I want to know your thoughts on that other topic."

"What topic?"

"You, setting a date to marry me."

Tonya's computer chirped.

"I think we're having a good day, and we shouldn't spoil it." Tonya sat back down in front of her computer screen and opened the message marked urgent. A save the date invitation from Joshua and Bella popped out of a virtual envelope. Tonya began to weep uncontrollably.

"Tonya, what is it?"

"Happy tears," Tonya managed to finally choke out. "It's my invitation plus one. Joshua and Bella are having a recommitment ceremony."

Ted's face lit up. "I'm invited too? I'm finally going to meet the family?"

"Yes!" Tonya said now laughing and crying at the same time. "That's you, you're my plus one! Oh, thank you, Lord Jesus! Thank you, Father, thank you! Thank you, Holy Ghost, I love you!"

"Wow, Bobby and Whitney are back together again. Who would have thunk it?"

Just as quickly as they had started, Tonya's tears dried up. She swung eyes filled with fury onto Ted. "Don't. Don't ever do that."

"Do what?"

"Don't come sideways at the people I love. Don't you dare run down my family. This is the answer to many, many prayers. This is God restoring what the locust and the canker worm have eaten away. And if you can't see that then you shouldn't come."

Ted held his hands up in surrender. He walked slowly towards Tonya. "Hold up, it was a joke, alright? Done in poor taste, I'll admit. But just a joke." Ted took Tonya's hand gingerly in his and led her back to the sofa. "I'm sorry, alright. I didn't mean any harm. Accept my apology?"

She nodded stiffly.

"I'm glad you're happy about Bella and Joshua getting back together. Believe me when I say I am too. But, baby, you weren't this excited when I asked you to marry me."

Tonya pulled back like she had been scorched. "I told you, this is the answer to many prayers."

"What about me, Tonya. Am I not the answer to your prayers?"

Tonya leveled him with a hard gaze.

"Fine. I see that this subject, like so many other topics, goes right inside the do-not-touch-or-else-our-relationship-will-explode-box. For the record, I'm not judging them or you. When's the ceremony?"

"I leave in two months."

"And will your beloved Michael be there?"

Tonya smirked. "Of course he will."

"Then Trust and believe me, baby, I'll be right there beside you."

CHAPTER 69

With wedding plans underway, it was a regular three-ring circus at the Keys's home. At Joshua's request, Melissa, Barbara, and Katie were only too happy to come down from Dallas for a spell to help Bella plan the wedding of her dreams. The older women had designated the dining room as wedding central and much to Joshua's relief, had pretty much told him to keep out.

Bella found Joshua in the home theatre playing video games with Mike, Marcus, and Jabari. All the males mumbled a greeting when she entered the room, but the four pairs of eyes remained glued to the giant screen. Bella plopped down next to Joshua and begin flipping through a bridal magazine. Joshua took his eyes off the screen long enough to glance over at Bella and the magazine in her hand. "Hey baby, where's my mom?"

"On the phone with the caterers. Do you think we should serve fish or chicken?"

Joshua shrugged. "What did my mom and Aunt Barb say? They're the experts on this type of stuff."

"Your mom, Aunt Barb, and Aunt Katie were unanimously in favor of serving chicken."

"Well, unless you have a burning desire for fish, you should serve chicken."

"So what do you think about having three different flavors inside of the cake?"

"Whatever you choose is fine with me."

"What about a carnation pink vest for you and the groomsmen?"

"Bella, your domain. We're going to show up, at the location of your choosing wearing whatever you want us to wear."

"Speak for yourself, bro," Mike said. "I can't do pink."

Joshua threw a pillow at his brother's head.

Mike ducked out of the way just in time. "Sorry, sis. I'm all for you having the wedding of your dreams but I gotta look fly."

Marcus shrugged. "I'll wear pink, Ms. Rose. Unlike my dad here, I look fly in whatever I wear."

Mike grinned at Marcus. "Oh, I see you got jokes."

Joshua slapped Marcus a high five. "My nephew!"

"I'm with Uncle Mike. I don't want to wear pink either," Jabari grumbled.

Joshua threw his son a look. "Hey, man, what'd I tell you?"

"It's mom's special day and we have to do whatever she wants us to," Jabari said.

Bella rolled her eyes. "Glad to know that this is only mom's special day. For the record, I don't even want pink. I just wanted to see if you were listening." Bella rose to leave, but Joshua pulled her back down onto his lap. He planted a kiss on her shoulder. "Any particular reason why you're trying to pick a fight with me?"

"I'm not. I'm trying to get you to take an interest in our wedding."

"We had an agreement remember?"

"Yes, but on the wedding channel—"

"Part of that agreement was that you would stop watching the wedding channel."

Bella folded her hands across her chest, "Joshua, I never agreed to stop watching the wedding channel."

"Fine, but you did agree to do this with my mom and the aunts and leave me out of it."

"Josh, brides and grooms are supposed to plan their weddings together."

"First timers, baby. All those dudes you see on the wedding channel picking out color swatches with their women, they don't want to do that."

"Maybe not, maybe they do it because they love her."

Joshua shook his head. "Naw, that ain't it. They do it because they're whipped, simple as that. That's not love. What you and I have, Bella, this is love."

Bella raised an eyebrow at him. "Oh, really? Please explain."

"It's simple, baby. You get to have the wedding of your dreams, and I don't have to participate in the planning of it. Everybody's happy."

CHAPTER 70

Josh, Bella, this is Natasha Kern. Natasha, meet my brother and sister-in-law, Joshua and Bella Keys."

"It's a pleasure to meet you, Mr. and Mrs. Keys," Natasha said, pumping first Joshua's and then Bella's hand vigorously.

"Please, Joshua and Bella is fine," Joshua said.

"Natasha and her public relations firm will be handling my wedding gift to you," Mike said.

Bella looked between Mike and Joshua. "I don't understand. Why would we need the services of a PR firm?"

"I can explain what I do in a word, optics. My firm specializes in controlling the media around celebrity families like yours. We believe that when you own your own image, no one, including the media can control it, or co-op it. But I'm getting ahead of myself, so please come in and have a seat," Natasha said, pointing to the large conference table in her office. After everyone had seated themselves around the large oval table, Natasha turned her attention to Bella. "Bella, I'd like to start by asking you a question. Is there anything that you've always wanted to do with Joshua that his fame never allowed you to do before?"

"Yes, walk down the street and hold his hand."

Natasha nodded her head knowingly. "And I can give that to you."

Joshua shrugged. "We can do that now. I'm not a ball player anymore. I'm a pastor. No one's interested in me."

Natasha looked at Mike.

He sat back in his chair at the conference table and shrugged. "Show him."

Natasha picked up the remote control and turned on the large sixty-inch screen that flanked the wall. She pulled up the YouTube clip entitled, *Joshua Keys's Passionate Pleas for His Family*.

"Eighty million hits and counting, twenty-five thousand daily views. The family reunion piece has even more than that. One hundred fifty million hits and forty thousand daily views."

"Wow," Bella said.

"There has also been a resurgence of fans posting old game clips of you from as far back as your college days. I know active players in the league who would kill for this kind of exposure. People are interested in you, Joshua. And it's only natural for them to be. Quite frankly, you're a legend. You're Houston's favored son, and you've locked the public out."

Mike spoke. "I want you to know that I thought long and hard about this. In the end, I decided that what I wanted you both to have was freedom. The freedom to take my niece to the park as a family without any problems. I don't want you to be a prisoner in your own city, bro."

Natasha nodded. "That's where my agency comes in. We can do that for you. I propose we start with the wedding."

Bella stared at Natasha. "Our wedding. You want us to let the media have access to our wedding?"

"Trust me, it would be very limited access, Bella. My proposal is that we take a different spin altogether with the media. Invite them in instead of locking them out. It's like you said earlier, Joshua, you're a pastor now. You're certainly not the bad boy everyone used to know. Show them the new Joshua. The pieces you want them to see anyways."

"So like reality TV?" Bella said.

"Something like that, but not quite. Reality TV is very stylized. What we do is more natural. More organic. With what I'm proposing we won't be invading your home with cameras. I noticed that you don't have a Facebook account."

"Nah, that's not really my thing," Joshua said.

"Not a problem, we'll set up one for you. We'll post some family pics and make some regular mundane but personal feeling posts from you. Bella, Michael tells me you love to cook, so we will have you do a few YouTube videos with Joshua making a candid appearance to taste something every now and again. The world will get a chance to see you as a normal couple, and your private life will remain just that, private. As for the wedding, we will allow one network of your choosing to film the wedding and we'll set up watch parties all over America so that fans will feel like they have a front row seat."

"We'd get to choose the network?"

Natasha smiled confidently. "Of course, Bella. Think of it this way. Your story represents something beautiful that has come out of a horrific storm. We've all heard about the tragedies that came out of Katrina and we've seen the documentaries. This is an opportunity to celebrate the rebirth of a love story. Trust me when I tell you, that there's not a network in America who wouldn't want to be a part of that. They'll be lining up to offer you all kind of sweetheart deals."

Bella raised her eyebrows. "You mean like money?"

Natasha nodded. "You obviously aren't hurting for money. But let me just say that on the reruns alone you'll make a fortune."

Mike winked at Bella. "This is the gift that just keeps on giving, huh, sis?"

Bella nodded. "I'll say."

Natasha spoke to Joshua. "You don't seem sold."

"You're right. I'm not. Right now, we're not in the limelight at all. What you're proposing, especially with the reruns, gives us a permanent front row seat there. That didn't work for us too well the last time."

"The reruns are the best part of the deal, Joshua. They create what I call overexposure. America will feel like they have a front seat into the lives of Houston's' favorite power couple on the most important day of their lives. We are literally going to saturate the American people with you. And when we are done, just like that, you won't be a novelty anymore."

Joshua smiled wryly at her. "You're saying they'll be sick of us."

Natasha smiled. "That's the plan. My firm has done it before. I'm confident we can do it again."

"Natasha can do this, Josh. She's the best in the business," Mike said.

Joshua looked at Bella. "What about you? You wanna do this?"

Bella nodded her head, "It really is my dream to walk down the street holding hands with you."

"Then we'll do it."

"Really? I mean are you sure?"

Joshua leaned in and kissed Bella softly. "It's my dream to make all your dreams come true. So, yeah. I'm sure."

Mike leaned back in his chair and grinned.

Natasha pumped her fist in the air. "This wedding is going to be the celebration of the century."

"Thanks, bro," Joshua said a half an hour later when the three of them were walking out of Natasha's office. "But you could have just gotten us a toaster."

"You already have a toaster, little brother," Mike said. "Besides, I should have done this a long time ago."

CHAPTER 71

Here's my eldest son now. Honey, please come and meet the baker. She makes the most fabulous cake I have ever tasted in my life," Melissa said.

The baker looked Mike up and down, appraising him openly. "Oh my, is this the groom?"

"Nope, just the best man. My brother's the one getting married. Michael Dutton, very nice to meet you." Mike said, extending his hand to the woman.

"AKA, the Man of Steel. So very nice to meet you," the woman gushed.

"Mikey, doesn't everything look great" Melissa beamed with pride.

Mike surveyed the skirted tables along the wall and the dining room table dressed with yards and yards of pink linens. "Yeah . . . what's the occasion?"

Barb walked into the dining room. She stood on her tiptoes and kissed Mike on the cheek. "Cake-tasting party's today, sweetie. Didn't Josh tell you?"

"I was told we were shooting hoops."

Katie chuckled.

"We understand that the family's privacy is paramount, Mr. Dutton, so we decided to set up the cake tasting here at your brother's home instead of in our gallery."

Mike nodded. "Cool."

"Yo, Mike, you ready?" Joshua called from the hallway.

"I'm in the dining room, bro. You might want to step in here for a bit."

Joshua walked in and looked warily around the room. "What's this?"

"It's a cake-tasting party. Bella saw it on the wedding channel," Katie chirped.

"This is my youngest son, the groom, Joshua," Melissa said.

The baker extended her hand to Joshua. "So very nice to meet you, Mr. Keys."

Joshua shook the baker's hand.

"Sweetie, the guests are going to be here in a moment, shouldn't you boys be getting dressed?" Melissa said.

"Excuse me for a second, Mom. Aunt Katie, can I speak with you for a moment please?" Katie followed Joshua into the adjoining parlor.

Joshua folded his hands across his chest and stared down at the older woman.

"What you looking at me for?"

"'Cause you slippin'."

"You think this was my idea? I told you she saw it on the wedding channel," Katie hissed.

"We had a deal, Aunt Katie. You're supposed to be the voice of reason during this process. Your job is to put down all foolishness."

"Hey, I thought we had a deal too. But here I haven't seen my new game controllers yet."

"They're not even on the US market yet. I had to order them from the designer in Japan. Your controllers are in the mail, they'll be here by the end of the week."

Katie's eyes lit up upon hearing this. "Okay, no more foolishness. I'll even fix it so that she can't watch the wedding channel. Just leave it to me. I have everything under control."

Joshua nodded. "Good, that's what I want to hear."

Joshua could hear Bella in the next room asking about him. Joshua and Katie walked back into the dining room. "I'm right here, babe. What's up?"

Bella looked at Joshua's and then Mike's attire, "Mike, why aren't you dressed? Didn't Josh tell you about the cake party?"

"All I know is that we supposed to be shooting hoops."

Jabari and Marcus walked in also dressed in shorts and t-shirts. Jabari had a basketball slung under his arm. "Cool cake!"

"My son and my nephew," Joshua said to the baker. To the boys he said, "Y'all want some cake?"

"Yeah, for sure, Unc," Marcus said.

Marcus and Jabari scooped up cake squares and popped them into their mouths.

"Wait. You guys can't just eat the cake. You have to mark the flavors you like on the card," Bella said.

"I like all of these," Jabari said with a mouth full of cake. Bella rolled her eyes.

"Are we ruining your cake-tasting party, Bella?" Joshua asked.

"Yeah, 'cause we can leave," Mike said quickly.

Bella sighed. "Joshua, can I have a word with you in the kitchen, please."

"We'll be in the car," Mike called to his back.

Joshua followed Bella into the kitchen and leaned up against the large center island.

"You're really going to go play basketball right now?"

"Yes."

"But you knew we had the cake-tasting party scheduled for today. I know you knew because I called Gertie and asked her to put it on your calendar."

"Yeah, and I asked her to change it."

"So that's it? You're just going to bail on all our friends? Pam and the girls will be here any minute. Micah and the guys too."

"The guys aren't coming. I called and told them they didn't have to come to this."

"This is . . . unbelievable."

"Believe it."

The doorbell rang. Joshua clicked on the TV and turned it to the security station. "Your friends are here. They'll be much better equipped than I am to help you pick cake."

"Josh, wait."

He sighed. *This woman was killing him.* "What?"

Bella walked over to him and wrapped her arms around his waist. She looked up at him with a pouty face. "You're really not coming to my cake-tasting party?"

"Bella, I don't even like cake. Why would I come to a cake-tasting party?"

She stuck her bottom lip out even further.

"Whose idea was it to wait till after the ceremony?"

"Mine," Bella muttered.

Joshua removed her arms from around his waist. "Okay then. A brother has to burn off this excess energy somehow."

"I'm not tryin' to cramp your style, Josh. I just wanted to get your opinion," she called to his back as he was heading out the kitchen.

"Chocolate," Joshua called over his shoulder.

Bella stomped her foot in frustration. "There are over 36 flavors of chocolate. That doesn't help me one bit!"

"So pick one!" he shouted on his way out the front door.

CHAPTER 72

Joshua leaned down and kissed Bella softly. "Morning, sleepyhead."

She could smell his freshly showered skin mingling with the soft masculine scent of his aftershave.

"What time is it?" Bella looked over at the clock and then scrambled for the baby monitor.

"Relax, Suri's fed and back down for her mid-morning nap."

"What's wrong with me? I didn't even hear her cry."

"That's because she didn't. I think my mom must have staked out in the nursery last night. All Suri had to do was gurgle and she was right there. She used some of the breastmilk in the freezer."

"I wish you would have woke me."

Joshua took a seat on the edge of the bed beside her. He brushed her hair from around her face. "I wanted you to sleep. Besides, you should use this time to build up your milk supply. Especially while my mom and aunts are here."

Bella yawned and sat up in bed. "I guess you're right."

"Big day today, huh?"

"Yep, dress hunting."

"And who's all going on this little dress hunting expedition with you?"

"Is my mind playing tricks on me or are you really asking me a wedding-related question?"

He smiled a full-on dimpled smile. "You like that, don't you? I'm taking an interest."

Bella pulled his face towards her and kissed his lips. "I do, gold star for you."

"How about you keep that funky little star and break a brother off with some real loving instead?"

Bella blushed. "Joshua, no, we're supposed to be practicing restraint remember?"

Joshua rose from the bed and continued getting dressed. "Yeah, yeah. Tell me about your dress party thingy."

"It'll be your mom, Maggie, Aunt Barb, Aunt Katie and Granny P."

"Tonya's not coming down?"

"Tonya will be video Skyping with us today."

"How she gon' help you pick a dress over Skype?"

"Don't ask. Boyfriend stuff."

Joshua grunted, and adjusted his tie in the full-length mirror. "Instead of taking a bunch of cars and wasting everybody's gas, why don't you call Jeeves and have him send over the Suburban."

Bella shook her head. "We're all going to pile into Granny P's new car. "

"The Deuce and a Quarter?"

"Yep, Granny P said that Mike got her a bumping new sound system to go with her hot new ride."

"What's the plan for Suri today?"

Bella rolled her eyes. Per Joshua's insistence, Serenity had only been to her uncle Mike's house and the doctor's office for check-ups. They hadn't even been to church as a family yet because Joshua didn't like the thought of so many people breathing on her.

"Don't you worry, Josh, Suri, the bubble baby, won't be leaving the house. The nanny is coming today."

He turned to stare at her. "What did you just call her?"

Bella laughed at the look of confusion on his face. "I called her the bubble baby because you act like she has no immune system at all."

Joshua shrugged. "It's too early to be exposing her to so many people that's all. By the way, did you check with the nanny to see if she's gotten the flu shot?"

"Yep, she's all clear."

"Good."

"But, Josh, do you think she'll be able to come to the baby dedication and the wedding next month?"

"Who, the nanny?"

"No, Suri."

He pecked Bella on the forehead on his way out the door. "Very funny."

CHAPTER 73

Bella came downstairs later that morning to find Barbara and Melissa attempting to work the FaceTime feature on Barbara's cell phone.

"Morning!" Bella sang out.

Melissa and Barbara both looked up briefly from their project and returned the greeting.

"Maggie called. She's on her way over," Katie said.

"Great." Bella reached for a piece of bacon from the plate on the counter and Katie smacked her hand.

"Ouch, Aunt Katie! What did you do that for?"

"This is the second day in a row I caught you nibbling at breakfast. You'll eat a full plate this morning. Breast feeding's the same as eating for two." Katie sat a full plate of grits, eggs, smothered potatoes, and bacon in front of Bella and glared at her.

"You don't have to be so violent. I just haven't been that hungry in the morning." Bella took a seat at the counter and started to eat the food on her plate.

"Bella, how in the devil are we supposed to fit six people in that tiny car of yours?"

"We're taking Granny P's car, Aunt Katie."

Pearl walked into the kitchen. "That's right, we're taking my new car. That grandson of mine just bought me a Deuce and- a Quarter. I can fit three in the front and three in the back."

Katie's eyes lit up. "Shut the front door. My late husband, Earl used to drive a Deuce. Boy did I love riding in that thing."

"Well, what do you know. My late husband's name was Earl, and he drove a Deuce too!"

"You're kidding me."

"I swear I'm not. You can drive it Katie, if you like. In fact, you all can. Got so much insurance on that thing the cat can drive."

Bella snickered as she drank her morning tea.

Barbara sighed. "Tonya, I don't know what to tell you. I can't figure this out. We're just going to have to call you when we get to the dress shop and put you on speaker phone."

Tonya's voice rang out in the kitchen. "No Mom, this family has kept me in the dark for far too long. From now on I want to see and experience everything."

"If you have to see and experience everything then you should have hopped your behind on a plane," Barbara muttered.

"Tonya, I wish you were here," Bella said, speaking into the receiver.

"I wish I was too, Bella. but I've spoken to everyone in my office, and they know I'm not to be disturbed because I'm cyber shopping today."

"Tell me again why you didn't just fly home for the fitting?" Melissa said as she paged through the directions that came with the phone.

"Auntie Mel, we've already been over this. The Children's Ministry is doing a program and Ted really wants me to be here."

"So, who is that on the phone?" Pearl whispered to Katie.

"That's my niece, Tonya. She can't be here today 'cause she's in an abusive relationship."

"I heard that, Aunt Katie," Tonya yelled through the phone.

"Good. I meant you to!"

҉ ҉ ҉

Mattingham approached the desk in the outer office at Home Court Advantage. His sister-in-law and former secretary looked up from her work when he called her name.

"Mr. Mattingham, what can I do for you?"

She said it like they weren't related at all. Like she hadn't been married to his brother for the last thirty years. Like he hadn't given her a job three years ago, when Lonnie got hurt on his job, and the two of them were about to be thrown out into the street. She said it like he was nobody.

Mattingham motioned towards Joshua's closed door. "Is your boss in?"

"Do you have an appointment?"

"No, Gertie, I don't, but I have some crucial information that he'll want to see. Trust me."

She eyed him suspiciously for a moment. "Wait right here. No promises, Marty. I will see if he's available to meet with you."

҉ ҉ ҉

The woman extended her hand to Bella. "Hello, I'm Vera, the consultant who will be working with your party today. This looks like a fun group. Tell me who do you have with you today?"

"This is my family," Bella said proudly. "I think everybody should introduce themselves."

Barbara pointed her cell phone outward so that Tonya could see the bridal consultant.

"I'm Tonya Malone, the maid of honor. I couldn't be there in person so I'm joining the festivities today by Skype."

Maggie spoke next. "I'm Maggie Trendale, friend of the bride."

"I'm mother-in-law of the bride," Melissa said.

"We're aunts of the groom," Barbara said pointing to her and Katie.

"And I'm Grandma Pearl, recently adopted into the family and just happy to be here," Pearl said.

"Well it's nice to meet you all," Vera said. "Welcome and please make yourselves at home in our showroom. I do have a question for the maid of honor. What city are you located in, dear?"

"I'm in New York," Tonya said.

"Well that's wonderful news. We can have you fitted at our Manhattan location and your dress shipped from there. Bella, I'm going to pull a few dresses and we can get you started."

❧ ❧ ❧

Joshua was at his desk signing documents when Mattingham entered. "I assume you have new information, that's why you're here."

Mattingham pulled a photograph out of the briefcase he carried. "I found the parents like you asked me to. The dad is in a state run nursing home. "This is him, right?"

Joshua took the photo from Mattingham's outstretched hand. He studied the photo. It was him alright, but it looked nothing like the crisped, polished minister he had always known Bella's father to be. This was not the man he had admired, the one who had been his mentor, nor was this the man Joshua had hated afterwards. This was just a broken shell of an old man. "What about Sylvia Leblanc?"

"Here's the part . . . you might not like so much. I found her in the morgue. Or at least I think I did. The coroner said they found her remains at the church. She drowned during the storm. They're still waiting on a relative to claim the body."

"And you're absolutely sure it's her?"

Out of pure instinct, Mattingham took a step backwards. Joshua's outward demeanor was calm but Mattingham could sense his agitation rising.

"As sure as I can be without a family member ID-ing the corpse. I would have gotten pictures, but they don't exactly allow that in the morgue."

Joshua dropped the photo of the minister down onto his desk and spoke into his intercom. "Gertie, I need you to cancel my day, and call down to facilities and get a flight for me. I need to leave for New Orleans right away."

"Shall I have them prepare the company jet, sir?"

"No, I need to leave within the hour. I'll take the helicopter."

❧ ❧ ❧

"Oh, Bella, you look so beautiful. I wish I was there. Mom, could you hold the phone still so that I can see the whole dress?"

"I'm doing the best I can, Tonya," Barbara huffed.

"Mom, this wouldn't be a problem if you would just read your manual."

"This isn't even my phone. We had to borrow a phone from Mikey so you could have this total experience."

"Barb, just cut that thing off if that girl can't be grateful," Katie said.

"Wait, Mom don't! I'm grateful. Very grateful."

"Really? 'Cause you could have fooled me. Do I look like I work for Ma and Pa Bell?"

Tonya's forehead wrinkled in confusion, "Who?"

Barbara rolled her eyes. "Oh, never mind. Talking 'bout this wouldn't be a problem if I would have read my manual. This wouldn't be a problem if you would have hopped your behind on a plane and came down here."

❦ ❦ ❦

The moment Joshua had landed in New Orleans a car and a driver was waiting for him.

"Where to, Mr. Keys?" the driver asked, as he scurried to get the door for Joshua.

"Philip T. Jones Retirement Center."

❦ ❦ ❦

Bella had finally decided on a dress, and when she came out of the fitting room wearing in her own clothes, Melissa presented her with a string of pearls.

"I wore these on my wedding day. My mother gave them to me. Now I want you to wear them."

Bella carefully examined the string of salt water pearls. "Oh my, these are the real deal."

"You bet your patootie they are."

"I-I couldn't, Mel. This is a family heirloom."

"Oh, of course you can. You need something borrowed, right? You take them now, and we'll both give them to Serenity on her wedding day."

Bella hugged her mother-in-law tightly. "I will wear them with pride on my wedding day."

Melissa smiled at her mischievously. "Actually, we were thinking you could break them in tonight."

All the women smiled knowingly as Katie held up a metallic gold three-quarter-inch trench coat and a pair of ruby-red high heal shoes for Bella's inspection.

"We figured what with the three of us living in your house these last couple of months that the two of you haven't really had the opportunity to—well you know . . ." Melissa shrugged and let her words trail off.

"Praise the Lord freely like you used to," Barb finished for her.

Tonya looked confused. "Praise the Lord... Mama, what y'all talking about?"

"She saying we ain't heard a peep coming from the master bedroom. No headboard knocking or nothing," Katie said.

Tonya gasped.

Bella turned bright red. "Oh, Mel, ladies, thank you. But this really is not necessary. Joshua and I are—we want to wait."

All the women stared at Bella like she had grown a second head.

Melissa was the first to find her voice. "But, honey, wait for what?"

"Did I hear that right? Did she say she ain't giving the boy any?" Pearl said.

Katie nodded. "That's what it sounds like to me."

Bella shot a pleading look over at Maggie.

"Don't look at me, Rose. I told you to drop the panties weeks ago."

Pearl's eyes bucked. "Weeks! Well how long has she been holding out?"

Katie shook her head. "As fine as my nephew is too."

"Ain't that the truth," Barbara said.

"Are you sore from the birth? 'Cause I've got an old remedy for that," Pearl added quickly.

"Well, no, not anymore. It's just that this is a new beginning for Joshua and me, and I kind of want it to be well you know . . . special . . . like the first time."

All the women looked at her for a beat and then burst into fits of laughter, tears-rolling-down-faces laughter.

"Now, hold up. All of you. I think, that if Bella wants to wait, I think she should. I think it sounds romantic."

"Thank you, Tonya."

"Oh child, please. Don't listen to her," Barbara said wiping the tears of laughter away from her eyes. "You better have sex with that man and plenty of it."

"Have some for me," Katie scoffed.

"And me," Pearl said.

"Ladies, I don't think this is appropriate conversation for a bridal shop," Tonya said.

"You know, I got up to go to the bathroom night before last, and I hear this noise. B*am-bam-whomp-whomp*! B*am-bam-whomp-whomp*! So I go investigate, you know? It's Joshua. He's upstairs in the middle of the night punching this big ole giant weight bag. I couldn't figure it out then. Makes sense to me now. The boy is frustrated. Bella you need to stop playing hard to get and give that man some," Katie said.

"No, what you need to do is show up at his job naked with this trench coat on and these high heels. I'll drop you off myself," Pearl said.

"We can all drop you off," Barbara said.

"And then we'll just keep on rolling," Maggie said.

The women howled with laughter.

"And if the two of you decide to check into a hotel somewhere tonight, the baby will be fine with me." Melissa's cornflower blue eyes sparkled mischievously. "Just make sure that under that trench coat you remember to wear these."

Bella shook her head. "Mel, not your mama's good pearls."

Melissa nodded. "I've gotten a lot of action with these pearls."

Tonya gasped. "Ooh, Auntie Mel, you so nasty!"

"Tonya, please. How do you think you got here? Back in the day me and your daddy—"

Tonya shook her head. "Mama, no. Please. I do not want to hear about you and daddy getting your freak on."

Katie laughed. "Last I checked the marriage bed was undefiled."

"Hum hun and wasn't nothing freaky about what went on between your daddy and me." Barbara paused for a second. "Well, actually, now that I think about it, we were known to get a little freaky from time to time."

The women cackled with laughter.

"My point is, Tonya, one day, when you are married, I hope you are blessed enough to have some very good sex. 'Cause your daddy. . . baby, let me tell you, he laid it down."

Katie stuck her face in front of the phone's camera. "Your uncle Earl did too. You might want to think about that before you marry that stick in the mud preacher."

Tonya closed her eyes and shook her head, "Aunt Katie, I'm going to try and forget you said that and Mom, I'm completely closing my ears now."

❧ ❧ ❧

Joshua walked into Rev. Leblanc's room and found the older man seated in a wheelchair dozing in front of the television.

"Reverend Leblanc?" the nurse called his name softly and his eyes popped open. "You have a visitor."

Leblanc took in Joshua standing by the door. He was quiet for so long that Joshua thought that perhaps with losing everything else the old man's mental facilities were gone too. However, the eyes that stared back at him told a different story. Though watery and jaundiced, they were still sharp.

"Joshua, my son," the minister finally pronounced. "Do my eyes deceive me or has my help finally come?"

Joshua nodded, but made no move to enter any further into the room. "It's me."

"You don't know how long I've prayed to see your face in person again. Bella and my grandson? I know that Sylvia met with them often, and that they were living in New Orleans during the flood. Did they—" The minister closed his eyes as if couldn't bear to finish the rest.

"They made it out. Thank God," Joshua said.

"Yes, thank God! Sylvia and I were separated during the flood. But the faithful among my flock, they are still searching for her."

"Actually, that's why I'm here. This isn't a social call. I hired a detective. He may have found Mrs. Leblanc's remains."

"My Sylvia?"

Joshua swallowed the sudden lump in his throat and nodded.

The older man wept. "Does Bella know?"

"I can't tell her something like this until I'm sure. I need you to come with me to identify the body."

CHAPTER 74

The female attendant rolled Reverend Leblanc out to the waiting car. The driver opened the left passenger door for the attendant and Joshua lifted the reverend from his wheelchair and set the older man inside the car. The reverend grabbed a hold of Joshua's arm with a surprisingly tight grip,

"Forgive me," he cried urgently.

Joshua looked at the minister's hand on his arm and resisted the urge to snatch it away. "I already have," Joshua said quietly. He closed the car door and rode up front with the driver.

❀ ❀ ❀

Pearl sped up to the front door of Home Court Advantage.

Katie reached across Bella and opened the front passenger door. "What are you waiting for? Go!"

Bella looked down at her clothes. She wore the string of pearls Melissa had given her and the cute little raincoat with nothing underneath. "Well, wait, you can't just drive off and leave me like this."

"Sure we can," Barbara said.

"What if he's not here? I should have called first."

"You can't call. That would ruin the effect," Maggie said from the back seat.

"I agree," Melissa said. "This is better."

"Rose, stop stalling and get out my car," Pearl said.

"Okay, but just—don't leave, let me see if he's here first."

"We won't leave until you give us the signal," Barbara said.

Gertie smiled when she saw Bella approaching her desk. "Mrs. Keys, it's so good to see you. What a beautiful coat. Were you planning on surprising the hubby for lunch today?"

Bella's cheeks colored. "Hum, yeah, sort of."

"I'm so sorry. He thought you'd be checking in with him at some point during the day by phone. He said I should tell you he would meet you at home tonight. He had to fly out of town today on urgent business."

※ ※ ※

"Mr. Keys wait!"

Joshua had just dropped the attendant and Reverend Leblanc back off at the retirement center. He was stepping into the limousine on his way back to the heliport, when he heard a woman calling at his back. Joshua turned around to see a petite dark-skinned woman with braids.

"I'm, Errol Davis, the director of this center, sir, and I really need to speak with you."

Joshua followed the woman back into the building and down the hall to her office. He took a seat in one of the uncomfortable metal chairs in front of Errol's desk.

"I'm going to get right to the point, Mr. Keys. Your father-in-law's bill is way overdue."

Joshua ran a hand over his face. "Doesn't he have insurance?"

"His insurance ran out months ago. We've only been able to keep him this long through the aid of donations, and that's only because of his standing in this community. But, as you can imagine, there are a lot of indigent elders left here in New Orleans after Katrina. That money needs to be used to care for them."

Joshua reached into his suit coat jacket and pulled out his checkbook. "How much? I'll pay the past bill and any future bills related to his care."

"Although that is very generous of you, I'm afraid it's not that simple. We need the bed."

Joshua sat back in the chair and stared at Errol. "Where do you expect him to go?"

"I am aware of the strained relationship between your father-and-law and your wife. I attended his church as a teenager. I was there the day you and the reverend had the uh. . . altercation."

Silence.

"So then you understand perfectly well why he can't come home with me."

Errol nodded her head slowly. "I understand that there are certain family dynamics at play here that need to be carefully considered. Mr. Keys, there are residential care facilities right here in New Orleans that would take your father-in-law in a heartbeat."

Joshua stood and buttoned his suit jacket. "Great, then pick one and send me the bill."

Errol stood too. "That being said, I've been in this business a long time, and I can tell you that elders get the very best care when they are housed in facilities in cities were their loved ones live. Mr. Keys, elder abuse is alive and real."

"Ms. Davis, I just identified my mother-in-law's remains today."

"I know, sir, I'm so sorry for your loss. My staff just told me."

Joshua nodded. "I have to go home and tell my wife and it's going to be a lot for her to take in. So if you can just give me a few days."

"Of course, but we'll have to make some definite decisions about your father-in-law's care by the end of the week."

"Thank you. That's all I ask."

CHAPTER 75

Since her plan to surprise Joshua at the office didn't work, Bella decided to put her clothes back on and treat her dress-hunting crew to a late lunch. It was after five o'clock when the women made it back to the Keys's residence, laughing and out of breath. Joshua was sitting on the couch in the family room waiting for Bella's return.

"Josh, is everything alright?" Bella had asked the question even though looking at him she could tell it wasn't. "Where's Suri, where's my baby?"

"She's upstairs sleeping." Joshua picked up the remote and flicked to the home security channel so that Bella could see the baby sleeping peacefully in her bed. "Suri's fine. Jabari is at Mike's house. He's fine too."

"Then Joshua what is it? Something is wrong, I can tell."

"Baby, a couple of weeks ago, I hired a PI. The same one I used to find you. I sent him to New Orleans to search for your folks. Your father is alive. He survived the flood."

"And my mother?"

"I'm so sorry, baby, she didn't make it."

※ ※ ※

Ted stopped by Tonya's office that evening on his way home. He knocked lightly on the door and entered when she didn't answer. Ted had peeked in her office a few hours

240

ago and found Tonya surrounded by takeout containers. She was having "lunch" with the ladies back home. She'd introduced him to Bella, and he had gotten a chance to say hello to her Aunt Katie, her godmother, Melissa, and Tonya's mother, Barbara. When Ted walked into the office this time, Tonya sat at her desk crying.

"More happy tears?"

Tonya shook her head, and Ted rushed to her, pulling her up into his arms. Tonya broke down completely then as she sobbed on his shoulder.

"What's the matter, darling?"

"They f-f-found her."

"Who, baby?"

"Bella's m-m-mother. In New Orleans. They found her remains in the church. When the flood waters got too high she ran to the ark of safety, only she drowned. I should be there right now! I should be with my family!"

Ted gripped her tighter. "Aw, baby, I'm so sorry." Ted kissed Tonya's hair and whispered into her ear, "I know you love them. I know you want to be there to comfort your friend, but the best thing you can do for her right now is pray. So can we do that right now together, you and me?"

Tonya nodded her head.

"Heavenly Father, we come to you lifting up Bella and Joshua as they receive this devastating news today. God, I simply ask that in the middle of this storm, would you give them your peace?"

Tonya dried her eyes and stepped out of Ted's arms. "I'm sorry."

He lifted a loose strand of her hair and tucked it behind her ear. "Don't apologize, I like comforting you. I'm sorry this happened. I really am, but I'll take any opportunity I can get to hold you."

CHAPTER 76

Joshua and Bella sat quietly together in an oversized leather chair in Joshua's office. Bella almost never came in here, but tonight she had padded barefoot into the room, still damp from her shower, and climbed wordlessly up onto Joshua's lap. Joshua immediately dropped the book he was reading and pulled her into his arms.

It had been three days since she'd learned about her mother's death. For three days, she lay balled up on a corner of their huge bed, rising only to go to the bathroom or to nurse Suri. And Joshua suspected that the only reason she ate and drank anything at all, from the trays his mother and aunts sent up to her daily, was so that she could continue to produce milk for Suri. She had fallen into his arms and accepted comfort from him during the initial hearing of it all, but as more information unfolded about her only surviving parent, Bella withdrew and asked Joshua for time and space to process the news alone. It was a lot for her to take in, especially all at once, so despite the ache in his own heart to hold her, Joshua complied with her wishes and gave Bella space to process her grief alone.

The smell of clean skin, her first shower in days, along with the ease in which she had climbed into his lap that evening, told Joshua that Bella was finally ready to make her peace with this. As the jazz from the house's internal sound system filtered into the room, Joshua absently played with her hair and thought about the unsaid. There was so much time sensitive stuff that needed to be discussed, but Joshua was hesitant to broach any of it right now, lest he shatter the mood and break her peace. And, yet these things, they had to be said.

"I'd pay a fortune right now just to know your thoughts." He placed a kiss at the base of her neck testing the solvency of her mood.

"I just keep thinking about the last thing I said to her. How I never said I love you. I never said goodbye."

"I'm sure if she had a do-over she would change that too." Joshua tugged a little harder on the line, this time testing the pliability of her mood. "I'll handle all the funeral arrangements. You just tell me where you want it to happen. Here or in New Orleans."

"It should be there. Everyone she knew was there."

"I'm going to be right there beside you the whole time. Nothing's going to happen, you know that, right?"

Bella leaned into him and released a heavy sigh. "I'm just so glad he won't be there."

He'd done it. He'd pushed too far too fast and broken the line. Before Joshua could think of a way to repair it, Bella had twisted her entire body around so that she was facing him.

"You said he was bedridden in a nursing home, that means he can't come."

"No, baby, I said he was wheelchair bound. He's still mobile."

Her body went stiff with this new piece of information.

Joshua exhaled and tried again. "He's going to be there Bella, she was his wife—"

Bella scrambled up from his lap. "She was my mother!"

"I know—"

"No, you don't know! He stole her from me! She chose him over me! And now you're saying I can't even have her in death?"

Bella was on her feet, screaming at the top of her lungs.

Joshua made it a point to remain seated and he lowered his voice to a quiet hum. He leaned forward in the chair and pulled Bella's hands into his. "If you're this adamant, I can arrange it so that the two of you will never be there at the same time. But as bad as this sounds, right now— even to me, I'll admit. . . baby, he's got a right to say his goodbyes."

Bella snatched her hands away from him. "No, you're right! You are absolutely right! So don't make any special accommodations for me. Let him say his goodbyes."

"Are you sure because—"

She folded her arms across her chest and glared down at him. "That's what I want."

The line hadn't broken, it had exploded. It was blown to smithereens. The mood was shredded beyond repair. Joshua saw no point in soft pedaling now, so he pressed on.

"There's one other thing we need to discuss. I put it off as long as I could but—"

Bella rolled her eyes and sighed hard.

"Errol needs an answer by tomorrow. We have to decide what we are going to do with your father."

"The answer is simple, Joshua. You let him rot."

Joshua studied his hands for a beat, then looked back up into her eyes. "I can't do that, baby. Deep down inside, I know you can't either."

"Watch me."

The office door slammed shut on her way out of the room.

CHAPTER 77

Bella came downstairs for dinner the next evening, without prompting. The first time in four days that she didn't eat in the bedroom alone. Katie, Barbara, and Melissa were a godsend to Joshua because they kept the conversation flowing from one mundane topic to the next. And just when it looked as if they would make it through the entire meal without a hiccup, Jabari asked a question about the funeral.

"It doesn't matter when it is because you aren't going," Bella said quietly,

"She was my grandma. I have a right to say goodbye."

"Not if he's going to be there you don't."

"Anybody up for dessert? We got apple pie for dessert," Katie said as quick as a whip.

Joshua shot her a grateful smile.

"Apple pie sounds fantastic Katie," Melissa said.

"Yes, why don't we all have pie?" Barbara said.

Joshua didn't even like pie, but for the sake of one night of peace in the Keys household he'd eat the daggone pie.

Jabari slouched down in his chair. "I don't even know him, what's the big deal?"

Joshua leaned across the table and spoke to his son in the same quiet hum he had been reserving for his wife lately. "Jabari, drop it for now, buddy, alright?" In a louder voice, he said, "Mom, Aunt Barb, Aunt Katie, thank you for dinner, everything is delicious."

Bella sent a weak smile across the table to the three elders. "Yes, thank you all for cooking breakfast, lunch, and dinner every day this past week."

Melissa patted Bella's hand. "It's our pleasure, sweetie. We know you've had a rough go of it these last couple of days. We're happy to help out wherever we can."

"You know Bella, we've been thinking. If you don't want to take Suri this weekend, we'd be more than happy to stay behind and watch her."

"Thanks, Barbara, that's very kind of you, but that won't be necessary." Bella's voice began to waver. "You see I'm not going to my mother's funeral." Bella shot Jabari a look. "Neither one of us will." Bella rose from the table and ran from the room.

Minutes later, Joshua found her in their bedroom curled up on the bed in a tight ball. Her go-to spot as of late.

"What do you think will happen if Jabari is there?"

"Josh, I don't want to talk about this right now."

Joshua took a seat on the edge of the bed beside her. "I know you don't, but the funeral is in three days, Bella, so we have to discuss this."

"I don't want him to ever see my son. I don't want him to ever lay eyes on either one of my children."

"This is about you saying goodbye."

"What's the point. She's already gone," she croaked.

Joshua stroked her hair lightly. "The point is you need closure. Jabari does too. Last night you were agonizing over the last words you ever spoke to your mother. And sweetheart, I don't want this to become something else you come to regret too. Go and say your goodbyes." Joshua kissed the crown of her head. He pulled a cover up around her and turned out the lights on his way out the room.

CHAPTER 78

As promised, Joshua handled everything. From the flowers, to the obituary, to the mauve-colored casket Bella's mother would have adored. There was a huge blown up photo of Sylvia Leblanc at the front of the church, looking stunning as ever as she held Bella's hand. The picture had to be taken when Bella was about six or seven. She could tell this immediately because in the photo she had been smiling, the light hadn't yet left her eyes. There were other photos there too. All photos of happier times. Photos meant to soothe her, of course. Instead, they only served to intensify Bella's extreme sense of lost.

During the service, somebody sang a song, somebody else read a scripture. And just about every black church in the city of New Orleans had a representative present who stood up and read a resolution. But when the officiating pastor asked if the family would like to say a few words, Bella stayed rooted in her seat. It was Jabari who got up confidently and approached the mic.

"When my mom and I lived in New Orleans, my grandma would take us out once a month to eat at this restaurant called Lucchini's. Those lunch dates were always fun. I know that I speak for me and my mom both when I say we will miss her a lot."

Bella's father came up next, wheeled by an attendant who lifted the microphone from the stand and placed it in his withered hand. And for the first time in Bella's life, Lamech Leblanc was too choked up to speak. The reverend laid his head atop the mauve-colored casket, and wept, heavy, pitiful tears over the remains of her mother. Bella closed her eyes and pressed her body even further into Joshua's. The remainder of the funeral went by in a blur.

Bella did open her eyes the moment she felt Joshua rise. He and Jabari both served as pallbearers, so despite what he had told her earlier, he did in fact, at some point during the funeral, have to leave her side. But the moment that Joshua and Jabari arose from their seats, Mike and Jack sat down in their spots. Two strong pillars anchoring Bella on both sides.

And just like that, it was over. She had made it through. Bella was just about to leave this church and this city behind her, unscathed, when she heard the right Reverend Lamech Leblanc call her name.

"Bella Rose, daughter, may I have a word with you?"

Mike stepped in front of her like a shield. Told him there was no way that was going to happen, not in this lifetime.

"I have to go to the washroom," was the only thing Bella managed to blurt out—she said this to Jack. He, like Mike, was glowering at the reverend.

"You go right ahead, darling," Jack said. "We'll be waiting right here for you when you get back."

Bella opened the door to the women's restroom and ran smack dab into the second last person on the planet that she wanted to see. Her father's former secretary. Sister Monroe, who'd never had a kind word to say to Bella in all the years she had known her, assaulted Bella with a crushing hug.

"It was a lovely service, Bella Rose. You put your mother to rest beautifully."

All those days you sat outside my daddy's office, didn't you hear me scream? "Thanks," Bella said woodenly.

"How you holding up?"

You had to have heard. You had to have heard me scream. "As well as can be expected."

"Well, I'mma get out your way."

Awkward silence.

"It was a beautiful service."

Bella turned to go into the stall.

"Bella, wait, I—" Sister Monroe laid her hand on Bella's arm and Bella felt herself choke back a scream.

"I know you and your daddy haven't always seen eye to eye. But what you're doing for him is right. Thank you for moving him to Texas."

Sister Monroe walked out of the bathroom, and Bella walked into the stall and emptied the contents of her stomach into the toilet.

CHAPTER 79

Mike knocked on his brother's office door at Home Court. Joshua was sitting on the large leather sofa in front of the fireplace with his Bible open.

"Am I interrupting?"

Joshua closed the Bible. "Naw, man, I just finished. What's up?"

Mike took a seat on the couch beside Joshua. "Just thought I'd stop by and check on you. You seemed distracted in the meeting earlier. I'm guessing that was about Bella. How is she?"

Joshua blew out a deep breath. "I can't seem to reach her these days. She's angry that's for sure. And the look on her face when she found out Leblanc was coming to Texas." Joshua shook his head.

"You figured she wasn't going to be too happy about that though, right?"

"I figured she'd be mad for a moment, yeah. But what I didn't anticipate was the pain. We're supposed to be renewing our vows in two more weeks. For all I know she may just serve me some divorce papers and call the whole thing off."

Mike shook his head. "She won't do that. A whole lot can happen in two weeks. She'll get it together by then. I'm praying for you."

Joshua raised an eyebrow and smiled at his brother. "Yeah?"

"Don't look so shocked, little brother. I do pray."

"Naw, I know. It's just. . ."

Mike smirked. "Just what?"

"Nothing, man. Thank you." Joshua held out his hand and the brothers gave each other their customary hug handshake.

"Listen, I've been thinking. This family has had enough grief lately. It's time to celebrate something. I'mma go ahead and make Marcus and Granny P's adoption official this weekend. I'mma have something formal at the house, but I'd love for you to be there for the actual event."

Joshua grinned. "Congratulations, man. You know I'm there."

"Good. I still want you and Bella to stand as Godparents. Selena will be there. I know Bella isn't really feeling her right now. But, for what it's worth, she got the baby a gift and she wants to apologize to Bella for what happened at Jabari's party a few months ago."

"So, you moving on?"

Mike shrugged. "I got to, man. The woman I'm in love with is in love with another man."

"I'm sorry I fired your girl."

Mike smirked. "Shut up, man. Don't lie. Besides it's better this way. She always wanted to go to law school. Now she can."

"I feel that." Joshua rubbed his chin. "Hey, you got plans tonight?"

"Nope just chilling at the crib, why, what's up?"

"I was thinking I could send the fam over to your place. Give me and Bella a chance to talk."

CHAPTER 80

Bella came downstairs to see Katie, Barbara, and their things waiting by the door. Jabari was making trips back and forth to the car.

"Jabari, did you get my controllers?"

"Yes, Aunt Katie, your precious controllers are already in the car."

"Good 'cause I don't play with nobody else's controllers."

Jabari laughed. "Is that the secret to your success."

Katie winked at Jabari. "That's one of them. If you show any promise, grasshopper, I might teach you a few more."

Jabari headed back outside, and Bella watched Melissa come down the stairs holding Suri.

"Getting your last hugs in before you get on the road?" Bella asked.

Barbara laughed. "More like, Grandma Mel is getting her last hugs in before she has to put Serenity in her car seat and straps her up and takes her down the road."

Katie sucked her teeth. "Bella, we came down here to plan a wedding. I ain't leaving until one happens. So you can just forget about trying to get rid of us."

Bella reached out and hugged the older woman. "I wouldn't dream of getting rid of you, Aunt Katie. I'm actually glad you're here."

For the past week, Bella had taken up residency in her old bedroom across the hall. Each night Joshua had gone to her sometime in the middle of the night and carried a sleeping Bella back to their room. They hadn't spoken to each other in a week. But every night, he'd hold her close all night long, and in the morning, he'd be a ghost, dressed, and gone to work before she awoke.

For the few waking hours where Joshua and Bella were home together, having the elders there acted as a nice buffer. They filled in the blank spaces of what would normally be awkward silence, and Bella didn't have to talk.

Melissa kissed Bella on the cheek. "We're going to get out of your hair for a bit. And we're taking the kids, too. It'll give you and Joshie some privacy."

"No, you can't. I mean, Suri can't go," Bella stammered. "It's still damp outside, and Josh really doesn't like for her to leave the house."

Barbara placed her hands on her hip. "Bella, this is happening. Serenity is packed, dressed, fed, burped, changed, and ready to go. Her car seat, diaper bag, and additional breastmilk are already in the car. So stop all this stalling."

"I'm not stalling."

"Use this time to talk to him, daughter," Melissa said gently.

"Talking is overrated," Katie said. "Go upstairs, put on them pearls and that trench coat and them high heels. Use this time to scream as loud as you want."

All the elders cackled as they rushed out the door.

CHAPTER 81

Minutes later Bella found Joshua in the kitchen. "Did you tell your mom Suri could leave the house?" This is what their conversation was like lately. When they did talk, it was always only about the kids. "Did you give Jabari permission to sleep over at Mike's?" or "Did you give Suri her bath?"

"Yes, I did."

"Can I ask why?"

"Because you and I need to talk."

Silence.

He peered into her eyes. "Is that alright with you?"

Bella shrugged. "Yeah, I'm just surprised you're letting the bubble baby leave the property."

A small smile played at the corner of his lips. "I wish you'd stop calling her that."

"Where are they going, Joshua?"

He shrugged. "Down the road a bit, to my brother's house."

"Uh huh, my point exactly."

"Come here, let me show you something." Joshua took her by the hand and led her into the parlor.

The room was aglow with candlelight, soft music flowed from the sound system, and a pretty, white, linen covered a table for two in front of the lit fireplace. A bottle of chilled red wine sat on the table.

"What's all this?"

Joshua pulled out the chair for her and handed her a warm towel for her hands. "I wanted to do something to make you feel special." He squatted down on his hunches and stared up at her. "Is it working?"

"That depends what's for dinner?"

He smiled at her, a full-on dimple smile. "My famous steak, potatoes, and asparagus, what else?"

Bella sighed. "Okay, I guess I'm starting to feel pretty special."

"Good, I'll be right back."

For the first twenty minutes or so, Joshua decided to keep the conversation light. He figured if dinner went well they could talk about the heavier parts later.

"Mike's doing the adoption ceremony this weekend. He's hoping you'll feel up to attending. He wants you and I to be godparents for Marcus."

Bella nodded. "For sure. I already told him I'd be honored to do that."

"They picked up Belinda. She got probation and mandatory treatment."

"You mean to tell me she stole a twenty-seven-million-dollar car and she's not going to prison?"

"If she completes the drug treatment program she won't." Joshua took a forkful of his steak and chewed slowly. "You disagree?"

Bella shook her head. "I'm just sick and tired of abusive people. Do you know that the morning we left New Orleans, we couldn't leave right away because Marcus had to go find his mama? And do you know where he found her? In the crack house. She bit, slapped, cussed, and scratched him while he carried her crazy behind out of the crack house. And if that wasn't bad enough she goes and pulls a stunt like this. She should have been prosecuted to the fullest extent of the law. She should be under the jail."

Joshua wiped his mouth with the napkin in his lap and stared at Bella. "How would that help Marcus to know that his mother was in prison?"

"He'd be free of her." Bella waved her fork in the air. "All y'all doing right now is enabling her."

"Baby, we got enough on our plate without us fighting about this. This is Mike's call. Don't forget this ain't his first time at the rodeo when it comes to situations like this."

Bella caught the pain in Joshua's eyes when he spoke about his brother. "No, I didn't forget," she said quietly.

"Good, because Mike is dealing with Belinda with the same care and compassion he showed to his own birth mother," Joshua said firmly.

"I know."

"Either she'll submit to the guidelines of her probation or she'll go to prison. It's as simple as that. But for now, she's got a chance to turn it around. She'll be a good candidate for Hebron House, the new community for ex-substance abusers that we're building, if she does."

"No, you're right. I'm tripping. It's wonderful that Mike is showing grace."

Joshua looked at Bella warily. It was either now or never. Given the way she'd been acting lately, she'd cut a complete fool if she got to the adoption ceremony and saw Selena there. For his brother's sake, this conversation had to happen."

"I almost forgot." Joshua stood and picked up a small gift from the mantle.

Bella raised her eyebrows. "You're really going all out tonight. Gifts too."

"It's for the baby from Selena."

Bella sucked her teeth. "Oh. Where'd you see her?"

"She gave it to Mike to give to me. They're dating. She'd like the four of us to go dinner. She wants to apologize for her behavior at the party."

Bella pushed the gift back across the table. "That won't be necessary."

"Selena's also going to be at the adoption ceremony this weekend. She's Mikes guest."

Bella's eyes narrowed. "That's what all of this is about isn't it? You're trying to butter me up?"

Joshua feigned ignorance. "What? No."

"And here I thought this was a genuine apology."

Joshua's nostrils flared. "Apology for what? What do I have to apologize—"

"You come in here with your romance, your wine, and your food, all this so that I don't cause a scene at the courthouse with that heifer!"

"Okay, yeah, I don't want you to cause a scene on the most important day of my brother's life. Is that a crime? They're seeing each other, Bella."

"You said that already, Josh!"

"And if they get married, then what? Me and my brother won't speak because you can't be civil to his wife?" Joshua could feel his temperature skyrocketing. This woman made him want to put his fist through the wall. He opted to pace the floor instead. "Nah, you better get this in order. Be the bigger person or whatever you gotta do. 'Cause me and my brother not talking is not an option."

Bella rolled her eyes. "She ain't into Mike like that, she wants you."

"Bella, nobody believes that but you!"

Bella folded her arms across her chest and glared up at him. "Like I said," she bit out slowly, "I am tired of abusive people having the right to walk in and out of my life."

Joshua stopped pacing. He stared down at her and prayed for patience to enter his soul. He took a seat on the coffee table in front of her and ran his hands over his face. "We both know this isn't about Selena. So why don't we just address the elephant in the room. You're still angry at me for helping your father. That's why you think I owe you an apology."

"Yes!" she hissed. Bella jumped up from the table, turning over her chair in the process. "You ask me what I wanted, and I told you to let him rot!"

"What did you expect me to do, Bella? God's law commands me to forgive."

"So you can just forget everything he's done?"

Joshua stood and stalked towards her, the muscles in his jaw and neck, bulging tight. "You think this is easy for me? Don't you know that every day I look at you and see the damage he's done, the pain he's caused right there in your eyes, that I want to get in my truck, drive across town, drag his feeble body out that bed and beat the hell out of him, again? Do you know how many times a day I fantasize about doing that? God's law is the only thing that restrains me!" Joshua backed away from her. "Trust and forgiveness aren't the same, Bella. I'm not in community with that man. I didn't move him into our home. I didn't give him access to our children. All I did was make sure he wouldn't be thrown out into the streets. Until you say so, he will never be a part of our lives." Joshua rubbed his hands over his face. "You've been so busy hating me for doing this, because you think that by obeying God that somehow I've betrayed you, but you've got to ask yourself, where would we be right now, Bella, if I couldn't forgive you?"

Bella's body shook as the sobs tore from her frame. "I don't hate you! I, I l-l-love you with all of my m-might. You just don't know everything he did to me!"

Joshua pulled Bella into his arms and for a moment, with his body encased about her like a hard protective shell, the unrelenting pain that had made its habitation with her for the last three weeks stopped.

"I will never know the fullness of the pain he caused you. It's not because I don't want to. I'm here, baby. You can tell me everything. Anything you need to in order to break free of this thing." He wiped her falling tears with the pads of his thumbs. "I won't shrink back. There's nothing you could tell me that would cause me to turn away from you. Nothing that would cause me to love you any less, because you are mine and I am yours. I love you."

"Joshua—"

"You gotta learn how to forgive, baby. For you." Joshua pressed his forehead against hers. And for a moment, Bella felt her tears mingle with his. He released her then and walked from the room.

CHAPTER 82

So Bella, what about you, how are you doing?"
They were at Jilly's house for their weekly Broken Vessels meeting, the accountability group that Joshua had mandated she join upon her return to Houston. A group that had become more than a bunch of strangers she was required to meet with, they had become her friends. All the group members had done their check-in, and so far, Bella hadn't said a word. A while ago, the Broken Vessels had decided to stop having their small group meet at the church but to instead take turns hosting their gathering in each of their homes. Bella was actually the next one in the rotation to host their weekly gathering. Normally, she welcomed the opportunity to play hostess, but with everything going on in her world right now she couldn't muster up the energy.

Bella sighed. "Thanks, Jilly, for taking my turn in the rotation. Our dining room has turned into wedding central since my mother-in-law and the aunts have moved in."

"That must be fun," Anna coaxed gently.

"It was. Up until about three weeks ago."

"When they found your mom's remains?" Renee asked gently.

"When I found out that my husband was harboring the man who raped me."

The room fell silent as the women processed this.

"These past nine months Joshua has been trying to figure out whether he could forgive me. Whether he could stay married to me, and now . . ." Bella shook her head. As she did the tears ran down her face.

"Now what?" Anna asked softly.

"Now I don't know if I want to be married to him."

Sadie shook her head vigorously, "Oh, no! The devil is a lie! We ain't even about to give up that fine bad boy turned pastor. Sister Bella you can't—"

"What? Walk away? I can, Sadie. I've done it before. Trust me, I can do it again. And you know what? I'm sick of people telling me what I can't do! Joshua telling me that I can't let my father rot! He deserves to rot, for what he did to me!"

Sadie folded her hands across her chest. "I was going to say that you can't let the enemy steal the victory from you in the final stretch."

Jilly bobbed her head excitedly. "Sadie's right, Bella. The finish line is right in front of you. This is your victory stretch."

Anna handed Bella a tissue. "Do you think he's not being truthful, that he wants to care for the man who hurt you?"

Bella shook her head. "No. Joshua was so disillusioned when he found out what my father did that he left the church. He says providing for my father is a part of his forgiveness process. I know he's telling the truth, but it still hurts."

"You know what, Bella? You're right. He does deserve to rot. You'll get no disagreement from me," Anna said. "What he did to you, to any child, especially as a father and a man of the cloth, is unconscionable. But this group is called Broken Vessels for a reason. Every one of us in this group has done some unconscionable things."

"Despicable things," Renee added.

"And we did them because we were broken," Jilly said.

"And God forgave us. Much," Anna said. "I'm not talking a little, Bella. He forgave us much. And I don't know about you. I can't judge your past, but I know my own and I'm telling you, I didn't deserve it."

"We've all been forgiven much. And here's the thing about forgiveness. A God who is generous enough to forgive us much, won't tolerate un-forgiveness inside of any of us. Forgiveness is for you," Thelma said.

Jilly, who was sitting right next to Bella, patted her hand. "Did you hear that, Bella? Forgiveness is for you."

"Yes, I hear, but why does everybody keep saying that?"

"'Cause it's true. Forgiveness keeps you out of the prison of your mind. Forgiveness will keep bitterness from taking root in your soul. Forgiveness will also keep you out of hell—now and in the afterworld," Anna said.

"You know what hell is, don't you, sweetie? Hell is having to live every single day with the memory of what he did to you. Every day outside the healing presence of God. Imagine doing that for eternity. Imagine having no relief," Jilly said.

Bella sniffed and wiped her nose. "If that's the definition of hell, I've been there every day for the last three weeks. Anybody got any tips on how I can break out?"

Thelma raised her hand. "Yeah, I got a tip for you. Try to remember that forgiveness isn't a feeling. I think that's where people get stuck. They think if they really, truly forgive from their heart, then immediately all the bad feelings surrounding that thing and that person should go away. But I read this book once, called *Doing Business with God*, and in it the author said something that stuck with me. She said that forgiveness is a tree that has to grow up. You have to water it, give it lots of care and attention, and tend it with your prayers."

Bella nodded and blew out a deep breath. "I started prostituting myself when I was fourteen. *Fourteen*. Not because I wanted to, but because I knew that if I were 'unclean' the good Reverend Leblanc wouldn't touch me anymore. And you know what? I was right. He called me a filthy, dirty girl. He beat me, and he cried. Cried because he said that from that day forward his body would no longer be joined with that of a whore's." Tears fell from Bella's face as she wept openly. "Now you tell me, where should my prayers begin?"

"The word of God says we don't even know how to pray. None of us do. It tells us that the Spirit prays through us with groans we can't even understand. Maybe you should just start there, with a moan," Sadie said.

Anna nodded. "And if the moan wants to turn into a yell, then you let it."

Renee stood up. "Well, come on. Let's do this then."

Bella blinked and stared at the women around the circle who were now all standing. "What, now?"

"Yes, now. We'll all moan and yell with you if we have to," Thelma said. "This is too heavy of a burden for one person to carry. It's eating you alive. You gotta get it up out of you, right now."

CHAPTER 83

Mike had set it up so that the adoption ceremony could happen at City Hall after hours. Melissa, Barbara, and Katie all got dressed in their Sunday best, and Jack flew in from Dallas for the celebration. Joshua and Bella stood in as godparents to Marcus. Walter and Maggie showed up as guests of Pearl's and Jabari was just super geeked to be getting a new cousin.

Bella kept watching the door for Tonya.

"Do you think her plane was delayed?" Bella whispered to Joshua.

"Whose plane, babe?"

"Tonya's. At this rate she's going to be late for the ceremony."

Joshua stared at Bella for a beat. "She's not coming."

Bella's forehead wrinkled in confusion. "Why not?"

Before he could answer, Selena came sauntering through the door.

Mike greeted her with a smile. "It's about time, girl. Now that the gang's all here, we can get this show on the road."

"Please, not even close," Bella huffed.

Joshua shot her a disapproving look.

Selena leaned into Mike and kissed him deeply. Next, she snaked her arms up and around Joshua's neck and hugged him tightly. "I can't thank you enough for allowing me to crash your family celebration."

"It's cool, we're glad you could make it," Joshua said with a smile.

Selena's eyes landed on Bella, "Bella I want to —"

Bella held up her hand. "Save it. 'Cause if it was up to me, you wouldn't be here." Bella turned on her heels and stalked off towards the judge's chamber.

Mike blew out a deep breath as he watched his sister-in-law's departing back. "Come on everybody. Let's go inside and make this legal."

CHAPTER 84

Bella was sitting on the edge of the bed rubbing cream on her legs. She looked up to see Joshua already dressed, standing in the doorway with his keys. "I can be ready in about five more minutes."

Joshua stared down at her, his face an unreadable mask. "I think you should sit this one out."

"Are you saying Mike uninvited me?"

"No. I'm uninviting you. Selena will be there, and we both know how you feel about her, so I think you should stay home."

There was a timid knock on the door. "Mr. Keys?"

"Come in." The nanny walked in with Serenity strapped snuggly in her carrier. Serenity's wide eyes stared up at Joshua and he smiled.

"Serenity's changed, fed, and ready to go. Her milk and diaper bag are already in your car." Lacy handed the baby over to Joshua.

"Thanks, Lacy."

"Anything else?"

"No, you may as well take off."

"Goodnight, Mr. and Mrs. Keys. Have fun tonight at the party."

"Thanks, Lacy," Bella called at the nanny's departing back. Bella spoke again when she was sure Lacy was well out of earshot. "I think I see how this works. First Tonya's out, now me."

Joshua shook his head. "That's just it, Bella, you don't see."

"And what exactly don't I see?"

"That this is Mike's day, not ours. That he can choose to have or not have whomever he wants there, regardless of how you feel about it. And most importantly Bella, you can't see that in the end, your inability to let go of the past only hurts you."

CHAPTER 85

From his position on the other side of the room, Mike saw his brother enter the ballroom with his niece cradled in his arms. Before his brother could get into the room good, his parents were there beside him, taking the baby from Joshua's arms. Mike greeted a few more of his guests before he made his way over to his brother.

Mike greeted his brother with their customary hug and handshake. "Where's, Bella?"

"Not coming."

Mike's eyes located Selena across the room. "Man, don't tell me she decided to hang back because of some beef with Selena."

"I uninvited her."

"You did what?"

"You heard me, I uninvited her."

Mike stared at his brother. "How is having Selena here and Bella not here going to make Bella feel any less threatened? You 'bout to marry this woman in seven days, man. What are you thinking?"

Joshua shrugged. "That this has gone on long enough and that I had to do something to get her attention."

The brothers both turned towards the door when they heard their father release a shout of exaltation.

"The party can start now! My daughter-in-law is here!"

Bella entered the ballroom wearing a black, off-the-shoulder evening gown. She was escorted into the ballroom by Mike's steward of the house, Jeeves. Jack bowed gallantly and kissed Bella's hand. Mike walked over and planted a kiss on Bella's right cheek. Joshua's eyes were trained on Bella the whole time, but he kept his hands in his tuxedo pockets and remained rooted in his spot.

"You feeling alright, Bella, baby? I heard you were a little out of sorts after the ceremony."

"I'm fine, Mike, thanks for asking," Bella said, her eyes glued on Joshua's. "Just needed a little time to myself."

"Come on, let's get you something to eat." Mike slung his arm around Bella's shoulder and the two of them filed past Joshua to the food tables.

Later that night, Selena approached Bella, while both brothers looked on cautiously from a distance. When they were sure that Bella wouldn't attack Selena, they went back to their conversations and relaxed.

"From the bottom of my heart I want to apologize to you for my behavior at Jabari's party. And I want to say that I am truly not interested in Joshua in any way. I'm sorry if anything I did led you to believe that. What I have for him is nothing more than professional appreciation."

Bella didn't believe this. Not for a minute. But the still quiet voice that used to speak to her as a child spoke like a whisper in her ear and said: ***agree with your adversary quickly.*** So that's exactly what Bella did. Bella took Selena's outstretched hand and smiled.

✻ ✻ ✻

Hand in hand, Melissa and Jack stepped onto the stage that had been erected for the occasion. Jack spoke into the microphone. "We'd like to get everyone's attention."

When the crowd turned towards them, Jack handed the mic to Melissa. "As the grandparents, we'd like to make the first toast."

"So, if you haven't got a glass already, get one and raise it high," Jack said.

Waitstaff moved through the room with goblets of wine on silver serving trays. Jabari and Marcus were standing near their dads when the wine tray passed by.

Jabari laid a hand on both Joshua and Mike's shoulders. "It is a special occasion tonight. You don't mind if Marcus and I have a little bubbly, do you dear old dads?"

Mike threw his brother a look. "You, hear this Josh, Baby Keys got jokes."

Joshua took a wine goblet from the tray offered to him. "I know one thing. Baby Keys and Baby Dutton both better kick rocks to that punch table over there."

Marcus pushed Jabari towards the punch table. "See what you started? That wasn't even me."

Melissa spoke into the mic. "Tonight feels like all my dreams are coming true. I've gotten a new sister." She smiled and waved at Pearl, who waved back. "I got a handsome new grandson, and an adorable granddaughter, all in a matter of a few months. And in a few more days my son and my daughter-in-law will be renewing their vows." The crowd broke into a round of applause. Melissa dabbed her eyes. "My joy is incredibly full."

"Be sure to catch the wedding on television if you're not one of the lucky ones to get an invitation," Jack said. "What network is that on Joshie?"

Joshua said nothing. His eyes had found Bella's, and they were staring at each other across the crowded room.

"You can check out the wedding on the Timeless Network," Mike called out.

"You heard it here folks." Jack and Melissa held their wine goblets up in the air. "Here's to family!"

The crowd responded back in an exuberant roar, "Cheers!"

CHAPTER 86

Later on that evening, Mike sat on the edge of the erected stage talking with Selena as servants moved back and forth through the mansion's massive rooms, clearing away the evidence of the night's festivities.

"I learned something about you tonight," Selena said smiling up at him.

"Yeah, what's that?"

"You never do anything small. When you told me you were having a little get together at your house, I just pictured, you know, a small gathering of family and a few close friends. Certainly, not a DJ, or a dance floor, a stage, exquisite cuisine, and a who's who A-list of Houston's top celebrities."

"It's not every day that I get to adopt a son. Marcus is an amazing kid. I wanted to make sure I properly introduced him to the world as my son." Mike removed his buzzing cell phone from inside his tuxedo jacket. He looked down at the screen and read the text from Marcus.

Dad, we hanging tonight? Or you chilling with your girl?

Nope. It's me and you tonight, chief. I'll be there in five minutes, let me walk her to her car.

Mike pushed the send button and slipped his cell phone back into his pocket. He caught the attention of one of the staff people moving through his house.

"Have Ms. Mason's car brought around front," Mike said when the young man ran up to him.

"Right away, sir."

"How'd your conversation with Bella go this evening?" Mike stood and took Selena's hands, causing her to have to stand up as well.

"I got an invitation to the wedding from Bella."

Mike's dark, handsome face broke out into a grin. "Yeah, no kidding?"

Selena nodded. "I think she's starting to warm up to me."

Mike leaned in and kissed her slowly. "I think I'm starting to warm up to you."

Selena giggled. "Is that a fact?"

"Yeah, it is." He lifted her chin to meet his eyes. "My family is the most important thing in the world to me. You keep this up and I might have to keep you around permanently."

CHAPTER 87

J oshua sat in the parlor, still wearing his tuxedo, watching the clock. Bella had left the party tonight at ten, at least a half an hour before he had. It was a little after midnight, and she still wasn't home. Every time he'd called it, her phone had gone straight to voicemail. Joshua heard the garage door open and then close, and he breathed a sigh of relief. Bella padded into the parlor in her stockinged feet, high heel shoes in her hand.

Instead of bombarding her with questions, like he wanted to, like the old Joshua would have certainly done, the first being, *where the hell were you?* Joshua decided to follow the leading of the Holy Spirit who counseled him not to speak but to let her talk. Joshua leaned back against the sofa. He unbuttoned the top buttons of the crisp white cotton shirt he wore and extended one long arm across the back of the sofa.

"I wasn't ignoring you. I'm not used to carrying one and I didn't have this on me," she said, motioning to the cell phone that was now in her hand.

"After I dialed your cell for the ninety-ninth time, I realized that."

"You didn't have to wait up."

Woman are you kidding me? Joshua stared at Bella until she looked away.

"I mean I'm glad you did, but you didn't have to." Bella walked over and stood in the space between the sofa and the coffee table. Joshua adjusted his long legs to make room for her. Bella sat down on the coffee table in front of him. "I went for a drive tonight and had a long overdue talk with Jesus. You were right. I still think Ms. Selena Mason is a lying wonder, but you were right. I have to learn how to forgive.

A small smile played at the corners of his lips. "Does that mean you still want to marry me again?"

Bella nodded. "I do in just seven days."

"What about your dream wedding? You and my mom and the aunts haven't worked on it in a while. You think you're going to need more time?"

Bella shook her head. "Whatever is not done won't be done, and I'm okay with that 'cause the real dream is to marry you."

"Can I kiss you now, or am I still in the doghouse?"

"You can, and you're not, because I forgive you."

Joshua's face broke out into a full-dimpled grin.

Bella raised her eyebrow at him. "You like that don't you? See, I'm practicing forgiveness right now."

"I do." Joshua pulled her off the coffee table and onto his lap. "Forgiveness looks really sexy on you." And he kissed Bella until she was breathless.

"Josh?"

"Yeah, baby?"

"I'm so sick of appetizers."

"Girl, you ain't said nothing but a word." Joshua picked Bella up and carried her upstairs to the master suite. He kicked the door shut behind them.

CHAPTER 88

After Ted and Tonya departed the plane and retrieved their luggage from the carousel, they saw him, the uniformed driver holding the large white sign that read: Reverend and Mrs. Theodore Maxwell. Not Reverend Maxwell and Dr. Malone, but Reverend and Mrs. Theodore Maxwell. Tonya was hot. Steam-coming-out-the-nostrils hot. Did he think this was funny? Was this Michael's version of some sort of cruel joke? Well, if so, then this was the last straw. Tonya was already upset that she had been the only person in their family not invited to Marcus and Pearl's adoption ceremony. She was just about to pull out her cell phone and give Michael an earful when she felt Ted's hands caressing her shoulders and her neck.

"So, what do you think of my little surprise?"

"You did this?"

"Yes."

"You told Michael's driver to—"

"I rejected his driver. I can find my own way from the airport. I don't need my woman's ex to provide a car for me. I just thought it would be nice for you to see your future in writing. I'm hoping this will motivate you to pick a date." Ted kissed her cheek, scooped their bags up, and headed towards the driver.

CHAPTER 89

"I'm sorry but check-in is not until 3 PM, sir."

"Yes, I'm aware of that, but I am the Reverend Theodore Maxwell, senior pastor of Now Faith International Church. I'll be staying in the penthouse suite this weekend. I'm hoping you can make an exception to your little check in rule."

"Normally we do try to accommodate most requests from our guests, Reverend Maxwell. But unfortunately, sir, we are booked solid what with the wedding."

"The wedding?"

"Haven't you heard? Joshua Keys, one of our local celebrities and his wife are getting back together. He found his family during Hurricane Katrina. Their wedding is happening right here in Houston this weekend. Everybody will be watching. We're having a viewing party right here at this hotel." The hostess's eyes lit up. "I can't do anything about the early check-in, but I can throw in two complimentary tickets to the viewing party if you like.

"That won't be necessary," Tonya said, smiling brightly at the woman.

"So your hotel is filled with guests of the wedding?"

The hostess shook her head. "Oh no, sir. The hotel is filled with fans. Folks have come in from all over hoping to get a glimpse of the happy couple. I tell you what, why don't you go grab a bite to eat and by the time you get back, you and the Mrs. can check into your room."

"Rooms," Tonya corrected. "We're not married."

The woman checked her computer. "I only have you down for one room, ma'am. If two rooms is what you need, you're going to be hard pressed to find that in Houston tonight. Every hotel room in this city is booked."

Tonya turned to Ted. "You told me your secretary booked two rooms."

"She did. It's a two-bedroom suite."

"Ted, we agreed."

Ted smiled at the hostess, at the counter, "Could you excuse us for a moment, Heather," he said, reading her name tag. He pulled Tonya off to the side. "Tonya, this was all they had. You just heard the woman say the hotel is filled with all of Joshua's cult followers. So could you please for once, cut me some slack and not make such a big deal out of this?"

Tonya folded her arms across her chest and stared at Ted. "I will absolutely not stay in a hotel room with you when we are not married."

"I see. But you'll stay at your ex-boyfriend's, right? You have no problem laying up in his mansion with him."

"My whole family will be there."

Ted looked her up and down. "One giant, incestuous orgy, huh?"

Tonya shook her head in disgust. She marched out of the hotel and got back into the waiting car.

About ten minutes later Ted came outside. He gave some directions to the driver, and then climbed into the car beside her. "You'll be happy to know that I called Martha. She is looking for alternatives right now as we speak."

"Here's an idea. Why don't you stay here and I stay at the mansion. I can't wait to get started on that giant orgy."

Ted rolled his eyes. "Don't be like that, you know I was only joking."

"Just make sure you don't joke like that in front of my family."

"Don't you mean in front of your precious Michael?"

"Not Michael, or Joshua, or Jack. I'm warning you, Ted, it won't go over well," Tonya said, agitation rising in her voice.

"Hey, are you sure you're over this guy? I mean, I'm not walking into some sort of a trap here, am I?"

"Ted—"

"I know he's your past, and I'm your future, but—"

Tonya shook her head. "No, he's not my past. Michael and Joshua are fixed components of my life. That will never change. That's why I need them to like you. I don't want them to have any pre-conceived ideas about you. That's why you can't go around making any off-color jokes today."

"Okay, I get that. I hear you loud and clear. But does he know it's over between the two of you?"

"Michael's moved on. He's dating someone else, Ted."

"So, why didn't he extend an invite for me to stay in his home with you?"

"Because he doesn't know you. I told you. Michael, is very private. He's extremely protective of the people he cares about and he would never have someone stay at his home who he hasn't personally vetted."

"Okay, fine, I can accept that, but what I can't accept is just how nervous my lady is about us traveling home to meet her ex. I can't help but wonder."

Tonya blew out a breath, "If you must know, my aunt Katie told Michael that you were abusive towards me."

Ted's face clouded with confusion, "What? Why would she say something like that?"

"Because she doesn't like you."

"But you told him that wasn't true, right?"

"I haven't spoken to him about it, but I'm pretty sure he doesn't believe it."

"How can you be sure?"

"Because you're alive, Ted," Tonya said bluntly.

Ted blinked hard. He took her words in and was silent for the remainder of the drive.

CHAPTER 90

The limo approached the Dutton estate, and Ted took in Mike's property for the first time. "This is like the fortress of solitude. Baby, look at all this! This place is huge!'

Tonya laughed. "I know. I guess it is impressive seeing it through your eyes."

"Baby, if Tatiana becomes a tithing member of my church, I could give you all of this."

Tonya stared at him doubtfully. "If Oprah Winfrey became a tither of your church, you might be able to give me half of it. But that's not the point. The point is, I don't want or need all of this to be hap—"

Ted held his finger up to silence her. "Hold that thought."

The guard at the iron gate said something to the driver, and the driver pulled off to the side of the road.

Ted knocked on the privacy window between him and Tonya and the driver. The driver lowered the window. "What's going on? Why are we stopping?"

"Their security team is only allowing authorized vehicles onto the property this weekend. Since this is considered an unauthorized vehicle, they have to perform a security check before they can allow us through."

Ted huffed. "You have got to be kidding me."

Tonya patted Ted's knee. "This is why Michael suggested he send a car to the airport for us. That way we wouldn't have to go through this extra step. You wanted to take your own car, so sit tight."

Twenty minutes later when Mike's people had run a full security check on the driver, the vehicle, and the contents of the trunk, they were allowed to enter through the large metal gates. At the next checkpoint they were asked to step out of the vehicle and go into the intake office.

"Is this necessary?" Ted asked when the intake officer confiscated his cell phone, camera, and wallet. "I'm waiting for a phone call."

"Don't worry, Mr. Maxwell, someone will bring you your phone in the event that you have a call. Your wallet and other personal affects will be stored in a safety deposit box until you leave the campus."

Tonya handed her cell phone over to the guard without being asked. "He's got children here. I told you with all the publicity this wedding is getting, Michael's staff would be on high alert."

Tonya walked up and stood on the raised black, metal square directly next to Ted's and held her arms out, preparing to be wanded by the guard. A tall muscular white man with a buzz cut stepped out of the office.

Tonya's face broke out into a huge grin. She waved excitedly to him.

He winked at her, and spoke to the guard preparing to wand her in a low voice. "Why the hell she on that box? You know family members are never processed."

The guard looked at Tonya and then back down at his screen. "Dr. Tonya Malone?"

"That's me."

He colored with embarrassment. "I'm sorry ma'am. I didn't recognize you with your um, baseball cap on."

Buzz cut folded Tonya into his arms. "How you doing, Squeeze?"

❧ ❧ ❧

"What did he call you back there?" Ted asked once they had settled themselves back into the car.

"Who?"

"The scary looking guy with the buzz cut."

Tonya smiled. "That's Caesar, he's not scary."

Ted snorted. "If you say so."

"He's Michael's chief of security, and he called me Squeeze."

Ted looked dumbfounded.

"Michael's security team has code names for the entire family. Some of them are pretty funny, and some are just self-explanatory."

"Like?"

"Well like for example, Uncle Jack's code name is Rascal. When Michael first hired the team, they used to follow the family around. Uncle Jack hated that, and he was notorious for giving his security detail the slip. Aunt Mel is Darla, Alfalfa's love interest from—"

Ted nodded. "*The Little Rascals*. Yeah, I get it."

"Aunt Katie is Mischief, which is pretty self-explanatory. My mom is Sweetheart, because, well let's face it, she's a sweetheart."

"Bella is Helen of Troy."

Ted smiled sardonically, "Let me guess, because of all the wars Joshua has fought over her?"

"You got it. And Jabari is Package because he was just the cutest little bundle of joy when we brought him home from the hospital."

"What about Joshua and Michael. Do they also have names?"

Tonya looked at him like he was stupid. "Bad Boy and the Man of Steel."

"Of course," Ted said drily. "And you're Squeeze, the only code name that doesn't really make sense."

Tonya turned her head then and looked out the window. "My code name is actually Main Squeeze, but most everybody on the team just calls me Squeeze for short."

"Huh. I see."

❧ ❧ ❧

Jeeves, the steward of the house, was waiting outside to greet them when the driver finally pulled up to the front door. The stately, older black gentleman gave Ted a firm handshake, and Ted noticed the cut and make of the man's suit. Obviously custom, nothing like what he'd picture a servant to wear at all. It fit the man's chiseled frame to perfection.

"Mr. Maxwell, on behalf of Master Dutton, I'd like to welcome you to the Dutton estate. We are most pleased that you could join us for the festivities this weekend."

"Thank you."

Next Jeeves took Tonya's hand in his and bowed low. "Mademoiselle, welcome home. Master Dutton and the rest of the family are eagerly awaiting your arrival."

Tonya beamed. "Where is everyone? I can't wait to see them too."

"The family is gathered in the courtside sunroom and the adjoining deck. Would either of you prefer to refresh yourself before you join the festivities? Mr. Maxwell, for your convenience, sir, we have a day room prepared for you. You can freshen up there and even rest for a spell if you like after your journey."

As if right on cue, one of the servants appeared seemingly out of the shadows, carrying Ted's luggage in his hand.

"Actually, that's not a bad idea. I'd really like to change out of these traveling clothes."

"And for you, mademoiselle, will you be staying in the main house this weekend, or shall I have your bags sent to the cottage?"

Tonya looked at Ted for a beat. "Actually, we haven't quite figured out where I'll be staying yet, Jeeves."

"Very well. Either place is ready for you when you do decide."

"Ted, I'm going to let you get settled in, and I'm going to go find everyone."

"Wait a minute. Aren't you going to change?" Ted's eyes combed over Tonya's attire. She wore a pair of hip hugging jeans and a fitted t-shirt. Large gold hoop earrings adorned her ears, and her hair had been combed into a long ponytail that hung out the back of the Rockets baseball cap she rocked. "You look so…"

"So, what, Ted?"

Delicious.

She looked downright good enough to eat. He surely didn't want her walking out there in front of her ex looking like that. "I just thought that when we got here, you'd naturally want to change into something more befitting a future first lady. For example, I'm wearing a suit."

Tonya shrugged. "Nobody else will be wearing one. But if you feel like you must, go right ahead."

"Tonya, I am the senior pastor of a seven-thousand-member congregation. You are my fiancée. We have a certain reputation to uphold."

"Maybe you do, but I'm home with my family and I certainly don't."

Jeeves cleared his throat. Ted had almost forgotten he was there.

"Shall I escort you, Mademoiselle?"

"No thanks, Jeeves," Tonya said, kissing his cheek. "Just get Ted squared away."

CHAPTER 91

"H ey family!" Tonya called as she walked into the sunroom.

"Auntie Tonya!" Jabari rushed over to greet her. Melissa, Barbara, Bella, Jack, and Joshua also rose and gave her hugs.

"You look good, Blackbird," Michael said when he pulled her into his arms.

Tonya smiled up at him. "You look pretty good yourself."

"Let me officially introduce you to the newest member of the fam." Mike waved Marcus over. "This is my son, Marcus," Mike proudly pronounced.

"Hello, Ms. Tonya."

Tonya had to reach up to hug the tall, lanky teenager. "I'd really prefer it if you just called me, Tonya, Marcus."

"Yes, ma'am."

Mike palmed his son's head playfully. "We made it official last weekend."

"I heard. I've been wondering why I didn't get an invitation."

Marcus leaned in and kissed Tonya's cheek. "Tonya, good to see you again. Dad, it looks like you're about to be chewed out, so I'mma make myself ghost."

Tonya and Mike both laughed as they watched Marcus walk away.

"He's charming. I can see you're already starting to rub off on him. That's not the same kid I met at Jabari's party five months ago."

"I can't tell you what it meant to me that he decided to take my name."

"I really would have liked to have been there, Michael."

Mike shrugged. "I didn't think your guy would feel comfortable with that, Tonya."

"Really, because I assumed it was because your new girlfriend was there, and she definitely wasn't feeling me the last time we met."

Silence.

"Is this how it's going to be from now, Michael? Should I expect to be excluded from family events?"

"Come on, Blackbird. You know I'd never let a female come between us. Josh mentioned that you couldn't make it for Bella's fitting so I figured—"

Tonya folded her arms across her chest. "You figured that meant I wouldn't be there for the most important day of your life?"

Mike looped his finger through the belt loop of her jeans and pulled her to him. "Hey, I'm sorry. Next time I'll ask, alright? I won't assume."

"Thank you."

Pearl entered the sunroom. "Oh, my goodness, look a here, we've got company."

"You remember Tonya, don't you, Granny P?" Mike said, as he and Tonya both simultaneously took a step away from each other.

"How could I forget the wife of your youth? We missed you at the adoption ceremony, sweetie." Pearl looked at Mike. "Why wasn't she at the ceremony?"

Mike rubbed his hand over the back of his neck. "Yeah, I already got chewed out about that. Tonya's traveling with her fiancé this weekend, Granny P, so you might want to cool it with the wife of your youth stuff."

Pearl stared at Tonya. "You sure about that? 'Cause I'm sensing a love connection all up through here," Granny P said, waving her hand between the two of them.

Tonya laughed. "Wow, you and my aunt Katie would make great friends."

"What you talking about, niecey-poo? Pearl and I are already friends," Katie said as she walked into the sunroom.

Tonya greeted her aunt with a hug and kiss. "Hey, Aunt Katie."

"Katie, your niece here says she's engaged," Pearl said.

"I know, to the jack-legged preacher I was telling you about. By the way, where is he?"

"Aunt Katie, could you please not do that this weekend?"

"Do what?"

Tonya turned to Mike. "She's your guest, please make her behave."

Mike smirked. "She's your aunt. Besides, you know as well as I do, no one can make Katie do anything."

Katie stared at Tonya's hand. "So it's official. You're wearing a ring."

Pearl's hand flew to her mouth, "Oh, you got a ring. I'm sorry, I didn't notice."

"Come see Tonya's ring everybody. The preacher man finally sprung for a ring!" Katie announced.

"It's no big deal everyone. Please, there's no need to make a fuss," Tonya said.

"We will too make a fuss," Melissa declared. All the women crowded around Tonya.

Katie peered at her hand. "Tonya, hold it up to the light. I can't see anything."

Melissa and Barbara both took out their reading glasses.

"Oh, there it is!" Barbara declared.

Joshua snickered and shot his brother a look.

Tonya snatched her hand away. "I heard that, Josh!"

"Hey, I didn't say a word, sis."

"He's not rich, okay?"

Katie rolled her eyes. "I don't know how come. He keeps bragging about his seven-thousand-tithing member congregation. The man had on Florsheims when I met him."

"Those aren't cheap," Pearl said.

"No they aren't. He's rich, alright, but he's cheap. I'll bet you five hundred dollars that he'll find a way to tell everybody here about his seven-thousand-tithing membership church before the night is over."

Tonya shook her head. "He's not going to bring it up, Aunt Katie."

"Put your money where your mouth is then. Five hundred dollars."

"Auntie, I don't have five hundred dollars."

"Tonya, you work at a church with seven-thousand-tithing members and you don't have five hundred dollars in the bank?"

"Ted puts most of his money back into mission."

"Yeah, and on his feet. His shoes cost more than your ring. Let me tell you something, honey. A man who puts that small of a ring on your finger will not be generous in bed."

"Katie!" Barbara gasped.

Jack howled with laughter.

Katie shrugged. "I'm just saying."

"Well, I like the ring," Melissa said, removing her reading glasses. "It's delicate."

Katie snorted. "It's invisible. Throw him back."

"I never would have brought Ted here if you all were just going to run him down," Tonya said.

"She's right," Mike said firmly. "Aunt Katie, Granny P, be nice, please. For me."

"I'll be nice when she takes my bet. I got five hundred dollars that says he tells us about his seven-thousand-tithing member church before the night is out. If I lose, not only will I cough up the dough, I won't say another mumbling word for the rest of the evening."

"You heard her, Blackbird. You gon' take that bet?"

Tonya glared at Katie. "As tempting as that sounds I really don't have the money."

"I'll spot you," Mike said.

"You'll spot me?"

"You believe in your man, don't you?"

Tonya's eyes met Mike's defiantly. "Of course I do."

"Then I got you."

"I think I'm gonna get in on this too," Pearl said.

"Which side, Granny P?"

"I'm putting my money with Katie, five hundred dollars."

"I'm in. I got five hundred dollars on Katie," Jack called out.

Mike looked at Tonya. "The pool just went up to 1500."

Tonya folded her arms across her chest. "I can't pay you back if I don't win."

"I thought you said this was a sure thing?"

"It is. I'm just saying on the off chance that I'm wrong I can't pay."

Mike looked her up and down. "I'm sure we can work something out."

Color rose to the surface of Tonya's cheeks. "Something like what?"

"If you win you take the pot."

"You're gonna give me 1500 dollars just like that."

"I'll call it an early wedding gift."

"And if I lose?"

"If you lose, then you dance for me. Here, tonight."

Melissa clasped her hands together. "Oh, that would be a marvelous treat."

"What kind of dancing does she do?" Pearl asked.

"Tonya is a classically trained ballet dancer," Barbara said proudly.

"Michael, I haven't danced in a very long time."

"That's a shame, Blackbird. You should dance every day of your life. So, do we have a deal or what?"

Tonya stared at him for a beat. "Yeah, I'm in."

A butler appeared in the doorway. He rang a small bell to get everyone's attention. All eyes took in Ted dressed in a three-piece suit with an ascot tied around his neck. Tonya closed her eyes and tried to will herself to disappear.

"How come he got on church clothes?" Jabari asked.

"Jabari, hush," Bella scolded.

"Dad, can I please get in on this action?" Marcus said.

Mike tried unsuccessfully to stifle his laughter. He spoke to the butler. "Let me finish this up real quick so you can introduce my man properly."

The butler nodded. "Of course, sir."

Mike turned his attention to Marcus. "We're the house, Marcus. You can't bet against the house."

"Yeah, you can," Joshua said. "With odds like these, I got you, nephew!"

"Thanks, Unc."

"That's five for Marcus and five for me." Joshua looked over at Bella. "Baby, you want in on this action?"

Bella looked over at Tonya then back at Ted standing in the doorway with his head lifted and his chest puffed out. "I'm in."

"Traitor," Tonya muttered.

"I'm sorry, girl, but Serenity be needing pampers and things. Baby stuff is so expensive."

"Dad, what about me?" Jabari said.

Joshua looked at his son for a beat as if considering it.

"An eleven-year-old boy, really, Josh. You're going to let him gamble?" Tonya said.

"Under normal circumstances, Tonya, you're right. I wouldn't. But this is more like finding money in the street. If he found five hundred dollars, I'd let him keep it."

Mike roared with laughter. "Okay, we got two G's from Josh."

"1500 dollars," a voice called out from the back of the room and another around of laughter began.

"Auntie Mel!" Tonya cried.

"I'm sorry, dear. I'm on your side really, I am, but I've got three grandchildren to consider now. I've got to start putting money away for their college funds."

"Well, Blackbird, the pot just went up to five thousand dollars. That's either going to be a nice little nest egg or one spectacular dance." Mike nodded in the butler's direction.

The butler cleared his throat. "Introducing, Theodore Roosevelt Maxwell the third."

"Call me Reverend," Ted corrected in a low voice.

Aunt Katie's hand shot up in the air. "I want to raise mine to a thousand."

"Excuse me, sir. Introducing, Reverend Theodore Roosevelt Maxwell the third."

"Pots closed, Aunt Katie," Mike said.

Tonya walked over to Ted and looped her arm through his. "Wow, you actually had him announce you," she whispered.

"Why wouldn't I? He asked."

"I know, but it's just a formality. Nobody ever actually does it." In a louder voice she said, "Ted, you remember my mother, Barbara. My auntie Mel and my uncle Jack.

"Howdy," Jack said.

"Good to see you again, Ted," Melissa said.

"And of course, you remember my auntie Katie."

"How could I ever forget dear, sweet, Aunt Katie," Ted said.

Katie rolled her eyes and let out a loud, "Humpf."

"This is Pearl, the newest elder of our clan, and over there is her grandson, Marcus."

"Nice to meet you," Ted said.

"That young, handsome guy beside Marcus is my godson, Jabari, and I would introduce you to Serenity, but she's sleeping and I haven't got a chance to officially meet her myself," Tonya said pouting.

"We can go check in on her if you want, Tonya," Bella said.

Ted's eyes poured over Bella. "Wait don't tell me. You must be, Bella. You are even more beautiful in person. You're stunning. Pictures do not do you justice."

Tonya's eyes darted nervously to Joshua who sat watching the scene with mild humor as opposed to annoyance.

"Huh . . . thanks," Bella said, somewhat taken aback. He kissed her hand.

"Ted this is her husband, Joshua Keys."

"Joshua rose and shook Ted's hand."

"The Bad Boy Joshua Keys in the flesh. Should I call you, Bad Boy?"

Tonya closed her eyes. *You just ogled his wife like she was a piece of meat! Trust me. Now is not the time to remind him that he's Bad Boy.*

"You probably don't want to do that," Joshua said, giving voice to Tonya's thoughts. "Just Joshua is fine."

"Well, I'm a huge fan of your work. Both on and off the court."

Joshua raised an eyebrow. "You've heard me preach?"

"Yes, you're over at New Horizons Christian Training Center, right?"

Joshua nodded. "That's right."

"What y'all running on a Sunday? About two thousand?"

Joshua grinned. "Something like that. You?"

Ted sniffed, "I'm doing a little more than that myself. I'm the head pastor at a church in New York city. Now Faith International Church. You may have heard of us."

"Can't say that I have."

"Well, we've got about ten thousand coming through the doors every week, and seven-thousand-tithing members."

Tonya closed her eyes.

Jabari and Marcus jumped up from their seats shouting and giving each other chest bumps. Jack slapped his knee and Katie and Pearl both cackled with laughter.

Ted turned around. "What's happening? Did I miss something?"

"Don't mind them, they're just horsing around," Mike said as he extended his hand to Ted. "Michael Dutton. Welcome."

Ted hesitated, taking in Michael's full stature. Michael was dressed casually in jeans and a t-shirt, but he looked every bit as poised and graceful as if an Armani suit clung to his muscular frame. Ted was a man of average looks and average height who always seemed to Tonya to be overly concerned with physical appearance. Right now, he was measuring himself up against this prefect specimen of a man and realizing that in every category, he fell drastically short. When would he learn that beauty was more than just skin deep?

What the heck is wrong with you, Ted?! Shake Michael's hand!!! Tonya screamed inside her head.

"Tonya talks about you so much, I feel as though I already know you," Ted said, finally shaking Mike's outstretched hand.

Mike raised an eyebrow and looked over at Tonya. "Does she now? Well, since you already know so much about me, I look forward to getting to know a little bit about you."

Translation: she don't ever talk about you, dude.

"Make yourself comfortable. I'm sure we'll have plenty of time to talk. Dinner will be ready within the hour. I hope you like steak."

Ted beamed. "I love steak."

"Good, waitstaff will let the chef know what cut of meat you prefer and how you want that prepared."

"What about Tonya? She doesn't eat red meat and she's allergic to onions," Ted said. He seemed to take delight in telling Michael this piece of information about her."

Mike smiled patiently at Ted as if he were indulging a small child.

"Michael already knows that, Ted," Tonya said quietly.

"I'm just checking, Tonya. I'm the new guy around here, alright? I'm not trying to offend anybody. Just looking out for my lady."

"No offense taken," Mike said. "That's your job. To protect her at all cost. Tonya will be having the pecan-encrusted salmon tonight, prepared on a separate grill so there's no chance of cross contamination."

Tonya looked up at Mike and smiled. "Sounds wonderful. Am I having lemon dill or the Jack Daniels sauce?" Tonya asked.

"Which would you prefer?"

"It's so hard to choose. I love them both."

"That's why they are both here." Mike motioned for one of the waitstaff to join them. "Make sure you get his order to the chef." Mike turned his attention back to Ted. "Enjoy the party," Mike said, as he walked away.

CHAPTER 92

Tonya was feeding Serenity a bottle when she heard the butler ring the bell again.

"Introducing Ms. Selena Mason." Selena stood in the doorway wearing a black, above-the-knee dress that looked like it was painted on.

Bella rolled her eyes and averted her gaze away from the door. "Great, just what we need today, another poser."

"I thought you said she wasn't coming," Tonya whispered.

"That's what Josh told me."

Selena sauntered over to Michael, wrapped her arms around his neck, and kissed him on the lips.

Mike looked down at his watch. "Don't you have a plane to catch?"

"I do. But I just couldn't leave town without seeing the bride-to-be. Is she here?"

Bella scooted down low in her seat pretending to be in deep conversation with Tonya.

Selena looked around the room. "Bella, there you are!" Selena's eyes settled on Tonya momentarily before dismissing her. "Bella, I can't make it to the wedding this weekend and I feel horrible about it. My aunt fell ill, and I have to fly out to see about her tonight. I know you are going to be a beautiful bride." Selena pulled a small gift out of her handbag. "I bought you something blue."

Bella locked eyes with Joshua who was nursing a bottle of root beer and watching her from across the room. Bella turned on her mega-watt smile and took the gift from Selena. "Thank you for coming, Selena. I hope your aunt feels better and that you have a pleasant trip."

"Believe me, I will. Mike is flying me first class." Selena turned her attention to Tonya again. "It's so nice to have a man who can do those types of things for you."

One of the servants appeared by her side. "The car is waiting, Ms. Selena. You really have to leave now if you're going to make your flight."

"Tootles, Bella. Please kiss my future brother-in-law for me," Selena said before casting Tonya a scornful look.

Tonya cracked up laughing after Selena walked away. "Tootles? Sounds like somebody has a new BFF."

"Oh, shut up," Bella snapped.

About twenty minutes later, the butler returned to usher the family into the dining room.

Serenity's nanny appeared beside Tonya. "I can take her, ma'am, while you eat."

"Oh, okay," Tonya said, reluctantly handing Serenity off to Lacy.

⸙ ⸙ ⸙

Marcus and Jabari got their dads' attention right before they were about to walk into the dining room.

"Hey dad, can we talk to you and Unc for a sec?"

"What's up?"

"We were wondering if we could skip this part," Marcus said.

Mike looked at his son and his nephew. "You trying to tell me that the two of you aren't hungry?"

Marcus shrugged. "I mean, yeah we are. We just don't want to eat in the dining room. The game is about to come on."

Joshua nodded. "The Heat and the Mavericks I sure would like to see that."

"You can, Unc. I can record it for you," Marcus said quickly.

Mike stared at the boys. "You know this weekend is important to your mom and your aunt, right?"

"We know, and we've been here, participating the whole time," Jabari said.

"So have we." Joshua and Mike said simultaneously.

Joshua smirked at Jabari. "What, y'all want a medal or something? You think we don't want to be somewhere chillin', watching the game?"

Mike gave Joshua a fist bump. "Word, that's all I'm saying, bro. If I got to be here, they got to be here too."

"But if we go watch the game now, then everybody wins," Marcus said.

Joshua rubbed his chin. "How you figure that, nephew?"

"The adults will get to hang out in peace. That'll make Aunt Bella happy, and you and my dad get to chill out and watch the game later after all of this is done."

"Please, it's the finals," Jabari begged.

Mike motioned towards the door. "Go."

Marcus and Jabari took off running.

"I don't want to have to fast forward through any commercials," Joshua called to their backs.

"I got you, Unc!" Marcus called over his shoulder.

⸙ ⸙ ⸙

"Well, how did I do?" Bella said. She walked up and looped her arm through Joshua's and the two of them walked into the dining room together. "I saw you grading me across the room. A plus right?"

"I'd say that was a solid B."

Joshua pulled out a chair for her, and Bella glared up at him. "Please, I was on point and you know it."

"No way. Too much teeth in your smile. I thought you were gonna bite her for a minute."

Bella rolled her eyes at him and took a seat in the chair. Joshua chuckled softy and planted a kiss at the nape of her neck. "I'll give you an A for effort though, considering it was a pop quiz."

❧ ❧ ❧

Just minutes after the food was blessed, a servant appeared beside Ted. "Excuse me, sir, but you have a call." Ted took his cell phone from the servant's outstretched hand. He sighed heavily into the receiver. "Two hours outside of the city." Ted stole a look at Tonya sitting next to him at the dinner table. "No, I don't think that's going to work. Thank you for trying." He ended the call and handed it back to the servant.

"I hope everything is alright, Ted?" Melissa asked.

"Thank you for asking, Melissa. That was my secretary. It seems when she booked our stay for this weekend she only booked one hotel room. And although she reserved the penthouse suite that has two bedrooms, Tonya doesn't think it would be appropriate for her to stay at the hotel with me."

"She's right. It wouldn't be," Barbara said. "You have your reputation to think about and of course the reputation of my daughter."

Ted cleared his throat. "Yes, well, be that as it may, it seems that the only other hotel available is two hours outside of Houston."

"I hope you know that's not going to work," Tonya said, not looking up from her plate.

"Yes, Tonya, I know. I already told her that."

"What's the problem? Why can't Tonya just stay here?" Pearl asked.

Everyone at the table, including Tonya looked at Ted. "Yeah, Ted, please do explain to everyone, why can't I just stay here."

"I didn't know this very private matter between the two of us was up for public debate, Tonya."

"Nothing's private in this family, son," Jack said.

Ted cast a quick glance in Mike's direction. "Well, given Tonya's extensive history with the host, I didn't think that she would feel comfortable, as a woman of God, staying in her ex-boyfriend's mansion."

"But it's perfectly okay for me to stay in a hotel room with my current boyfriend," Tonya said.

"You mean your fiancé," Pearl said.

"Yes, don't you mean your future husband?" Ted said.

"Ring's so small, she probably forgot," Katie said.

Barbara shot her sister-in-law a look of disapproval.

"We're not married yet," Tonya said.

"For crying out loud, Tonya, it's a hotel suite with two bedrooms. You act as if I'm trying to deflower you. Believe me, I'm not. Besides, I strongly suspect that job was taken long before I got here."

Katie's fork paused in mid-air. "Did he just call my niece a ho?"

"That's what it sounds like he said to me," Pearl said.

All eyes flew to Ted.

"No—I would never. Forgive me, that was a very . . . bad joke. Seriously, folks. Tonya and I are good." Ted laid his hand on top of Tonya's and patted it weakly. "Tonya's always telling me how people don't get my humor. I guess I should listen, huh?" Ted looked around the table at the shocked female faces. Then at the men. Jack appeared mildly amused. Joshua's face was as hard as stone. Mike's face was an unreadable mask.

"So, we're good, right?

"Naw, player, we not good," Joshua growled.

Jack leaned back in his chair. "Ted, apparently Tonya didn't explain our family dynamics to you."

Tonya shook her head. "I tried to tell him."

"The boy's about to get his teeth kicked in, and we haven't even finished supper yet, sweetheart. So, I'd say, you didn't do too good of a job."

Ted met Joshua's eyes across the table. "I apologize. It really was a joke. I meant no harm."

"You're new around here, so let me fill you in on the parts you've missed. That's my sister sitting beside you. The only one I got."

Tonya's eyes met Joshua's across the table, and she gave him a little smile.

"I'm real sensitive when it comes to her. So, if we gon' keep things breezy this weekend, I'mma need you to remember a couple of things, Ted."

Ted nodded. "Okay, Joshua, what would those things be?"

"First, take some of the bass out of your voice when you speak to her. I don't like your tone. Second, don't ever joke like that in my presence again."

Silence permeated around the dining room table as the two men locked eyes.

Finally, Ted relented. "Fair enough."

Melissa blew out an audible sigh of relief. "Well that's good, because we certainly want to keep things nice and breezy this weekend."

"Yes, we do," Barbara quipped. "Ted, trust me there are no worries. Whenever I come to Houston I stay at Michael's. There are plenty of rooms here in the main house. Not counting the cottage and the pool house. We'll all be here together. Tonya will be fine."

"Auntie Barb's right, we have plenty of room," Mike said.

Ted locked eyes with Mike. "For Tonya, you mean?"

"That's right, for Tonya."

"Don't forget we have space at our house too," Bella said.

"Also for Tonya," Joshua added firmly.

"Then I guess it's settled. I'll be retiring to the hotel tonight alone," Ted said.

"Just let me know when you're ready to bounce. I'll have my driver drop you," Mike said evenly.

Jack winked at Ted. "See why we handle everything around here family style? The more heads the more fun."

"Tonya, have you decided what song you are going to be dancing to this evening?" Barbara asked.

"Not yet."

Ted looked at her. "You're dancing?"

"Is that going to be a problem too, Ted?"

"No, no problem, I just thought we agreed."

"Agreed to what?"

"Forget it, Tonya. Never mind."

"I'm curious to know what the agreement is," Melissa said.

"It's nothing, Auntie Mel. I agreed that I wouldn't dance in his church on the liturgical dance team."

Katie shook her head. "All them lessons, and the man don't even want the girl to dance."

Barbara's face clouded with confusion. "I don't understand. Tonya's a classical trained dancer. Dancing has always been her passion. Why wouldn't she dance for the Lord?"

"It's not that I don't want her to dance for the Lord, Barbara. Tonya's a marvelous dancer. But as my future wife, she has to learn to present herself in a manner that is appropriate for a first lady—"

"Of a 7000-tithing-member church," Joshua finished for him.

"Exactly." Ted beamed. The sarcasm in Joshua's voice having flown right over his head.

"So, you're saying that if my niece marries you, she can't ever dance again."

"Of course, she can dance. Anytime she wants, Katie. Just not in public."

All the women at the table reared back as if they'd been slapped.

Pearl shook her head. "Sounds like a whole heap of bondage to me."

Mike studied Tonya from his position at the head of the table as she picked at her food. "How's your salmon, Blackbird?"

"It's prefect," She muttered.

"Then why haven't you eaten any of it?"

"Honestly, I think this whole conversation is making me sick."

"Then let's change the subject," Mike said firmly.

Ted raised his hand in the air. "I have a subject change. What's with this secret language between the two of you? He calls you, Blackbird, but no one else around here seems to. Another code name I should be aware of? Can I call you, Blackbird?"

"Not if you expect me to answer."

"Okay. Tonya's angry with me. Again."

Bella glared at him. "Why wouldn't she be? You asking her not to dance is like asking a bird not to fly. It's like asking a painter to paint but telling them that they can never show their creations to the world."

"Do you paint, Bella?" Ted asked.

"I do, and I'd be mortified if my husband told me that because of his position in our church or his ego that I couldn't share my gift with the world."

"I doubt if your husband would ever say anything like that to you at all. You're prefect in every way. Any man, especially a pastor, would be blessed to have a woman like you by his side. Tonya could learn a lot from a woman like you."

All eyes at the table flew warily over to Joshua, who was studying the man across from him with an annoyed expression.

Mike's fork clattered to the table. "That's it. That's game for me. I can't do this anymore. I just got one question for you, Blackbird."

Tonya looked up from her plate and held his eyes.

"Why are you with this clown?"

"I told you it's an abusive relationship," Katie chirped.

Barbara closed her eyes. "Oh come, Lord Jesus be our guide."

"Jack, do something. Neutralize this situation, please," Melissa muttered.

"Everybody just relax. Despite what, Aunt Katie thinks, I am not being abused. However, Ted is being a class A jerk right now, and I apologize for his behavior."

Ted pushed his plate away from him. "Well, Tonya, if you feel like that, I guess I shouldn't have come."

Mike's eyes never left Tonya. "So now you're going to apologize for his behavior."

"Michael, what do you want me to say?"

Mike wiped his mouth and threw his napkin down on his unfinished plate. "You don't have to say another word. I'mma take it from here."

Tonya jumped up from her seat at the table and ran to Mike. "Michael, wait—"

"This man just disrespected you. In my house. You, my brother, and his wife. You think I'mma let that ride? Baby, you ain't just now meeting me." Mike moved Tonya out the way and strolled down to the other end of the table where Ted was sitting. "I don't know how y'all do it in New York, but I damn sure don't get down like that. Raise up, let me holler at you."

Joshua rose from his chair too. Bella stood quickly. She placed her hands on Joshua's broad chest. "Whoa, baby, you cannot get arrested on the night before our wedding."

Joshua wrapped his arms around her and kissed the tip of her nose. "It's cool. We just gon' talk to him."

Jack sighed. He threw his napkin down on his plate and stood up. "Boys, I say we let the ladies finish the rest of their meal in peace and the four of us go somewhere to talk."

CHAPTER 93

The four men filed into Mike's home office and Joshua closed the door behind them. Mike walked over to a leather seating group in front of the fireplace. He and Joshua both took a seat in the two leather arm chairs opposite of Jack who sat down on the cognac colored leather sofa. Jack motioned to Ted, "Have a seat, son."

Ted took a seat beside Jack. "Look fellas. We seem to have gotten off to a bad start. It was not my intention to insult you, Joshua, or your wife, and Mike it wasn't my intention to, in anyway, disrespect your home. The truth is, Tonya and I were already arguing before we arrived. I should have handled my business before we got here, and I should have never allowed what was going on between us to come into your home."

The two brothers shared a look.

"I've known Tonya all my life," Joshua began. "She's always been headstrong."

"And mouthy," Jack said, smiling fondly.

"She's got a brain and opinions. That doesn't make her mouthy," Mike said.

"She's not going to back down from an argument, and she won't bite her tongue just to keep the peace," Joshua said.

"'Cause she's mouthy," Jack said.

Mike glared at his father.

"What? I'm not saying anything's wrong with it. Hell, your mother's the same way. Why do you think I married her?"

"It takes a certain kind of man to deal with a woman like that. It's not a job for everyone," Joshua said, focusing his attention on Ted, and tuning out the conversation going on between his brother and his dad.

Ted seemed to relax a bit. "She is a challenge. You got her number, man, spot on."

Joshua returned Ted's smile with one that didn't quite reach his eyes. "I know, I've got a woman just like her."

"Bella, really? I never would have suspected that."

Joshua nodded. "She's gon' say and do whatever she wants to, whenever she wants to, and it ain't a damn thing I can do to stop her. So, I'm wondering what you mean when you say you should have handled your business with my sister before you got here?"

Ted swallowed hard, taken aback by the subtle mood shift inside the room. "I'd really like to answer your question, Joshua, but I don't think I understand what it is that you're. . . implying."

"The question is, are you putting your hands on her, *motherf*—" Mike said quietly.

Honest to God, Ted would have handled it better had Mike yelled at him, but the deadly calm in the ex-ball player's voice made the minister want to reach inside his shirt collar for the crucifix he wore tucked beneath his suit and back up out of the room speaking in tongues.

"Mike . . ." Ted stopped. He cleared his throat, making sure his voice wouldn't falter. "I don't know what you've heard, but I have never hit a woman in my life. I'm not about to start now. No matter how frustrated I get. If things were to ever deteriorate to that point, I'd walk away from the relationship first."

Mike leveled the man seated before him with a hard gaze. "I don't like you, but you're Tonya's choice, and out of respect for her, I'm willing to tolerate that choice."

"I know you don't like me, Mike. I also know that there is nothing I could ever say or do that would change your opinion of me. No matter how desperately she wants this great friendship to happen between the two of us, it's never going to happen, is it? Because you're still in love with her."

Jack rolled his eyes. "Is that your big reveal, pal? Mikey's in love with Tonya? You mean to tell me my dinner is getting cold for this? Joshie, hurry, alert the media!"

Joshua chuckled. "Be cool, Dad."

Mike shook his head. "The only thing that matters is how Tonya feels about you. So, let me be clear, I don't like you because you're not good enough. You got a pearl in your hand and wanderlust in your eye. You're still checking for crabs on the ocean floor."

"Okay, I see. This—this is about the little exchange between me and your girlfriend, Selena, earlier. Again, my apologies. I wasn't trying to push up. Just paying a beautiful lady a compliment." Ted's eyes moved to Joshua. "We're men of God, but we're still men. Right?"

"Problem is, you don't look like a man in love," Joshua said.

"Let's cut the crap, okay? That's my goddaughter out there," Jack said pointing to the door. "I made a promise to her daddy on the day he died. So, Ted, if you hurt Tonya, I'll kill ya. I'll get my gun and I'll blow your effing brains out. Now you think about that real carefully, son, 'cause I'm a white man. You're black, this is racist America, and my sons are rich. Well, Joshie over here is a man of the cloth now, so we may just decide to leave him out of this altogether, but Mikey would get me off."

"You damn straight I would," Mike growled.

Joshua nodded. "Yep, I would too."

"You see that, Ted? My sons and I are simple men, we love our family, and that girl happens to be a part of our family. So if you don't love her, walk away now while you still can. And if you do love her, man the hell up, and start acting like it."

"I do, sir. I love Tonya very much," Ted said contritely.

"Well, good. I'm glad to hear that. 'Cause I'm ready to eat some pie."

CHAPTER 94

Tonya paced back and forth across the room.

"Daughter, you're going to wear a hole into the carpet. Sit down," Barbara said.

Tonya plopped down on the couch beside Melissa. "What is taking them so long. They've been in there for nearly an hour."

"Well, I hope they are whipping his a— good."

Bella laughed. "Ooh, Aunt Katie, you are so bad!"

"No, they are not doing that. Jack promised they were just going to talk to him," Melissa said.

Pearl shook her head. "If they ain't whipping it, they're tearing him a new butthole that's for sure. That grandson of mine was furious. I've never seen that side of him before."

Melissa brushed a lose strain of hair behind her ear. "It doesn't surface too often, but when it does, watch out."

"Well, I knew it was about to hit the fan when the preacher first started talking crazy. Michael had this strange look on his face."

Katie snapped her fingers and pointed to Pearl. "Pearl, I saw that too!"

"Then the man start going on and on about how good you looked, Bella. And that's when I knew, Joshua Keys was a man of God for real. 'Cause there was a time I'd turn on my TV and all you could see was Joshua punching somebody's lights out."

"Pearl, what you talking about? Back in the day preacher man would have been laid out for much less than that. He would have got the word Bella out his mouth and *capowie!* Josh would have laid him out like a thanksgiving turkey." Katie cackled. "Boy, I sure do miss those days."

"Katie!" Barbara and Melissa cried.

Katie waved them away with her hand. "Oh, hush, up you two. I'm glad the boy is saved. I just meant the excitement of it all."

"All I know is when the preacher started going on about how Tonya could learn a thing or two, that grandson of mine went clean off," Pearl said.

"Now wait a minute, you missed a part now, Pearl. 'Cause it had already started to get thick in there when the preacher man said, 'I've got a subject change.'"

Pearl nodded. "Oh yeah, that's right. Then he said, 'Can I call you Blackbird?'"

Melissa looked at Barbara. "Well one thing's for sure. Nothing wrong with their memories."

"And Tonya, you said, 'Not if you expect me to answer.'"

"Then the preacher man got mad and threw his fork down like a little girl."

The women all laughed when Katie demonstrated the action.

"Then, Tonya you were like, 'Just ignore him, Michael. That's what I do,'" Pearl said, imitating Tonya's voice.

"No what she said was, 'I apologize for his behavior,'" Bella corrected.

Pearl nodded. "Oh, that's right. She did do that, didn't she? That's when Michael said, 'Tonya, this man is sitting at my table eating my food, disrespecting my brother, his wife, and my woman, and I ain't havin' it!'"

All the women fell out laughing.

"He did not! He did not call me his woman!" Tonya said, laughing so hard tears flowed from her eyes.

"We're paraphrasing, okay? Just reading between the lines. That's what he meant," Pearl said.

Katie sat down on the other side of Tonya and put her arm around her. "See there, babygirl, we just wanted to make you laugh."

Barbara looked at her daughter earnestly. "Michael asked a very good question tonight, baby. What in the world are you doing with this man?"

Tonya sighed. "Believe it or not, Mama, there is another side to him."

There was a knock on the doorframe then, and Ted peaked his head around the corner.

"May I come in?"

Tonya rushed to him. "Ted, are you—"

"I'm fine. All we did was talk. They pulled my coattail and rightfully so. But, we're good now."

Tonya stared at him doubtfully. "Really?"

"No, really. I think in time, the three of us will become the best of friends. I'm getting ready to leave for the hotel, but before I go, I was hoping we could go someplace private and talk?"

Katie cleared her throat.

"Or, I can just say what I have to say right here in front of everyone," Ted amended quickly.

"That sounds like an excellent idea," Barbara said.

"Tonya, sweetheart, I owe you and your entire family a tremendous apology. I guess it was more intimidating than I wanted to admit coming here and meeting your folks, and frankly, I acted like a complete jackass. I hope you can all find it in your hearts to forgive me."

"Of course, we can, Ted," Melissa said. "We're all good Christian women here."

Katie rolled her eyes.

"Thank you, Melissa."

"Ted, will we be seeing you at the wedding tomorrow?" Barbara asked.

"Yes ma'am, if Tonya will still have me, you will."

Tonya grabbed Ted's hand and spoke to the women in the room. "I'll be right back. I'm going to walk Ted out."

CHAPTER 95

B y sunrise the next morning, a golden portico was being constructed on the grounds of the Dutton estate. Work crews moved back and forth on the east lawn, hauling things in and out of trucks in preparation for the evening's festivities.

By ten o'clock that morning, there was a knock on Ted's hotel room door. Ted opened the door to see a man dressed in a suit.

"Reverend Theodore Maxwell?"

"That's me." Ted took the envelope from the man's gloved hand.

"Mr. and Mrs. Joshua Keys request the honor of your presence at their vow renewal ceremony this evening."

Ted opened the invitation and read the contents quickly.

"Do you accept this invitation, sir?"

"Yes of course. But I don't see an address."

"The ceremony will begin at 8:00 PM. A car will arrive precisely at 7:00 PM tonight to pick you up."

※ ※ ※

Two local news celebrities from WKTV, Shelia Jackson and Bill Mulligan, stood outside on a busy street corner in downtown Houston handing out chocolate covered almonds wrapped in wedding tulle. "Happy wedding day, folks!" the news reporters called to people on the street.

"Happy wedding day!" was the response that many of the residents of the city cheerily called back.

"Here, have a wedding favor, compliments of WKTV," the two reporters said to the residents who actually stopped to chat with them for a while.

Actually, the wedding favors had been compliments of the Kerns Agency, the public relations firm Mike had hired to handle the event. Natasha's team supplied local businesses and shops all throughout the state of Texas with the colorful wedding favors to pass out to all their patrons, in celebration of the famous couple's pending nuptials.

Right now, Natasha and her staff all stood in the agency's large conference room, milling around the wall-mounted screen, watching the live pre-wedding footage play out.

"Well, today is the big day and everyone who is anyone is talking about the wedding of the century. I'm Shelia Jackson and this is my co-host Bill Mulligan, and we are reporting live from downtown Houston."

Bill furrowed his eyebrows and looked into the camera and started in on his and Sheila's usual banter. "Wait a minute, isn't that supposed to be the other way around? Aren't I the host and you the co-host?"

Shelia rolled her eyes playfully. "Maybe in the second half of the segment, Bill. But for now, I think I'm going to take the lead."

Bill grinned. "Shelia, I know how you ladies feel about weddings, so take it away, my friend."

"Sources close to the couple say that this morning 150 guests will receive hand delivered invitations to the wedding."

"That sounds very cloak-and-dagger. Is it true that the guests don't have to drive to the event?"

"Not only is it true, Bill, but the guests aren't even being told in advance where the ceremony is being held.

The bride and groom aren't taking any chances. There will be no wedding crashers at this event today."

"This is exciting."

"It is exciting. All of Houston is celebrating the fact that this couple has found their way back to each other."

"And that's why we are out on the streets of Houston today. To hear what our fellow Houstonians have to say." Bill stopped a couple walking by. "Here, have a wedding favor. Happy wedding day."

"Happy wedding day to you too, young man," the woman said.

"I don't want to make any assumptions," Bill said speaking to the couple, "but are you two married?"

"Thirty-nine years," the man said proudly.

"So, tell us, will you be watching the wedding tonight?" Sheila said.

"Are you kidding? We wouldn't miss this for the world," the woman gushed.

"Where do you think the wedding is going to be today?"

The man scratched his head. "I think it's going to be at a church. Bad Boy is a pastor now, so I think he'll say his vows in a church."

"I got my money on the church," another man said.

"And you, ma'am, what do you think?"

"I think they are going to say their vows on a private island, Tahiti, or someplace like that. Get as far away from Houston as they can."

"The church."

"The church."

"The church," one citizen after another said.

"I mean, come on. He's a pastor now. We live in the Bible Belt. I think there is some rule or something that says he has to get married inside of a church."

Bill shook his head. "No, sir, I don't think there is."

"Are you and your sweetie going to the church today hoping to catch the bride and groom?" Shelia cut in.

"Nah, I'm going to be watching from the comfort of my home. Besides, those two have been through a lot. If fans love Bad Boy like they claim they do, then they'll let them have their moment. They have the right to their special day."

Shelia smiled at the man. "I think you're absolutely right, sir, they do." Shelia turned her attention back to the camera. "In just a moment we are going to be rolling a clip of another special moment. WKTV was there, live, ten months ago on August 5th, 2005, almost one year ago today, for Hurricane Katrina, the most shocking storm of our lives. We were there to witness this special moment." The words *Looking Back* scrolled across the television screen. An image of Joshua standing at a podium at a press conference at his company, Home Court Advantage, appeared on the screen next.

"My wife, Bella Rose Keys and my son, Jabari Keys were living in the New Orleans' lower ninth ward area when the storm hit." Joshua held up a photograph of Bella, and Jabari. "Those of you from New Orleans may know them as Rosemary and Matthew LeBlanc. I am offering a one-million-dollar reward to anyone with information that will lead to their safe return. To my wife and my son, if you are still in New Orleans, I want to say to you, just hang on. Be tough. Don't quit." Joshua's voice quivered. He lowered his head to compose himself. When Joshua looked up again, he was staring directly into the camera. "I love you. Hang in there. I will come for you, Bella, my beautiful Rose. I will come for you, and I will find you, baby, just like I always do."

The camera cut back to Bill and Sheila. "Wow. You know, Sheila, as a husband and a father, I can only imagine that had to have been the most horrific moment in the Houston Rockets' hall-of-famer's life.

"I'm sure it was," Sheila said. "WKTV was there to bear witness to that, and we were there to celebrate this next moment too." Another clip appeared on the screen. This time of Joshua walking towards Bella in a crowded Astrodome. A sea of reporters surrounded Bella. The moment they saw Joshua, the sea of reporters parted, and they allowed him room to walk through to her. Reporters fired questions left and right. "Joshua, what's it like to be reunited with your wife and your son after so long?"

"Mrs. Keys, will the two of you reconcile?"

"Joshua, now that you have your family back, will you consider returning to professional ball?"

"No comment," Joshua said, never once taking his eyes off of Bella. Finally, when he was standing directly in front of her, he looked down at her, enfolded her in his arms, and closed his eyes. Joshua kissed the crown of her head and rocked her in his arms as the world looked on. Then suddenly, Joshua pulled away and looked into Bella's eyes. "Remember the drill?" Bella nodded her head and Joshua picked her up and carried her out of the Astrodome.

"Yes!" Natasha Kerns said as she pumped her fist in the air. Applause rang out throughout the entire Kerns Agency as the team members celebrated in the conference room.

CHAPTER 96

"You mean to tell me those two still aren't up yet? They're missing all of this," Jack said, pointing to the television screen in Mike's kitchen.

Mike and Tonya sat at the kitchen table having breakfast, while Barbara, Katie, Melissa, and Jack sat around the kitchen island watching the pre-wedding day footage and drinking coffee.

Mike took a swallow of his orange juice. "I think it's okay if they missed this part, Dad. After all, they were there when it happened."

Jack rolled his eyes. "I know they were there, you big lug. That's not the point."

Tonya shrugged. "What is the point?"

"The point is that it's two o'clock in the afternoon and those two are up there sleeping their lives away on the most important day of the year," Jack said.

Tonya looked at Mike. "Is it just my imagination or have I heard that before?"

Mike ate his eggs. "Yep. Every day growing up. If one of us had the audacity to sleep past eight o'clock we'd be accused of sleeping our lives away."

Tonya laughed. "Oh, the horror. Growing teenagers needing rest."

"Did you two forget that we are having a wedding here today?" Melissa said.

"The wedding isn't until eight o'clock," Mike and Tonya both said simultaneously.

Barbara folded her arms across her chest. "We planned this wedding. We know what time it is!"

"Auntie, all I'm saying is that maybe you all should dial it back a little," Mike said.

Tonya snorted. "Yeah, like way back."

"My people are on it. Everything will be ready. The only thing Josh and Bella *have to do* is show up this evening."

"That's all well and good Mikey, but haven't you ever heard that it's bad luck for the groom to see the bride right before the wedding?" Melissa said.

"Yep, and let's face it, those two don't need any more bad luck," Katie said.

Tonya rolled her eyes. "That is some superstitious mumbo jumbo. Besides they're already married."

"That is tradition, missy," Barbara said.

Melissa nodded. "That's right, and it's the maid of honor and the best man's job to uphold all wedding traditions. So the two of you need to march up those stairs and get those two up."

Tonya and Mike both stared at each other for a beat, then shook their heads.

"Nah, not gon' happen," Mike said.

"You all seem stressed," Tonya said, looking back and forth between the elders. "Maybe you should switch to decaf or something, just for today 'cause. . ."

"That's not gon' happen," Mike finished.

CHAPTER 97

"Joshie, are you decent?" Jack whispered.

Joshua opened one eye to see his father standing on the left side of the bed peering down at him and Bella.

"Dad, how'd you get in here? The door was locked."

"We were concerned, honey, so we had one of the servants unlock the door."

Joshua opened his second eye to see his mother, his aunt Barbara, and his aunt Katie all peering at them from over the foot of the bed. In her sleep, Bella moaned and nestled her body closer to him.

"We're fine. Get out," Joshua said flatly.

"We came to collect the bride. It's bad luck for you see her before the wedding."

CHAPTER 98

Joshua and Bella renewed their vows in a candlelight ceremony on Mike's estate. The garden was aglow with hundreds of white candles perched securely atop outdoor candelabras. And each of the one hundred fifty guests in attendance that evening had been given a small communion candle which they also then lit. The flowers, the candles, and the moonlit night, all worked together to give the garden an ethereal glow.

The bride had chosen for her wedding colors, classic black and white. The groom and his best man donned black Armani tuxedos, and the bride and her maid of honor both were stunning in white. Tonya walked in first as the maid of honor. When Tonya got halfway up the aisle, Mike left Joshua's side to give her his arm and escort her the rest of the way. Bella came down the aisle next, looking more beautiful than Joshua could have ever imagined her on his father's arm.

Bishop Micah Ford performed the ceremony. He told the people assembled there that the lit candles they'd each been given upon their arrival were a symbol of God's light. He talked about how the flame needed to be both fanned and protected. He talked about a city set upon a hill and the Christ King who would one day return for His bride, the Church, who, would ultimately be transformed by that same light.

Next, Bishop Micah Ford called for baby Serenity. "Not only have we gathered to witness the renewing of this couple's vows, we have also gathered to dedicate their precious daughter to the Lord as well."

Like her mother, Serenity was also outfitted in white. Melissa handed the baby to Joshua. And, as her godparents, Tonya and Mike stepped forward and surrounded Bella and Joshua as the Bishop prayed.

"Children are a blessing from the Lord. An inheritance from Him. Blessed is the man whose quiver is full. It is my great privilege to present this child to the Lord. Serenity Wildflower Keys, we dedicate your life to the Master of the Universe. We present you as a holy offering to the King of Kings."

After the couple had finished exchanging vows that evening, Joshua presented Bella with one more precious thing. Joshua turned to Mike, who held out a cobalt blue, velvet jewelry box. And when Joshua lifted the solid gold clasp on the velvet box, a cameraman from the network zoomed in close for all of America to see.

Inside the box was a triple strand pearl necklace, with four five-carat diamonds placed at the joints. A 22-carat diamond-encrusted sapphire hung in the center.

"You already have a ring. To get you another would be somewhat redundant. To celebrate our union today, I wanted to give you something else."

"Josh—is this my necklace? The one I made? I — how did you—?" Bella's hands flew to her mouth and her knees almost buckled, as she examined the necklace closer. "Oh, God, that's—It's not the same one."

Joshua smiled wryly down at her. "No, it's definitely not the same one. Bella, a necklace like this brought you back to me. One that you created with your own hands. But this necklace was created by a master jeweler—"

Bella felt herself beginning to hyperventilate. "Francisco Marquis. Seventeenth century. There's only one like it in the whole wide world!" She gushed.

Joshua raised an eyebrow at her. "Bella, you wanna handle this part or will you let me?"

"No, no, you do it." Bella said excitedly. "You're doing great."

The one hundred fifty guests present that evening all roared with laughter.

Joshua waited for the crowd to settle down before he began again. "Bella, this necklace represents what can only be created in the hands of a master. Every time you wear it, I want it to be a reminder to you of God's ability to make us better than we can ever make ourselves. He alone turns us into something priceless and rare. That's exactly what you are to me. You are worth far more than diamonds, sapphires, or rubies to me, Bella. My heart trusts safely in you."

Bishop Micah Ford's voice bellowed from atop of the golden portico. "I present to you Mr. and Mrs. Joshua Keys. Go ahead, son, salute your bride."

Joshua removed Melissa's strand of pearls from around Bella's neck and handed them to Tonya. He placed the sapphire necklace around her neck then he cupped her face between his two large hands and kissed her passionately.

CHAPTER 99

Bella awoke the next morning in their bed to find Joshua staring down at her. She smiled up at him. "Good morning, Mr. Keys."

He leaned in and kissed her softly. "Good morning, Mrs. Keys."

"What time do we fly out?"

"Whenever you want."

"Is the house still empty?"

"Last I checked it was."

"No kids, or grandparents, or aunts?"

"Nope."

"Can you promise with absolute certainty that your mom and your aunts aren't going to bust in here any minute and drag me away from you?"

Joshua chuckled. "Bella, I promise, everyone is exactly where we left them last night."

"I can scream as loud as I want?"

"As loud as you want."

Bella wrapped her arms around Joshua's neck and pulled him on top of her. "Well, in that case, my vote is that we stay in bed a little longer."

CHAPTER 100

Three hours later, Joshua held the door open to the car that had arrived to take them to the private airfield. Bella hesitated before getting in.

"What's the matter?"

"Josh, I think I need to do something before we go. End one chapter of my life before I—we start the next. Do you mind if we stop by the nursing home?"

"Of course not."

Joshua gave instructions to the driver, and twenty minutes later, they arrived at the nursing home. The driver opened Bella's car door, and Joshua walked around and met her on the other side.

Bella laid her hand gently on Joshua's arm. "I have to do this next part, alone."

The look on Joshua's face told her, Nah, he definitely wasn't feeling that, but he pulled Bella close and kissed the crown of her head and told her he'd be waiting in that exact spot until she got back.

Bella walked into the building, up to the front desk. She signed in. Received a visitor's pass and directions to her father's room. Then she made the longest walk down the shortest corridor she had ever taken in her life. Reverend Leblanc was perched in his wheelchair, which looked more like a throne. He sat in front of the television, watching the footage from Bella and Joshua's wedding. The door to his room, which looked more like a small apartment, was ajar.

"Daddy."

Reverend Leblanc looked up at Bella standing in the doorway. He stared at her for a long time, without a word. Then he turned his attention back to the television.

Bella walked into the room and took a seat in the chair across from him.

"Where's Joshua, my son? Does he not wish to see me?"

"He's outside waiting for me. I came today, Daddy, because I needed to see you."

"I see he married you again. This wedding is the only thing they're playing on the television today."

"I forgive you Daddy."

Silence.

"Only thing playing on every channel. I suspect they'll be playing it for the rest of the week."

"I just need you to tell me why."

"People 'round here calling what the two of you have the greatest love story ever told. Guess they've never read the Bible."

"Daddy, I need to hear you say that it happened, and that it was wrong. My mama's gone. Your church is gone. Nobody's here but me and Jesus. I just need you to say that it happened and that it was wrong."

"I guess the folks that hold to that notion have never read the Bible."

"But you won't, will you? You're so empty that you can't even give me that."

"I gave you life!"

"And when I was eight years old you took it away."

"I had such high hopes for you, Bella Rose. The greatest of which was that you would be saved. Looks like your soul will rot in hell after all."

"I am saved, Daddy."

"You aren't fit for the kingdom. The Bible says to honor your mother and father so that your days may be long upon the earth and yet you dishonor me with your despicable accusations!"

"It's because of that Bible that you quote so well that you aren't out on the streets."

Spittle flew from the reverend's mouth. "I don't believe this was your idea for a moment! My son did this for me! Not you! My son!"

"Yes, he did, Daddy. For me. He did it to sow good where you have sown evil. He did it to recompense me."

"I don't have to listen to this. Nurse!"

Bella rose to leave. She had made it all the way to the door when Reverend Leblanc called her name.

"I pray for your soul."

"I'm praying for your soul too, Daddy."

Joshua was waiting beside the car when Bella came through the nursing home's sliding doors. His whole body tensed for a fight when he saw the unshed tears glistening in her eyes. She ran to him, threw her arms around his neck and he caught her in the air.

"You alright?" he growled.

A sob tore from her throat, and Joshua clutched her tightly to his chest.

"I'm better than alright, Josh. I'm free."

Author's Note

Dear Reader,

You have just finished, *The Fire This Time*, book three of the Redemption's Price series. Thank you for taking this journey of forgiveness and redemption with our hero and heroine. Although this concludes our story of Joshua and Bella, the story continues with the last book in the series, book four, *Flight of the Blackbird*.

In *Flight of the Blackbird*, our story picks up five years later. It tells the story of Tonya Malone, and Joshua's tall, dark, and handsome brother, Michael Dutton, AKA, the Man of Steel. Please look for *Flight of the Blackbird* to be released in the Fall of 2019. In the meantime, call a friend, make a pot of tea and sit back and enjoy the discussion questions at the end of this book.

I love hearing from my readers, so if you have any questions or just want to drop me a line, please send an email to doingbusinesswithgod@gmail.com

Oh, and just in case Fall of 2019 feels like too long of a wait, after the discussion questions, you will find a short preview of the next book. I pray God's blessings upon you and all who you hold dear.

Sincerely,

Catrina J. Sparkman

Discussion Questions for Book Groups

1. Discuss the role family and community played in this book. Do you think Bella could have experienced the level of change she received in this series without the aid of family and community? How important was it for Bella to have community with the women of her church?

2. In chapter six, Bella prays to God and asks him to send an angel to get rid of the creatures she sees riding on her parents' backs. The creature on her father's back reaches into his pocket and hands the angel some type of document. Discuss what you think that document might be?

3. Which character did you connect with or identify with the most? Which character did you connect with or identify with the least? Why?

4. Consider Bella's forgiveness journey. What evidence do you see (if any) of God softening her heart and adjusting her perspective? Why is forgiveness essential to the Christian walk?

5. Do you agree with Joshua's decision to relocate Reverend LeBlanc to Texas, why or why not?

Chapter One

Tonya sat in Ted Maxwell's office, gripping the arms of the chair. She was sitting across from Ted and his fiancée, which was impossible because he was the senior pastor of Now Faith International Church, and her fiancé.

"I've put this decision to much prayer." That was Ted speaking. "As a founding member of Now Faith, you are an integral cog in this machine. This ministry doesn't work without you. We'd like for you to stay on in the ministry. What you've done with the children's ministry has been nothing short of phenomenal."

"What we don't want, is a church split over this," that was the fiancée speaking. A model turned actress who only went by her first name. Would she still be just Tatiana after she and Ted married, or would she now be Mrs. Tatiana Maxwell?

"Tonya, you know things haven't been good between us in a while. What with you studying for the boards. And I get it. Your career as a child psychologist is important to you. I only wished being the first lady of this ministry would have been as equally important." Ted sighed. "Tonya, don't you have anything to say at all?"

He was probably wondering why she wasn't fighting, why she hadn't raised her voice one time. In fact, during this whole meeting Tonya hadn't said a word. She just stared at their hands entwined with one another and the engagement ring on Tatiana's finger, the one Tonya has seen the model turned actress sporting at least a week ago on her right hand. It had to be two, maybe even three, carats. Aunt Katie had been right. Katie's husband, Earl, had been a shoe salesman for the better part of his life. Aunt

Katie had insisted that Ted didn't love her. She'd taken one look at the small, murky diamond Ted had placed on Tonya's finger and said, "Throw him back, his shoes cost more than your ring."

"Well, this is a lot to take in at once. Perhaps I shouldn't expect you to say anything at all."

Tonya finally met Ted's eyes. Her lips curled up into a pleasant smile. Ted shifted uncomfortably in his chair. Of course, this was not the Tonya that Ted knew, the overreactor, always so over-the-top with passion. Tonya knew her silence had to be unnerving to him, but she wanted him to believe, no, she needed him to believe, just how unfazed she was by his dismissal.

"Listen, the people love you. They expected you to be their first lady. So, I really need for us to be Christ-centered about this. Present a united front. I was thinking that we should make an announcement to the congregation this Sunday, saying that we sought the will of God, and have decided to remain friends."

Tonya tuned out Ted and began to play the tape back in her own head. She had relocated for this man. Had turned down graduate school at John Hopkins to help build his ministry. And when she did graduate with her doctorate, he couldn't attend because he was at the Oscars with the woman sitting across from her right now. Then, there was the part that she didn't dare think about. The most important piece she had given up. Tonya pushed the thought out of her mind. She couldn't think of that, not now in this space. She would not think of him, or what she had thought she had heard God say. If she did, she would fall to the floor and weep, and Ted would think she was weeping for him. No, she would leave this place with her dignity intact.

"Just so you know, we plan to marry quickly," Tatiana said.

Ted's free hand was massaging the back of Tatiana's neck, but his eyes were trained on Tonya, like she was a time bomb about to explode. "I don't want that to be an additional shock to you. And since the three of us are now a team, and I know how much you care about this ministry, for the sake of full disclosure I should also tell you that Tatiana is pregnant. Of course, that was never my intention for that to happen but—"

"But when two people love each other as much as we do, it's just impossible to wait," Tatiana finished for him, staring brazenly at Tonya.

Translation: You didn't love him anyways, Boo-Boo. If you did you would have given up the panties a long time ago.

Thank God for a revelation of holiness.

"Tonya, I want you to know that I've repented for this, I've cried out to God, and he's shown me the error of my ways. He also showed me that I am a David. Tatiana is my Bathsheba, and this baby will be my heir, my Solomon."

"Wow." Tonya thought she had only spoken that inside her head, but she had actually said that part out loud. "Is there anything else?"

"Only that I know how much you care for the people of this flock. In many ways, you've been more a pastor to them than I have been and—well, frankly you and I both know that something like this would break their hearts."

"My lips are sealed."

Relief spread across Ted's face.

Tonya stood to leave.

"I'll walk you out." Ted followed Tonya into the outer office where his secretary, Martha, usually sat but today was conspicuously absent. "Tonya." He had said her name barely above a whisper. When she didn't respond he cleared his throat and spoke louder. "Tonya."

"What?" This time Tonya turned and faced him.

"I'll need the ring back, just so there's no confusion."

Tonya handed him the tiny, murky diamond, and Ted grabbed her hand.

"I want you to know that I really did love you. A part of me always will. I don't want you to think I'm going back on what God said, it's just that I believe God gives us choices. You are the perfect woman to help me reach my destiny but Tatiana . . . well she's the perfect woman for me."

He released her hand, and Tonya walked out of Now Faith International Church for the last time. She went back to her apartment, loaded up her car and hit the road, all the while thanking God who had provided for her a way of escape. On a whim, she had applied for a job at a school a few weeks ago and had gotten the news yesterday that they would like to hire her as their new child development psychologist. Even if it meant returning to the last place on Earth she wanted to run to right now, Tonya was grateful for a way of escape.

<hr>

The plan was simple. Work maybe three, at the most six, months. Then apply, apply, apply, and get the heck out of Dodge or, rather, in this case Houston. Texas was the place where she was born and raised. It was where most of her family called home, with the exception of her jet-setting aunt Katie, who declared herself to be a citizen of the whole world. Houston, in particular, was the place where Michael lived. Tonya hadn't thought about how she was going to get in and out of Houston without her family knowing her whereabouts. Especially since Tonya talked to someone in her family at least once a week. She had, however, been unreachable during her move, and she knew that if she didn't start leaving messages with the quickness, they would send a search party after her for sure. Tonya continued unpacking her new office and rehearsed aloud what she would say to her mother.

"I took a temporary job somewhere, but I'm not at liberty to tell you where." *Yeah, nah that won't work.*

"I'm back in Houston. Just for a minute, so please don't tell Michael. Or anybody connected to Michael. Don't tell his mother, your best friend, who also happens to be my godmom." *Okay, I guess that won't work either.* "I broke up with Ted, I need some time to disappear. I'm fine. Don't call me, I'll call you." *They would send a search party for sure.* Tonya heard a knock on her door.

"Come in."

Julie, the school nurse, peeked her head in. "I know this is your first day, but are you ready to get your feet wet?"

"Sure."

Julie took in the entire room. "Wow, you work fast, Tonya. I like what you've done to the place. Okay, we have kind of a special case. She's five years old. Cute as a button, but she's a fighter. Her dad's a high-profile celebrity. She got into another fight today, and Headmistress Stone is calling for a three-day suspension."

"I thought you said the child was five."

"Her teacher thinks the child may have anger issues. When I tell you who the father is, you'll see why."

God, please, out of all the schools I could have chosen to take a job at, please don't let this be Serenity's school.

"Her father is Bad Boy Joshua Keys," Julie said, measuring Tonya's response.

Tonya knew all the rumors that had circulated about Joshua and his wife Bella, but she kept her face as neutral as possible. "Julie, are you suggesting that the dad is exhibiting violent behavior towards the child?"

"Oh gosh, no. Nobody would dare say anything like that. Anybody with eyes can see that he loves that little girl to pieces. First of all, let me say I'm one of his biggest fans. I don't believe any of those rumors. I think he is one of the sexiest men on the planet."

"Good, because he's a pastor now, so I'm guessing he doesn't advocate violent behavior in his children, but even if he wasn't, it's really unfair to target the child because of her father's profession."

"I know, and I agree. I just think Cindy, that's Serenity's teacher, may think that this anger thing may be genetic. Do you think that's possible?"

"If her father was Charles Manson, maybe that theory would work, but since he's just a retired basketball player, I don't think so. Serenity will have to be judged on her own record, not her father's."

"Would you be willing to see Serenity before her father gets here?"

"I'll tell you what. Let me take a look at her file before you send her in."

Little Serenity's eyes lit up when she saw Tonya. Tonya put her finger to her mouth, a signal to be quiet. The teaching aid who had delivered Serenity, closed the door on her way out, and Suri ran into Tonya's arms. Tonya scooped the child up and hugged her tightly.

"Auntie Tonya, what are you doing here?"

"I'm going to be working at your school for a while. At school I'm not Auntie Tonya, okay? You must remember to call me Ms. Malone. It'll be our secret."

"Okay," Suri said.

So much for her quiet entry and escape plan.

Flight of the Blackbird coming Soon!

www.ingramcontent.com/pod-product-compliance
Lightning Source LLC
Chambersburg PA
CBHW032055180726
48284CB00002B/300